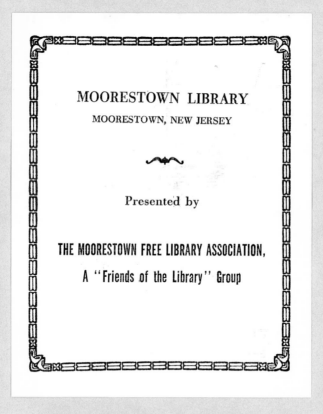

THE TREE OF HANDS

THE TREE OF HANDS

Ruth Rendell

THORNDIKE PRESS • THORNDIKE, MAINE

Library of Congress Cataloging in Publication Data:

Rendell, Ruth, 1930-
  The tree of hands.

  1. Large type books. I. Title.
[PR6068.E63T7 1985b]   823'.914   85-8148
ISBN 0-89621-639-X

Large Print edition available through arrangement with
Pantheon Books, New York, N.Y.

Cover design by Mimi Harrison.

For Francesca, my godchild, with love

BOOK I

1

Once, when Benet was about fourteen, they had been in a train together, alone in the carriage, and Mopsa had tried to stab her with a carving knife. Threatened her with it, rather. Benet had been wondering why her mother had brought such a large handbag with her, a red one that didn't go with the clothes she was wearing. Mopsa had shouted and laughed and said wild things and then she had put the knife back in her bag. But Benet had been very frightened by then. She lost her head and pulled the emergency handle, which Mopsa called the "communication cord." The train stopped and there had been trouble for everyone involved, and her father had been angry and grimly sad.

She had more or less forgotten it. The memory of it came back quite vividly while she

9

was waiting for Mopsa at Heathrow. Though she had seen Mopsa many times since then, had lived under the same roof with her and seen how she could change, it was the scarved, shawled, streamered figure with its fleece of shaggy hair that she watched for as she waited behind the barrier among the tour guides with their placards, the anxious Indians, the businessmen's wives. James wanted to come out of the stroller, he couldn't see down there and he wasn't feeling well. Benet picked him up and set him on her hip with her arm round him.

It ought to have been exciting, waiting here. There was something dramatic about the emergence of the first people from behind the wall that hid Customs, almost as if they had escaped into freedom. Benet remembered once meeting Edward here and how wonderful that first sight of him had been. All those people streaming through, all unknown, all strangers, and then Edward, so positively and absolutely Edward that it was as if he were in color and all the rest in black and white. Waiting for Mopsa wasn't like that. Waiting for Edward, if such a thing were conceivable, wouldn't be like that now. There was no one in her world that waiting for would be like that except James, and she couldn't see any reason why she and James should be separated. Not for years and years anyway. She dug in her bag for a tissue and wiped his nose. Poor James. He was beautiful though, he always was, even if his face was wan and his nose pink.

A couple came through, each pushing a tartan suitcase on wheels. The woman behind them held a small suitcase in one hand and a small holdall in the other. It would be hard to say which was carry-on baggage and which had been checked. The cases matched; they were of biscuit-colored stuff you couldn't tell was plastic or leather. She was a drab, colorless, washed-out woman. Her pale, wandering eyes rested on Benet and recognized her. It was that way round – otherwise would Benet ever have known?

Yet this was Mopsa. This was her mad mother who was kissing her, smiling, and giving a dismissive wave of the hand when James, instead of responding to her, buried his face in Benet's shoulder. This was Mopsa in a dowdy gray suit, a pink silk blouse with a gold pin at the collar, her hair cut brusquely short and faded to tarnished silver.

Benet put the cases on the stroller, using it as a baggage trolley. She carried James, who snuffled and stared, round-eyed, curious, at this new unknown grandmother. Mopsa had developed a brisk, springy walk. Her carriage was erect, her head held high. In the past she had sometimes slouched, sometimes danced, swanned and swayed in her Isadora Duncan moods, but she had never walked briskly like an ordinary woman. Or perhaps she did when I was very young, thought Benet, trying to remember a girl-mother of twenty years before. It was too long ago. All she could recall now was how she had longed for a normal mother like other girls had and took for granted. Now, when she was twenty-eight and it no longer mattered, it seemed she had one. She stopped herself staring. She asked after her father.

"He's fine. He sent his love."

"And you really like living in Spain?"

"I don't say it hasn't its drawbacks but Dad hasn't had a sign of his asthma in three years. It keeps me fit too." Mopsa smiled cheerfully as if her own illness had been no more than a kind of asthma. She talked like one of those neighbors in Edgware had talked. Like Mrs. Fenton, Benet thought, like a middle-aged housewife. "I feel a fraud coming here for these tests," Mopsa said. "There's nothing wrong with me anymore, I said, but they said it wouldn't do any harm and why not have a holiday? Well, I'm on holiday all the time really, aren't I? Are we going in the tube? It must be seven or eight years since I went in the tube."

12

"I've brought the car," said Benet.

In her teens, she used sometimes to say over and over to herself, I must not hate my mother. The injunction had not always been obeyed. And then she would say, But she's ill, she can't help it, she's mad. She had understood and forgiven but she had not wanted to be with her mother. When she went away to university, she had resolved that she would never go back and, except for short holidays, she never had. Her father had retired and her father and mother had bought themselves a little house near Marbella. Mopsa's face and the backs of her hands were tanned by the sunshine of southern Spain. Benet shifted James onto her other hip and he sniveled and clung to her.

"He's got a nasty cold," said Mopsa. "I wonder if you ought to have brought him out with a cold like that."

"I'd no one to leave him with. You know I've just moved house."

There was a baby seat in the back of the car in which James usually sat contentedly. Benet strapped him in and put Mopsa's cases in the trunk. She would have been grateful if her mother had offered to sit in the back with James, but Mopsa was already in the passenger seat, her seatbelt already fastened, her hands, in rather clumsy black leather gloves, folded in her lap. It didn't seem to occur to her even to talk to James. He was miserable in the back, sneezing sometimes and grizzling quietly. Benet talked to him as she drove, pointing out people and dogs and buildings, anything she thought might be interesting, but she soon became aware of Mopsa's resentment. Mopsa wanted to talk about her own troubles and her own hopes, about Spain and their house and about what she was going to do while in London. Something struck Benet that she had never thought of before, that one always assumes that when mental illness is cured or alleviated one will be left with a nice person, an unselfish, thoughtful, pleasant, sensible person. But of course this wasn't so. Why should it be? Underneath the psychosis there might just as well be normal nastiness as normal niceness. Not that Mopsa was nasty, far from it. Perhaps what she meant was that Mopsa was, had been, used to be, mad – but when the madness lifted, it revealed a solipsist of a very high order, someone who believed the world to revolve around herself.

The house in Hampstead, in the Vale of Peace, still seemed an alien place to return to. It was only three days since Benet had moved in. Benet slid the car into the narrow lane between high banks which led into this hamlet on

14

the edge of the Heath. For half her life, since the day she had come with friends to the fair that is always held on public holidays just off the Spaniards Road, she had dreamed of living here. Then, when it need not be fantasy any longer, when it was possible, she had planned for it. But Mopsa seemed never to have heard of this celebrated enclave, enbowered by chestnuts and sycamores and Monterey pines, where blue plaques honored poets dead and gone, a painter, an impresario or two. That Shelley had sailed paper boats on the pond and Coleridge had begun, while sitting on a log on the green, another magical epic never to be completed, were items of literary lore that had never reached her. Getting out of the car, she eyed Benet's tall and narrow Victorian villa with something like disappointment. What had she expected? An art deco palace in the Bishop's Avenue?

"Well, I don't suppose you wanted anything too ambitious, just you and the baby on your own."

James wasn't really a baby anymore, Benet thought, unlocking the front door. He was a year and nine months old, saying a good many words, understanding more. He clambered up the flight of steps, happier now that he was home, probably remembering the treasures awaiting him, the toys that littered the floor of the big basement-kitchen-playroom. Mopsa stepped over him to get to the door. Benet wondered how soon it would be before she began on his fatherless state. Or was she, in spite of the enormous improvement, not quite enough, never to be quite enough, of the conventional suburban middle-aged woman for this to weigh with her? Benet hardly expected to escape without the mention of Edward, the disadvantages of illegitimacy, the threat to a boy's normalcy of growing up only with a mother. She ought to be glad, she told herself, that it was Mopsa who had come and not her father. He was still expressing shocked disbelief over James's very existence.

The house was not yet set to rights. Boxes and crates of still unwrapped ornaments, kitchen utensils, china and glass and the unending hundreds of books were ranked along the hallway. Leaving for the airport, Benet had come from her task of setting books on the shelves she had had built in the room that would be her study, from attempting some sort of cataloguing system. Spread across the floor in all its sixteen foreign-language editions lay her best-selling novel, the source of her affluence, of this house, *The Marriage Knot.* She closed the door to keep James from rampaging among the welter of paperbacks.

Though James seemed even farther from rampaging than he had been in the car. Instead of doing what Benet had expected and rushing back to his newest toy, a xylophone with its octave painted in colours of the spectrum plus one in gold, he had taken himself to his small wicker chair and sat in it, sucking his thumb. His nose had begun to run, and when Benet picked him up, she could hear his breath moving in his chest. It wasn't wheezing exactly, just a sound of his breath moving where there should be no sound. It was warm and cozy in the big basement room, and on a sunny day like this one, bright enough. Benet had had all the kitchen part-fitted with oak units and the floor carpeted in Florentine red and a big cupboard built for James's toys.

Mopsa, having deposited her cases on the bed in the room Benet had got ready for her, came downstairs quite jauntily and said: "Now I'll take us all out for some lunch."

"I don't think I ought to take him out again. He doesn't seem very well. We can eat here. I meant to give you lunch here."

Mopsa showed her displeasure. "It isn't *cold* even by my Spanish standards." She laughed, a metallic, rather cracked sound not unlike that made by striking the lowest key of the

17

xylophone. "You must be a very devoted mother."

Benet made no answer. She too was amazed by what a devoted mother she had become. Of course she had meant to be that. In having James, in purposefully setting out as an unmarried woman to have a child, she had planned a perfect devotion, an ideal childhood, the best of love and of material things. She had not guessed how little she need have calculated, how absolutely committed to him she would be within a moment of his birth.

She made lunch — soup, wholemeal bread, duck pâté, and salad for her and Mopsa, scrambled eggs, fingers of toast, and chocolate ice cream for James. Up at the other end of the room, in the window seat with the little front garden and the stone garden wall rising up behind it, Mopsa sat reading the paperback she had brought with her on the plane. She hadn't attempted to take James on to her knee. Benet repressed her indignation, told herself not even to feel it. James's favorite lunch didn't tempt him beyond a few mouthfuls.

"He needs a good sleep," said Mopsa.

Probably she was right, though Benet thought she said it more from a desire to be rid of him than for his own benefit. James's bedroom was the room in the house she had seen to first, the only one without a still unemptied crate in it. Benet put his favourite toy, a squashy tiger cub with dangling limbs, into his hands and laid him gently in the cot. James didn't like being put down to sleep in the daytime and usually if this was attempted sat bolt upright at once, putting up importunate arms. This time he lay where he was put, clutching the tiger. His face was flushed as if he might be cutting those awaited back molars. Benet thought there couldn't be much the matter with him. She had had him immunized against every possibly threatening disease. His chest had always been a bit troublesome when he had a cold. It growled now when he breathed in. She sat with him for five minutes until he slept.

"I didn't imagine you'd have all that much maternal feeling," Mopsa said. She had been up to the chaotic living room and found bottles that hadn't yet been put away and poured herself some brandy. She had never been a hard drinker, never approached alcoholism, but she liked a drink and it sometimes affected her strangely. Benet remembered, from years back, her efforts and her father's to deflect Mopsa from the sherry bottle. Mopsa smiled her vague silly smile, parted lips trembling. "It's often the case that you don't want them but you come to love them when they arrive."

"I did want James," said Benet, and to effect a change of subject, one she knew her mother would be happy to embark on, "Tell me about these tests you're having done."

"They haven't got the facilities to do them in Spain. I always did say there's some enzyme or something that's missing in me, that's all it is, and now it looks as if they're coming round to my way of thinking." Mopsa had for years denied that she was ill at all. It was others who were ill or malicious or lacking in understanding of her. But when realization that she was not normal was inescapable, when in lucid periods she looked back on nightmares, she had come to lay the blame not on psychosis but on a defect in her body's chemistry.

"Take the case of George III," she would say. "They thought he was mad for years. They subjected him to hellish tortures. And now they know he had porphyria and just giving him what his body lacked would have made him sane."

Perhaps she was right. But whatever vital substance she might lack, it now seemed that the deficiency had lately and by natural means made itself good. As Mopsa talked lucidly, and with a good deal of intelligent grasp of detail, of the tests and the complicated processes that would follow them, Benet thought her saner

20

than she had been since she herself was a child. Even the glaze that lay on her greenish-blue eyes seemed to have lifted and been replaced by a more normal inner light.

Mopsa was looking round the room. "Where's your television?"

"I haven't got it."

"You mean you haven't got a set at all? I should be lost without the TV, not that it's very good in Spain. I was looking forward to English TV. Why haven't you got it? It can't be that you can't afford it."

"I write when James is asleep, so that means I mostly write in the evenings and television wouldn't be much use to me."

"He's alseep now. Do you want to do some writing now? Don't take any notice of me. I'll keep quiet and read my book."

Benet shook her head. The peculiar conditions necessary for writing — some measure of solitude, a contemplative atmosphere, a certain preparation of the mind — she felt unable to explain to anyone not involved in the process, least of all Mopsa. Besides, she was in the highly unusual position of someone who had written down some reminiscences and observations — in her case the time in India with Edward — made them into fiction largely for her own amusement, and suddenly finds she has produced a bestseller. An immediate and enormous bestseller. Now she had to write something else, if not to match *The Marriage Knot,* at least to put up a creditable showing beside it. She was the author of what might prove to be a one-time success faced with the hurdle of the "second book." It didn't come easily even when she was feeling tranquil and James slept.

That reminded her, he had been asleep for nearly two hours now. She went upstairs to look at him. He was still sleeping, his face rather flushed and his breathing rough. She could see Edward in his face, especially in the curve of his lips and the modeling of his forehead. One day, when he was grown up, he would have those "English gentleman" looks Edward possessed, flaxen hair, steady blue eyes, strong chin — and perhaps something more than just looks, something more than his father had.

Waiting for him to wake, she stood by the window and watched the setting sun. The sky would become red only after the sun had gone down. Now it was a dark gold, barred with gray, the waters of the Vale of Peace pond sparkling with points of light. A row of Monterey pines on the farther bank stood black and still against the yellow and gray marbling. A

22

good place to live, a fine place for James to grow up in. She had chosen wisely.

Was there some feature of that view, the row of pines perhaps, the sunset, or simply thinking of childhood and an environment for it, that brought back that awful afternoon with Mopsa? She hadn't thought of it for years. Now she remembered it very clearly, though it was nineteen or twenty years ago, but did she remember what had really happened? It had been the first manifestation of Mopsa's madness, her paranoid schizophrenia, that Benet had known. She was eight and the cousin who was with them only three or four. Mopsa had taken them into the dining room of the house they lived in in Colindale and locked the door and bolted it, and then phoned Benet's father at work to say she was going to kill the children and then herself. Or had Mopsa only threatened to remain shut in there with the children until some demand of hers was met? The true version was something between the two probably. Why, anyway, would a dining-room door have a bolt on it? But Benet could very clearly remember Mopsa taking knives out of a drawer, the little cousin screaming, Mopsa pulling heavy pieces of furniture, a sideboard, some other sort of cabinet, across the French windows. Most of all she remembered the door coming down, splintering first, and her uncle breaking through, then her father. They had brought no outside aid; shame and fear of consequences had no doubt prevented this. No one had been hurt, and Mopsa had become quite calm afterwards so that one wouldn't have guessed anything was wrong with her. Until she had started the compulsive stealing, that had been the next thing. It became impossible to say you wanted anything – anything within reason, that is – without Mopsa stealing it for you. Benet remembered her father admiring a record he had heard in someone's house, a popular, even hackneyed classical piece, Handel's *Water Music* most likely. Mopsa had gone to great pains to find that identical recording in a shop, and when she had found it, she stole it, though she could easily have afforded to buy it. She stole to make gifts to those she loved and the element of risk involved in the theft rendered her gift, so some psychiatrist had said, more valuable in her own eyes. Since then the manifestation of her condition had been many and various: sporadic violence, divorcement from reality, inconsequential "mad" acts. . . .

James turned over, sat up and gave an angry yell, rubbing his eyes with his fists. His cries turned to coughing with a rattle in his chest.

Benet picked him up and held him against her shoulder. His chest was a sounding box that made almost musical notes. An idea which had been taking shape of asking people round for drinks – a way of passing the evening and quite a good way now Mopsa was behaving so rationally – no longer seemed feasible. James had a bad cold and would need her attention all evening.

The house felt very warm. She was glad she had had the central heating system overhauled before she moved in. Mopsa, unpacking her case, her bedroom door open, looked the epitome of a sensible, rather ordinary housewife. No doubt it was a part she was acting, had perhaps been acting for years. Roles of various kinds had been common with her in the past, all of them seemingly having coalesced into this form. Or was this the real Mopsa, emerging at last from shed layers of psychotic personae?

Now it was even as if her true name, the mundane Margaret, would have suited her better than that which evoked connotations of wildness and witchcraft, ancient familiars, ducking stools, eye of newt and toe of frog. It was not from *Macbeth* though but *The Winter's Tale* that she had named herself when playing the part of Mopsa in a school production at the age of fifteen. Familiar with it as a mother's name, as others might be with a Mary or Elizabeth, Benet nevertheless suddenly saw it as fantastic, incongruous, something that should have been disposed of at the same time as that fleece of blonde hair. Mopsa's face, a thin and pointed face, always witchlike, though in Benet's childhood that of a young and beautiful witch, had undergone some blurring of the features that was perhaps part of an ageing process. The jawline was no longer hard and sweeping, the lips were less set. The dowdy haircut made her look very slightly pathetic, but possibly no more so than any woman of her age who had no particular purpose in life and was not very well or much loved or needed.

Benet was surprised to find her down in the kitchen making tea for herself. Mopsa generally expected to be waited on wherever she was. Once James was better, Benet thought, they would all go out together. He was almost old enough to be taken to places of interest, to begin anyway. Lunch somewhere nice after Mopsa had been for her hospital appointment, and then if the weather were as good as it had been that day, they might go to Hampston Court. Little children became ill and well so quickly, she had already learned that. It wasn't going to be easy getting through this evening. In a day or two she might come to find hiring a television set essential.

"When is his bedtime?" Mopsa said.

"About six-thirty usually, but it obviously isn't going to be tonight."

"You spoil him."

Benet made no answer to that and Mopsa began to talk of the complexities of getting to the hospital where the first tests were to be carried out. It was such a long way and the underground system had "all changed" since she had lived in London. She studied a tube map and a street guide. Benet said of course she would take her by car, and if James wasn't well enough to come, she would find someone to sit with him.

When she had been living in her flat in Tufnell Park, a baby-sitter had sometimes been arranged, but that was from the block of flats next door, where teenage girls abounded, all wanting to earn. Here it was different. She knew no one. She didn't even have friends with small children, except Chloe, who was currently away on holiday.

Mopsa, never lacking in intuition of a kind, went part of the way towards reading her thoughts. "Can't you find someone now? I should like us to go out to eat."

"I couldn't leave him."

Benet decided to ignore Mopsa's sullen look.

Anyway, it was becoming a question not of whether she should stay with James or leave him but of taking some more positive step. His forehead felt hot and damp. His breath strained and sometimes a honking sound came from his chest. He had made an attempt to play with the xylophone but had soon come back and climbed on to Benet's lap, the difficulties he was having with breathing making him break into miserable choked cries.

"I'm going to have to ring the doctor."

"It's seven o'clock. Surely you wouldn't bother an overworked man like that just because the baby's got a cold."

"It's a woman," Benet said, and she said no more. In the old days it had always been useless getting cross with Mopsa, still less losing one's temper. It threw her at once into a desperate, frenetic panic. That was years ago now, but old habits died hard. Benet reached for the phone and as she did so it rang.

"That'll be your father."

It was. Mopsa looked complacent. Signs of care and attentiveness towards herself always disproportionately gratified her.

"Hello, Dad, how are you?" Benet had to move the mouthpiece away from James's loud, unhappy crying. "Sorry, that's poor James giving tongue. He's got a cold."

Though there had never been anything so dramatic as casting her off from the bosom of the family, though in fact no positive denunciation of her had ever been made, her father had been shocked and outraged by her pregnancy and the birth of James. The situation was made worse by her being an educated person and now a well-off one, living in a society where much was available to prevent the births of children outside wedlock. He had never yet actually referred to James by name. When James, as had lately happened, became interested in the telephone and wanted to speak to whomever was on the line, his grandfather had been embarrassed and had spoken gruffly, had barked out a series of hellos and goodbyes and positively panted to get back to Benet. Now when she explained about James's cold, he said only: "Ah, well." An awkward pause followed. "How's your mother? Got there all right, did she?"

"She's fine. Do you want to speak to her?"

The pause was briefer this time, but it was there. No doubt John Archdale had loved his wife once. Since then he had had a lot to bear. It wasn't her fault, she was to be pitied, she was just as helplessly ill as if she suffered from multiple sclerosis; but now, instead of love, what he felt was duty; he bore a cross that yearly grew heavier. At the moment he was probably having a little well-earned respite with those expatriate cronies of his, a game of bridge, a drink in the bar of the Miramar. The sound of his wife's voice would not make that evening pleasanter. Benet could do nothing.

"I'll just have a word," he said.

From time to time in the past, Benet had heard her mother hurl at him a variety of epithets, of which "bag of shit" and "filthy murderer" was among the mildest. Now Mopsa took the receiver and spoke into it in her sensible housewife role.

"Hello, dear."

There was a short interchange. Benet couldn't help feeling indignant that James's name wasn't once mentioned. He was quiet now — that is, he had stopped crying — and leaned heavily against her, the rasps of breath louder than ever.

"Yes, quite a nice flight. One thing you can say for air travel, it doesn't go on for long, it's soon over. I was met and brought here in style. Yes, in the morning, ten in the morning. You'd better phone again tomorrow, hadn't you? I'll say goodbye then."

She put the phone down and stood staring at Benet with James in her lap. That trembly look, rather as if she were going to cry, which

Benet knew of old as presaging a change of mood, had settled on her face. Suddenly Mopsa began to speak in a high and rapid, though not mad, voice.

"I wasn't a good mother to you, Brigitte. I know that. I neglected you – well, I didn't pay enough attention to you. I was ill, you see, I was ill long before you and Dad realized. It was this hormone or whatever it is that's missing, it was missing then, it was affecting me. I wasn't a good mother. I was a lost soul, you see. Can you forgive me?"

Emotional outbursts from Mopsa always embarrassed Benet. She felt awkward, farouche, not least because of the use her mother always fell back on, in times of stress particularly, of the hated given name which, for once following in Mopsa's footsteps, she had divested herself of immediately she left home. Benet was rather angular, long-legged, with pointed features and straight dark hair. How could she have borne to suffer afresh, with a new set of friends, the inevitable mirth and amazement consequent upon being called after Bardot?

She was embarrassed but she had to conquer that embarrassment for poor, pathetic Mopsa's sake. And Mopsa stood there waiting, hungry for love, for reassurance, her breathing fast and nearly as shallow at James's.

31

"Can you forgive me, Brigitte?"

"There's nothing to forgive. You were ill. Besides, you weren't a bad mother." Holding James, pressing him against her shoulder, Benet forced herself to get up and put the other arm round her mother. Mopsa was trembling; she quivered like a nervous animal. Benet held her arms round her mother and round James. She kissed Mopsa's cheek. The skin was hot and dry and slightly pulsating. But Mopsa's water-blue eyes were clear and steady and sane. "I haven't anything to forgive, believe me," Benet said. "And now let's forget it, shall we?"

"I'd do anything in the world for you, anything to make you happy."

"I know."

Benet sat down by the phone again, settled James on her lap, and dialed the doctor's number.

2

"He's got croup."

An onomatopoeic word, roughly the sound James made when he breathed. Benet knew by the immensity of her relief – she could have thrown her arms around Dr. McNeil's neck – how worried she had been.

"I thought that was something Victorian children got."

"They did. Children still do. Only we can do more for them these days." Causing Benet's relief to plummet like a lead weight, the doctor said, "I'd like him to go to hospital."

"Is that absolutely necessary?"

"To be on the safe side. They'll have the equipment. I don't suppose you could achieve a steam-filled room here, could you?"

Dr. McNeil was sixty; she was due to retire in a week or two. Was she old-fashioned? Benet wondered. A steam-filled room? She imagined a shower turned on full, crashing nearly boiling water into a bath, the door and window of the bathroom shut. But one of the bathrooms here didn't have a shower at all and the other had one that was hopelessly furred up, waiting for a replacement.

"What exactly is croup?"

"If you had it, we'd call it laryngitis."

Benet left the doctor to make phone calls. She carried James down into the kitchen, where Mopsa, very practical in apron and rubber gloves, was washing up cups and saucers. Relief had returned. Croup was only laryngitis.

"I'll come with you," Mopsa said.

Benet would have preferred her mother to stay here but she didn't know how to say so. And perhaps Mopsa shouldn't be left alone, especially at night and in a strange place. It was unfortunate Mopsa happened to be here at this particular time. Benet could not help reflecting that, when people said they would do anything in the world to make you happy, they never meant things like keeping in the background, not interfering, acceding to your small requests.

At any rate this time Mopsa sat in the back of the car, holding James. The night was clear but moonless. Benet realized suddenly that it

34

was Halloween. She carried James, wrapped in a big fleecy blanket, into the big old vaulted Gothic vestibule of the hospital and then they were sent up to the ward in the lift.

Not very familiar with hospitals — she had been in one only once, and that when James was born — Benet had expected a long ward with beds close together and ranged along both sides. But Edgar Stamford Ward was all small rooms with a wide corridor down the center. The building, she had heard, had once been the old workhouse, but this part must have been gutted to make the children's department, for nothing nineteenth-century remained except for the windows with their small panes and pointed arches. In James's room, a tent over a cot into which steam was being pumped awaited James. The nurse called it a croupette. He had been in it for about ten minutes, protesting at first, then lying quietly and clutching Benet's hand, when the doctor arrived to look at him. In the doorway he took off his hospital jacket and laid it across the sister's desk.

"They get white-coat phobia if we don't do that," he said. "Won't even go in the butcher's with you." He smiled. "My name's Ian Raeburn. I'm one of the registrars here."

There was a bed beside the cot. She was sitting on it. She had noticed it was made up with sheets and blankets.

"Can I stay here with him?"

"Sure you can if you want. That's what the bed's for. And you've got a bathroom next door. We're rather proud in here of encouraging parents to stay – a change from the bad old days."

"I'd like to stay."

Mopsa said in a small, lost voice, "What about me?"

"I'll leave you to decide about that," said Dr. Raeburn. "I think you'll find James will be easier now he's in the tent."

The fingers clutching her finger had not slackened. "You can have a taxi back, Mother. I'll come down with you and call you a taxi. You'll be all right."

Mopsa's face had grown soft, putty-like, tremulous. Her lips shook. The bedroom was very dimly lit, a single low-wattage bulb gleaming from a fitting on the wall above the washbasin, and in this gloom the glazed look had come back into her eyes. It was the first time since her arrival that Benet had seen that look.

"I'm never left on my own. It was bad enough being alone in the plane, I mean, without anyone I know. I can't be all on my own in a strange house."

"It would only be for one night."

"Why do you have to stay with him? He's asleep; he won't know whether you're there or not. Parents never used to stay in hospitals with children; it was unheard-of, the staff wouldn't have put up with it."

"Things have changed."

"Yes and for the worse. Your father wouldn't have let me come if he'd known you were going to leave me on my own, Brigitte. I'll be ill if you leave me on my own."

Benet carefully disengaged her finger from James's grasp. He did not move. She was filled with an intense dislike of Mopsa, something that verged on hatred. When her mother was rational like this, though exhibiting all the signs of solipsism – indifference to others' wishes, deep selfishness – the feeling that all her madness was an act put on to gain attention was inescapable. Of course it wasn't, it was as real as a physical paralysis. And if it were an act, wasn't that in itself a sign of madness, that anyone would take an act so far?

I must not hate my mother. . . .

"You'll be quite safe. There are bars on the ground-floor windows, there's a phone on each floor. It's not exactly a rough area, is it?"

"I'm not going without you, Brigitte. You can't make me. I can sleep in the chair here. I can sleep on the floor."

"They won't let you," Benet said. "They'll only allow parents. Look, I'll drive you home and then I'll come back here. I'll come home again first thing in the morning."

"I have to go for my tests first thing in the morning."

Mopsa's face was stubborn and set. All the pointed, sharp witch look had come back. Her clouded eyes were fixed not on Benet but on a point in the far corner of the room. Benet looked at James. He was asleep, and the vaporizer was gently and steadily puffing steam into the croupette. She picked her coat off the bed. She thought she saw surprise, perhaps a little more than that, in the ward sister's expression when she said she wouldn't be staying overnight. Mopsa, who had spent long stretches of her life in hospitals, wasn't happy here. She darted wary glances from side to side as they walked towards the lift, especially at the sign pointing in the direction of the psychiatric clinic.

The house had a welcoming feel in spite of the crates still waiting to be unpacked. It was warm and bright and comfortable. Yet for Benet the night was almost a sleepless one. She could not rid her mind of the image of James waking up in that steamy hothouse and finding her gone. What use was she to her mother?

Mopsa had taken a sleeping pill the moment they got back to the Vale of Peace, had fallen asleep ten minutes later and had been sleeping ever since. Passing her door at six in the morning on her way to make tea, Benet heard Mopsa's regular breathing with a hint of a snore in it.

She phoned the hospital, spoke to the staff nurse on Edgar Stamford Ward, and was told James was much the same. He had passed a restless night. The staff nurse didn't say if he had called for Benet or cried for her and Benet could not bring herself to ask. She knew he must have done. He had never before been parted from her. If only Mopsa's tests were being done at the same hospital! Instead she was going to have to drive her miles across the sprawl of north London suburbs and fight her way back again through the traffic before she could go to James. For the first time in her relationship with James, she felt guilt, she felt she had failed him.

Mopsa appeared at eight, dressed in the skirt of the gray suit and a harebell blue angora sweater with a string of pearls round her neck. This morning she was not so much the sensible housewife as the svelte businesswoman. Even her hair, probably from the position in which it had been pressed into the pillow, looked less uncompromisingly chopped off. Discreet make-up, pinkish and mauvish, lessened the years and the ducking stool image. She didn't ask about James and Benet didn't tell her she had phoned the hospital. She was full of the prospect of her tests. Did she look all right? Should she wear her blue raincoat or the jacket of the suit or both?

James might not have existed. Benet felt an actual physical pain at this neglect of him; she couldn't eat, she was choked with resentment at Mopsa's attitude and with love for him. She wanted to get hold of Mopsa and shake her and shout into her face, This is my child, this is my son, don't you realize it? It would be useless, it would be cruel and pointless.

I must not hate my mother....

Once they were in the car, driving along Hampstead Lane, she found a practical, calm voice.

"I'm going to leave you at the Royal Eastern and go to James. You must take a taxi either back home or to the hospital where James is. It's quite simple and you'll be fine. I've written down both addresses for you."

She waited for the storm of protest but none came. Mopsa was in euphoric mood, anxious to please, graciously prepared to be unselfish. Of course she would have a taxi, of course she would be all right. She was sorry she had insisted on Benet's coming back with her the night before, but things felt different at night, didn't they? On a bright morning like this one you could hardly believe how bad you had felt at night, how disoriented and alone and afraid.

Benet came back by the same route, the same short cut through back streets, as that by which she had taken Mopsa to the Royal Eastern Hospital in Tottenham. The traffic piled up as she was waiting to turn out of Rudyard Gardens into Lordship Avenue – there were roadworks in progress at the junction – so, taking her place in the slow-moving queue, she was able to look around her at this district where she had once lived.

It was very much changed. The trees in Rudyard Avenue had been pollarded and had become an avenue of beheaded trunks. The rows of houses were no longer inhabited, their doors and windows boarded up with sheets of corrugated metal. Mopsa would have called it a slum. On the far side of Lordship Avenue the sun shone out of a hard blue sky onto the blocks and terraces and single tower of a housing estate called Winterside Down. When she and Mary and Antonia had shared their attic in Winterside Road, the estate had not yet been built. There had only been their road overlooking a stretch of desolate land extending from the gasworks to the canal.

Her car and the three ahead moved slowly up to the junction. A black Doberman pinscher was strolling over the pedestrian crossing. It reached the Rudyard Gardens side and the traffic began to shift again. Just at this point, Benet remembered, she had used to catch the bus that took her down into the city and the offices of the magazine she had been working for. If it hadn't been for James, for hurrying to be with James, she would have turned into Winterside Road and parked the car, for just as the traffic began to move she saw someone she knew. Tall, heavily-built, fair, getting on for forty now probably – what was his name? Tom something. Tom Woodhouse. He had had the garage next to the house where their flat was and once or twice she had rented a car from him. Benet wound down the window, called his name, and waved, but the traffic roar drowned her voice. She watched him in her rearview mirror as he went across the zebra crossing and got into the cab of a parked van.

James wasn't in the croupette or even in his room but in the children's playroom chalking on a blackboard. When Benet came in, he didn't run to her or hold out his arms but only smiled a radiant and somehow mysterious smile as if he and she were together in some secret conspiracy. He said to a small girl: "That's my mummy."

"We'd like him to have one quiet night in here before he goes home," the sister said.

Mopsa arrived at twelve. She looked pleased with herself, almost jaunty. They had done no tests on her at the Royal Eastern, only examined her and questioned her and made a new appointment for three days' time.

"I shall risk it on my own in your house tonight."

"It would be a great help if you could." Benet felt absurdly grateful. "It's very brave of you."

Suddenly Mopsa had become the sensible, no-nonsense woman who stayed by herself in strange houses night after night. "I shall take a pill. I shan't know a thing till morning."

James ran about playing all day. By six he was asleep, rather pale, breathing heavily, exhausted. One more night and he could go home.

"I ought to be there now," said Mopsa, looking at her watch. "I expect your father's been phoning. I expect he was worried when I wasn't there."

"I'll come down with you and help you find a taxi."

"I thought I might drive your car."

It was dark. The streets here were narrow and congested. Mopsa had held a driving license for thirty years but not driven for the past fifteen.

"I'd rather you practiced in daylight first," Benet said.

Mopsa argued about it while putting her coat on, she argued about it in the lift, surprisingly giving way without another word when Benet said she had left the car keys up in the room and the spare set at home. The night was black and damp with a smell of gunpowder in the air. Children had been letting fireworks off in advance of Guy Fawkes Day. Mopsa waved from the taxi window; she leaned out and waved as if she were going away forever.

James's crying awoke Benet after about three hours. She had been dreaming of Edward, the first time she had dreamed of him for months. She was telling Edward she was going to have a child, his child, and no, she didn't want an abortion, she wanted the child, and the alternative was not marriage, she didn't want to marry him or even be with him anymore....It had been very much like that; things in reality had been very much like that dream. Waking up was a shock because she had thought the dream was real. James was sitting up inside the croupette, crying and sobbing.

Benet picked him up and held him and he stopped crying, though his breathing was rough again. She wondered if this would count against a "quiet" night. The next doctor or nurse to look in would probably ask her, and she couldn't lie to them, for James's sake she wouldn't dare. The room was not dark; it was still lit by the single dim wall light. It was very quiet for a hospital, silent but for a distant faint metallic clattering. She started thinking about Mopsa. She was aware that it was a mistake to admit anxieties into her mind at this hour, but, once there, they stuck, they refused to go away. Had she been wrong to let Mopsa go off alone? Suppose she hadn't been able to find the key? Or once she was in, suppose the lights had fused? Benet was sure her father would never have allowed Mopsa to be alone. And if Mopsa had got into the house safely, had answered the phone and spoken to him, was he too lying sleepless down there in the south of Spain, worrying about his wife, furious with his daughter, thinking of all the things that might happen?

James was sleeping now against her shoulder. She laid him back in the cot inside the tent and put her hand through the opening in the zipper so that he could hold it. When the nurse came in at four he was still sleeping and Benet said nothing about the disturbance of two hours before. She went to sleep herself; she had no more dreams. The room was beginning to lighten, a gray dawn showing through the slats of the blinds, when next she woke. A siren had awakened her, and when she knelt up and looked out of the window, she saw an ambulance passing with its blue light on.

As soon as it got to eight Benet thought she would phone the house in the Vale of Peace. It was not yet half-past seven. Mopsa was not a late riser; she was always up and about by eight. Inside the steamy tent James slept, lying on his back, the vaporizer puffing away. They would let her take him home before lunch. Then a week or two for convalescence, and once Mopsa had gone back, there was no reason why the two of them, she and James, should not go away for a holiday. Why not? She could afford it now. She could afford any amount of holidays, or tax-deductible working trips, as her accountant called them.

"You don't have holidays anymore, Miss Archdale."

They could go somewhere warm, North Africa, or the Canaries. James wouldn't get croup there. Her American publishers wanted her to go to California as part of a promotional trip and she could pay a visit to Universal Studios, where they had begun shooting *The Marriage Knot.* . . .

James had opened his eyes. He was moving his head from side to side, rubbing his eyes with his fists. The floppy-legged tiger cub lay sprawled on the pillow beside him. Benet ran the drumstick down the painted octave of the xylophone, *do-re-mi-fa-so-la-ti-do.* Usually that alerted him. He would reach for the stick and want to play the notes himself. She unzipped the tent. He put out his arms and said, "Mummy," but he didn't lift his head from the pillow.

Benet lifted him onto her lap. His forehead was hot and he was breathing the way he had done the evening she had brought him in. He very obviously wasn't over it yet; he was less well than he had been the day before.

"You're my poor lamb, aren't you? It's giving you a really hard time."

The nurse came in with a thermometer. Benet left James with her and went down the corridor to the pay phone. The time was just on eight. In the house in the Vale of Peace there was a phone on each floor; you didn't have to run downstairs or up when the phone rang. Benet dialed her own number, wondering what kind of storm would break when she had told Mopsa that James was going to have to stay in hospital for more days and more nights, and she was going to have to stay with him.

The phone started ringing. It rang and rang. Benet put the receiver back and tried again in case she had misdialed. Still there was no answer. It was early yet; it was possible Mopsa was still asleep.

Breakfast had arrived. Cornflakes, a boiled egg, and bread and marmalade for herself, milk, baby cereal, and an orange for James. James wouldn't eat. He clung to her, clutching her round the neck while she tried to eat cornflakes. The day sister came in, said she would like him to be in the croupette, would Benet please try and keep him in the croupette, and Dr. Raeburn would be along to see him in about an hour.

James pushed the milk away with his arm, spilling it over Benet's jeans. She got him to lie down inside the tent by inserting the upper half of her own body in with him. The vaporizer puffed away steadily.

"He's got a little temperature," the nurse said, filling in his chart. "It would be good for him to have a little sleep."

Finally he did sleep and she went back to the phone. She dialed her own number and it started to ring. She was aware of a tight feeling of anxiety beginning to knot inside her. The phone rang ten times, fifteen times. She put the receiver back and she didn't dial again because there was a woman in a dressing gown and with a bandaged leg waiting to use it. Benet recalled how, when she herself had been about thirteen, Mopsa had disappeared without warning and been found two days later wandering in Northampton (in a sleeveless dress) having apparently lost her memory. No one ever found out how she got there or where the dress, which was not one of her own, had come from.

Mopsa might never have gone back to the Vale of Peace last night. As soon as she was out of sight, she might easily have altered the directions to the taxi driver. Benet wondered if she should phone the police, then dismissed the idea as extreme. Later in the day, especially if James got up and played with the other children as he had been doing, she would take the opportunity to rush home for an hour.

Mopsa had seemed so sane, so ordinary, so normal. But perhaps she had always been at her sanest, or appeared to be so, before a bout of madness. If she hadn't gone to the Vale of Peace, where would she go? She knew no one in London now except those old neighbors the Fentons, and very likely they too had moved away by now.

The woman with the bandaged leg finished

her call and Benet dialed again. There was no reply. Benet found it impossible to imagine her mother going for a walk or getting a taxi to come here, but how well did she know her mother? What did she know of her except that she was totally unpredictable? Once Mrs. Fenton had found her lying in a bath in reddening water, her wrists cut....

It took Benet a long time to get hold of a London telephone directory A-K, but at last she did and found the Fentons' number. They were still there at number 55 Harper Lane, or Mrs. Fenton was. The number was listed in the name of Mrs. Constance Fenton, so perhaps her husband had died in the meantime. Benet dialed her own number again and, when there was no reply, Mrs. Fenton's. A young woman's voice answered.

"That was my daughter," Constance Fenton said when she came to the phone. "I've got my daughter and my son-in-law and my grandson staying with me till their house is ready." She was a woman who had the rather pleasant habit of talking to you as if the last time you had conversed had been yesterday and not ten years before.

Benet asked her, warily, tactfully, if by any chance her mother was there.

"Your *mother?*"

Then Benet knew at once Mopsa wasn't there, hadn't been there. Constance Fenton wanted to know all about Mopsa. Was she in London? When was she coming to visit? What a delightful surprise it was; how much she looked forward to seeing Mopsa!

"I know she'll be in touch with you very soon," Benet said. She put the phone down. She had begun to feel sick with dread. Mopsa might be anywhere, a danger to herself and others.

3

The Chinese bridge spanned the canal from Winterside Road to the path that crossed the green lawns and penetrated the estate. Barry had wondered why they called it Chinese until he had seen one just like it on an old willow-pattern plate round at Iris's. Winterside Down was a little world that had everything in it you wanted and plenty you didn't. The streets were all named after people from the Labour Party's past. There was a square in the middle of it called Bevan Square with a shopping center, a post office, a unisex hair stylist, a video store, and a take-out Turkish restaurant. Most of the people were of Greek or Irish or West Indian origin, though there were some Indians too. It was all quite new, the oldest houses only six years old, and it hadn't yet settled down. They had built one tower block and then apparently decided people didn't want tower blocks and were frightened of living in them, so that single tower stood out of the middle of Winterside Down like an enormous lighthouse, surrounded by the pygmy houses that people did want to live in.

The Isadoros lived in two, they were such a big family. The council had put an arch between the hallways so that you could go through from one house to the other without going outside. Carol's was just an ordinary single house, part of a terrace, one of the oldest. When you came into Winterside Down by way of the Chinese bridge, the first part of the estate you saw was the back of that terrace, and if Carol was at home, you could see her lights on. It seldom happened that Barry came home later than Carol, but if he did, or thought he was going to be later, he would look for her lights as soon as he came to the crown of the bridge. Her house was the eighth from where the path came into Summerskill Road. He would count, two-four-six-eight, and if the lights were on feel a surge of joy, a leaping of the heart.

Mostly he got home first. It had been home to him for the past six months, not the kind of place he would have chosen to live in, but home because Carol was there. When she worked evenings at the wine bar, he didn't come the Chinese bridge way but by the main turn-in from Lordship Avenue. Sometimes the Isadoros looked after Jason in the daytime and sometimes his grandmother, Iris, did or, rarely, his aunt Maureen. Barry called round at Iris's place on his way home, but Jason had fallen asleep watching the TV and Iris had put him to bed. He might as well stay the night, why not? She was having him in the morning anyway.

Barry walked home across Bevan Square. He went into the tobacconist, open till eight, and bought twenty Marlboros. He had never used to smoke, but being with Carol so much and Carol's family, he was on to twenty a day now. The square was paved in pinkish-red with flowerbeds surrounded by low brick walls and with a statue in the middle of it that looked like a piece of car bodywork from a scrapheap but was by quite a famous sculptor and called *The Advance of Man.* A smell of garlic and fat hung about the Turkish place. The eldest Isadoro girl and a boy Barry didn't know sat on one of the flowerbed walls, eating kebab and chips out of paper cones.

It was dark, the place painted with the brownish-yellow light from the sodium lamps that stood on concrete stilts above Winterside Down. The light turned everything to khaki and yellow and black. Of the boys who huddled or lounged over their motorbikes all round the statue, one had red and yellow hair in a crest like a hoopoe's and another had dyed his blue, but the light turned all to yellow-brown and glittered like crumbling gold leaf on their black leathers. Those boys were not much younger than Barry, they were almost his contemporaries, but he felt immeasurably older than his twenty to their seventeen or eighteen. In taking on Carol, in becoming, so to speak, the father of a ready-made family, he had leaped half a dozen years.

Her husband's photograph, in a plastic frame from Woolworth's, stood on the shelf over the living-room radiator. It was the only photograph in the house. Dave. He was dead, killed when the lorry he had been driving went over a mountainside in Yugoslavia. A tall, thin, dark-haired man, Dave had been, with blue eyes and an Irish mouth. Barry didn't look like him but they belonged to the same type, Carol's type. Soon after they had first met and he had gone home with her, Carol had told him he was her type and shown him the photograph of Dave.

Barry dusted the photograph. He dusted the few ornaments in the room and the phone and the back of the television set, and then he got the vacuum cleaner out and vacuumed the bit of carpet that had been Iris's before she went mad (as she put it) and had wall-to-wall. He kept the house clean for Carol; it was the least he could do. Before he had moved in, it had been a mess, which was only what you'd expect in the home of someone who had three kids and two jobs.

There was nothing demeaning or emasculating to Barry in house-cleaning. His mother, had she known, would have sneered and called it woman's work. But Barry belonged to a generation in which the girls resented menial tasks even more than the boys. He might take it for granted that his mother cleaned and washed and polished, but not the woman he lived with. Why should she? She worked as hard as he did.

He cleaned the hall as well and stripped the bed and changed the sheets. The only nice furniture in the house was in this bedroom, Carol's bedroom and now his too. The cupboard which Dave had built in when they first moved here and the house was new had its doors made of mirror. It was on the wall facing the bed. Carol liked to sit up in the mornings and look at herself. It brought her a childlike pleasure that warmed Barry's heart, to look at herself in mirrors.

Barry put the sheets and pillowcases into a plastic carrier with a pile of smelly diapers of Jason's and took the lot round to the laundrette in Bevan Square. Blue Hair and Hoopoe and the rest of them were still there but clustered now round an old American car, a Studebaker, parked on the edge of the precinct with its windows open and its radio playing loud rock music. Barry felt old, but in a way he felt proud too and responsible. He and Carol had met in a laundrette, though not this one. His mother's washing machine had broken down and he had taken a couple of pairs of jeans to do himself. Carol had come in with two loads. She had had Ryan and Tanya home for the weekend and Four Winds didn't like it if you sent the kids back with a lot of dirty washing.

Those two big children — he had thought they were her brother and sister. He had thought her the same age as himself or younger. It wasn't possible she was twenty-eight. Maureen said Carol had a face like a doll and in a way that was true, but dolls were made that way, to look like beautiful children, that was the idea, wasn't it? Carol's face was round and her upper lip very short, her skin pink and white china and her hair the kind of golden curls that cluster baby-like over forehead and temples, ring curls, coin curls, damp-looking like a child's. And her sea-blue eyes had met his and she had smiled.

He fell in love with her, he often thought afterwards, even before she spoke. When she did speak, it was to see if he had any change for her second machine. He hadn't — who ever has enough in a laundrette? But he told her where change was to be come by.

"Get your sister to go next door but one to the paper shop. They've always got change."

She looked at him sideways, charmingly. She lowered her long, dark, curling lashes.

"Flattery could get you a long way, d'you know that?"

He hadn't known what she meant, and when she explained, he couldn't believe it. It was hard for him to believe his luck too, that he had met Carol and she liked him. Two days later he was in her house and he was asking who the man in the photograph was and she was saying: "You're the same type really. I always say that's *my* type."

Rolling up the clean sheets, stuffing them back into the bag, he set off home to wait for her. After six months he still got excited thinking about her coming home, waiting for the sound of her key in the lock. Still? It was stronger now than it had been at first. Best of all, he liked coming home at night over the

Chinese bridge — on whose wooden parapet he had joined the other graffitists and printed in paint: *Barry Loves Carol* — and counting the houses and seeing the lights in the eighth one and knowing she was there, longing for him as he was longing for her.

Just before eleven-thirty he thought he heard a car outside, but he must have been mistaken because Carol never had a taxi or a mini-cab; they couldn't afford it. It was coincidence, that was all, that a minute or two after he heard the car Carol's key turned in the lock. He had been watching television and he turned it off as she came in.

She had had quite a bit to drink. Who wouldn't have, working six hours in a wine bar? It was only human nature. Her cheeks were flushed pink and her greeny-blue eyes very bright. She came a little way into the room and took an extravagant pose, lifting up her arms, turning slowly round to twirl the skirts of the black and white zig-zag striped dress above her red boots.

"That's new," said Barry. "Where did you get that?"

Carol began to laugh. "Nicked it. How about that?" She pulled him into the armchair and sat on his knee. "Mrs. Fylemon went out to have lunch with her mum so I whipped round quick with the Hoover and got done by two and then I got on the bus and went down Shopper's Heaven. There's this new boutique I've had my eye on. They only let you take two things in the changing room with you. The girl said how many had I got there and I said two though I'd got three. I'd put a black one on the hanger over this one. I put this one on and my jumper and skirt over it and I didn't hang about. I took the other two back and said they were too big and just sailed out though I was laughing inside fit to kill myself."

"That was clever," said Barry admiringly. "I wouldn't like you to get caught, love."

Carol stroked his hair, and rubbed his nose with her nose. "I won't get caught. I'm too careful." Her fingers moved over the nape of his neck. "Dennis Gordon was in Kostas's. He kept on about my dress, wanted to know if I'd ever done any modeling. Modeling, I said, what's that supposed to mean?"

"You don't like him, do you, Carol?" said Barry.

"He's okay. I don't fancy him if that's what you mean. He was a pal of Dave's. He reminds me a bit of Dave, him being on the lorries too. D'you know, he told Kostas he makes so much doing the Turkey run he can't afford to live here really, he ought to live in one of them tax havens. How about that?"

"I wish he would. I wish he'd go and live in Jersey or Ireland or somewhere."

"I believe you're jealous, Barry Mahon!"

"I'm not ashamed to admit it. Wouldn't you be jealous of me?"

She snuggled close to him, put her lips against his ear. "I reckon. Let's go to bed, lover."

His voice grew hoarse. "I won't say no to that."

On the stairs she remembered Jason.

"Stopping the night with your mum," said Barry.

That was a relief to her. She danced into the bedroom and peeled the new dress over her head. Underneath it she wore only tights, black, see-through. Carol seldom wore a bra; she didn't need to, her breasts were as firm as the buds of large white flowers.

"You're going to marry me, aren't you, Carol?" he said, holding her, touching the warm, damp, creamy flesh. The bedlamp was on, the clean sheets turned back.

"Maybe," said Carol, teasing. "I reckon. Some day. You've got a pretty face and Christ knows you're a great stud."

"But you do love me?"

"Haven't I said?"

Barry had had quite a lot of girls before he met Carol but he might truthfully have said

61

that, before he made love to her, he had never made love. It was something different, it was something he hadn't known there could be. And it was not without its frightening side, for the passion he felt and its fulfillment brought him not so much satisfaction as awe. He lost himself in Carol and found something he couldn't name. He underwent a mystical experience such as he imagined you might feel under the influence of certain kinds of drugs of a curious mind-altering intensity, but this experience had no side-effects except to heighten his love.

When, afterwards, they composed themselves for sleep, Carol curled up against him and held his hand in her hand between her breasts. He was supremely happy then; he was happier than he had ever been in his life.

4

When she had tried to phone Mopsa again and there was still no answer, Benet walked back to James's room and found Ian Raeburn with him. Once more he had taken off his white coat so as not to create a phobia in James. He had his stethoscope held against the small, rapidly rising and falling chest.

"He seems to have got a secondary infection," he said, emerging from the glistening folds of the croupette. "It's not responding to the antibiotic. I'm sorry to disappoint you, but you won't have him home for a while yet."

Benet had known it, but it was still a blow to have it confirmed. She sat down on the bed and put one hand up to her forehead.

"You're not worried, are you?" he said.

"Oh, not about James, no. I know he's being looked after here. It's my mother. My mother's staying with me and she's not very well and she really shouldn't be left on her own."

But she had left her, and where was she now? He asked no questions about Mopsa. Perhaps he had already discerned it was mental instability she was talking about.

"Couldn't you find someone else for your mother to stay with? To take a load off your mind?"

The Fentons? Could she ring Constance Fenton and ask her to have Mopsa for a day or two? It would have to be fixed so that Mopsa didn't know it was a put-up job. What was the use of even thinking of such a thing when she didn't know where Mopsa was? Ian Raeburn was looking at her, not a doctor-to-patient's-mother look at all. Benet thought she recognized that look as of a man taking an interest in her as a woman. No man had done that for two-and-a-half years, there hadn't been the opportunity or, on her part, the wish for it. He was rather a personable man, she noticed for the first time — tall, thin, inclined to be but not markedly sickle-faced, his hair a reddish-blond. She wondered what he was going to say.

"You are *the* Benet Archdale, aren't you?"

"I suppose so. Yes, I am."

So much for his being interested in her as a woman. She almost laughed.

"I liked your book very much. It must be the worst cliché a writer hears when people say they don't have time for reading. I made time to read it and I hope my patients didn't suffer."

She was so warmed and delighted by what he said that it carried her for a few moments above her worries over Mopsa and James. It was somehow as gratifying as getting her first good review had been. She smiled with pleasure. How could she have been so foolish, so female in the worst possible way, as to fancy she would have preferred sexual attention to *that?*

"How do you come to know so much about India?"

"I was there for six months with James's father. He was planning a series of articles about an Indian mystic." She began telling him about Acharya the Learned One and his 40,000-mile walk.

A nurse came in to say he was wanted. Could he come now? Benet had forgotten to ask him if it would be all right for her to go home for an hour to look for Mopsa. But now she could see that this would in any case be impossible for her. James couldn't be left. He lay on his back, listlessly holding the tiger cub. His eyes were wide open, unblinking in their distress at the shallow, noisy breaths he was forced to take. At this time yesterday she had been in the children's playroom with him while he trundled a wheel-barrow full of bricks and drew on the black-board.

They said now that he had a virus infection. There was a drug to treat it but it was very new and still in use only in certain teaching hospitals. It might be thirty-six hours before James began to respond to the drug. After a while he cried to be taken out of the tent. Benet lay on the bed and held him against her, rocking him gently. It was wrong to keep him out of the tent. The more he was kept in there, even against his will, the more quickly he would recover. And he must recover soon, he must be up and about and playing by tomorrow so that she could put an end to the imprisonment that kept her from her responsibilities to Mopsa. Somehow she knew that one day he would see it that way too, he would share in the burden his mother and grandfather had. She imagined him a teenager, becoming responsible, and talking to him about his grandmother, teaching him to understand.

If Mopsa were still alive when James was a teenager. If she were still alive now. . . . He fell asleep, lying against her, and she put him gently back into the tent, hating that breathing of his, physically hurt by it. But he was sleeping and the vaporizer was steaming up the tent and the anti-viral drug had begun its work. She left him and went back down the corridor to the phone.

A young woman with a child on her lap was using it. The playroom door was open, so she went in and sat on one of the chairs for five-year-olds that were set round the table. There was a dollhouse in the playroom, a bookcase of books, boxes of toys, a cage with two gerbils in it, and, all over the walls, posters and drawings and collages. Paper cut-out witches riding up the window panes on paper cut-out broomsticks reminded her of Mopsa, though she needed no reminding. On the inside of the door a dozen or so children had written, or had had written for them, their names underneath the heading: *We have had our tonsils out*. The dominating collage was a piece of bizarrerie, the brainchild evidently of someone with a B.Ed. and flair, a mural whose paper base sheet filled half a wall.

Benet, when she had seen it the day before, had immediately dubbed it a tree of hands. She had liked it then; it had even made her smile. Now it seemed to her sinister, Daliesque, haunting, something about which one might have bad dreams. On the white paper base sheet had been drawn a tree with a straight brown trunk and branches and twigs, and all over the tree, on the branches, nestling among the twigs, protruding like fungus from the trunk, were paper hands. All were exactly the same shape, presumably cut out by individual children using a template of an open hand with the fingers spread slightly apart. And the children must have been allowed to decorate them as they pleased, for some were gloved, some tattooed, some ladies' hands with red nails and rings, one in mittens and another in mail, mostly white but some black or brown, one the stripped bone hand of a skeleton. And now to Benet all those hands seemed to be held upwards, to be straining upwards in silent supplication as if imploring mercy. They reached out from the tree begging for relief or freedom or perhaps for oblivion. They were horrible. There was an essentially mad quality about them. She found that she had got up from the low chair and gone close to the tree of hands to stare at it with fascinated repulsion. As soon as she realized how hypnotically she was staring, she pulled herself away and went out into the corridor to the phone, which was now free.

The repeated hollow ringing had a dull meaningless sound. Benet listened to the ringing; she let it ring on and on. An idea had come to her that Mopsa might simply have decided not to answer the phone, but she would have to if it rang long enough. She let it ring forty times, fifty times, until going on any longer became absurd.

The best that could have happened to Mopsa was that the change of scene, the new ways, being abandoned to look after herself, had been too much for her and she had wandered off in the manner of the Northampton escapade. Looking out at the clear hard blue sky and the racing wind, Benet hoped she hadn't done it in her nightgown. But that was the best. There were other options. The overdose of sleeping pills and the rest of the brandy or the sleeping pill ten minutes before she took a bath or the barricading of herself in one of the rooms with a can of paraffin and a box of matches. Surely there hadn't been any paraffin in the house, or matches either, for that matter. . . .

If she phoned the police, they would want her to go to the police station and fill in a "Missing Persons" form. Of course she could ask them to come here and collect her key and let themselves into the house in the Vale of Peace. But would they do that? She must try, that was all. As soon as Dr. Drew, the ear, nose, and throat specialist, had been to see James, she would go back down the corridor and phone the police.

He came at two, accompanied by Ian Raeburn and a couple of house officers. Dr. Drew was shortish, thick-set, wearing a brown tweed suit and gold-rimmed glasses. James began crying at the sight of the white coats, which the house officers hadn't remembered to take off. When he cried, it made him choke.

Drew was one of those doctors of the old school who never tell a patient or a patient's next-of-kin anything if they can help it. If they can't help it, they talk to them as if they were illiterate half-wits or simple-minded peasants. He said nothing at all to Benet, talked to Ian Raeburn in polysyllabic words of Greek etiology, and walked out leading his little procession. James put out his arms to be picked up but the nurse said he had to stay inside the croupette. The hectic flush had faded from his cheeks and he had become pale again. His pulse was taken again and Benet asked what it was.

Was there ever a nurse born who would answer that question? "He's not a very well little boy, are you, sweetheart?"

When they were alone again, Benet put her hand inside the tent for him to hold. Her hand held no interest for him. He let her take his, he suffered her touch. All his energies, all his will, seemed concentrated on maintaining his own breathing. Benet held his hand and came as close to him as she could. To leave him and phone the police, to leave him even for those few short minutes, she could see was out of the question. If Mopsa were wandering, she would be found, and if she were dead — well, she was dead and it was too late. Benet took James's wrist and began to count his pulse beats, looking at her watch. A hundred, a hundred and ten, twenty, forty, sixty, eighty. . . . He couldn't have a pulse rate of a hundred and eighty a minute; she must have counted wrong. His forehead was cool and dry, his temperature was normal.

So perhaps he was not so very ill. The first infection had passed off quickly, so it was very likely this secondary one would too. If only he wouldn't breathe in that awful way, puffing like a little weak, feverish, anxious bellows, the way she had never heard anyone breathe before. The door opened, the procession came back, Dr. Drew leading it.

"Now then, this is James, isn't it? And you are the mother? I'm going to have to do a little operation on James to relieve his breathing."

Benet stood up. She felt as if a heavy stone, for some while lodged in her throat, were slowly rolling down through her body.

"An operation?"

"Nothing too serious. Just to relieve the breathing. For a few days he'll be breathing through his neck instead of his nose and mouth."

The stone rolled out of her, leaving her with a sick, dry, bruised feeling. "Do you mean a tracheotomy?"

Dr. Drew looked at her as if she had no business to know the word, much less utter it. It was Ian Raeburn who answered.

"It will be a tracheotomy, yes. The larynx in a child of James's age is very narrow, only about four millimeters across. If you get a millimeter and a half swelling on one side and a millimeter and a half on the other, you haven't much space left to get air through. Now James's larynx is closing up and we aren't able to dilate it sufficiently with the ventilator."

A nurse came up with the form for her to sign consenting to the operation. Her hand wasn't very steady.

"Dr. Drew is very experienced," Ian Raeburn said. "Only a week ago he had to do a tracheotomy on a child with diphtheria, so he's had some recent practice."

"Can I be in the operating theater with him?"

"He'll be under anesthetic; he won't know whether you're there or not. Dr. Drew would say he doesn't want two patients on his hands."

It took her a moment to understand what he

meant. "You mean I might be sick or I might pass out?" She tried to smile. "It's possible. How does one know?"

He took her hand and held it. He held it tightly. "You can be just outside. It won't take long."

The nurse unzipped the tent and lifted James out. Benet put out her arms to him, was about to say she would carry him herself when the door swung open and Mopsa walked into the room. Benet stared at her, stunned. She looked serene and happy, years younger. Her hair was covered by a pink and red scarf and she wore a rather dashing bright-red coat.

"I've been trying to get you on the phone," Benet said. "I've been trying for hours."

"Have you really? I heard the phone ringing when I first woke up and then I thought it couldn't be you, you'd be too occupied with him to bother about me. So I thought I'd find your spare car keys and come down here and get your car and practice driving. And that's what I did. I've been doing it all morning. I'm quite an expert now."

Benet said nothing. It was better not. It was always best to control one's temper with Mopsa. She turned away, first managing a strained smile. Her mouth felt dry and there was a pain pressing on the bone above her eyes. James, his skin bluish, was taking a breath every second now. For one brief instant she thought of, she pictured, that tiny narrow passage, no thicker than a darning needle, a thread, the stem of a daisy, through which all the air for James's lungs and brain and heart must pass, and then she pushed the thought away with such force that she made a little sound, a stifled "Ah!" Mopsa looked at her. They were going up to the operating theater in the lift, all of them.

"Croup? He has to have an operation for croup? I can't believe it. There must be something they're not telling you."

Ian Raeburn said, "There is nothing more complicated than a swollen larynx."

Benet noticed a harsh, even ragged, edge to his voice she hadn't heard before. Did he too find Mopsa almost unbearably irritating? He went between the double doors into the theater and the nurse carrying James went with him. Dr. Drew was already there. Benet wondered if she should have insisted on going in there with James. He would be having the anesthetic now, though; it would soon be over.... There was a kind of waiting room here, comfortless like all waiting rooms, with armless chairs and unread magazines. Four floors higher than the children's ward, it overlooked a panorama of roofs and spires. The old workhouse windows showed a spread of the top of London with a horizon of Hampstead Heath, so green it hurt the eyes. The sunshine looked warm because it was so warm inside, a still, constant hospital heat, smelling faintly of limes.

"He's going to be all right, isn't he?" Mopsa said. "I mean he's not in danger?"

Benet felt sick. "As far as I know, this is just routine. I don't really know any more about it than you do."

"Mrs. Fenton's sister had one of those trach-whatever-they-are things done. She had cancer of the throat."

I must not hate my mother. . . .

"Your father phoned when I got back last night. He was very worried about me. He'd been phoning all the evening. I didn't say anything about James. I thought it best not to."

Pointless to argue about that. A waste of time even to attempt to find out why Mopsa thought it best not to. Benet picked up one of the magazines but the print was a black-and-white pattern, the illustrations meaningless juxtapositions of colors. She found herself thinking of the tree of hands, all the hands upraised, supplicating, praying.

The double doors opened and Ian Raeburn came out. He stood there for a moment. Benet jumped up, still holding the magazine, her nails going through the shiny paper. His face was as gray as James's had been. He took a step towards her, cleared his throat to find a voice, and began apologizing, saying he was sorry, they were all sorry, beyond measure sorry. He stopped and swallowed and told her James was dead.

The floor rose up and she fell forward in a faint.

5

Every other Saturday, Carol was allowed to have Ryan and Tanya home and sometimes they stayed overnight. It was usually Barry who went over to Four Winds at Alexandra Park to fetch them. Carol liked to have a lie-in on Saturdays. She had a bath every morning anyway, it was a rule of life with her, but on Saturdays she made a special ritual of it, putting avocado-and-wheatgerm bubble bath in the water and rubbing body lotion on herself afterwards, washing her hair and giving it a blow-dry and painting her nails. There wasn't a mark on Carol's body from having had three children. It was white and firm, with taut muscles. The only scar of any kind Carol had was a curious curved pit on her back just below the left shoulder blade. She told Barry how she had come by it.

"My dad did that when I was a kid He was always belting us up, me and Maureen. I reckon we deserved it, kids can be a real pain in the arse. He went a bit too far that time though didn't he? That was his belt buckle done that, cut right through to the bone."

Barry had been horribly shocked. He would have liked to have got hold of Knapwell, wherever he was — he had walked out on his family when Carol was ten — and cut him to his bones with a steel buckle. He loved Carol even more for her generosity of spirit, her ability to forgive. Though how she could say any child deserved that, he didn't understand. Carol didn't like children much, he was forced to admit that. It was her misfortune, really, that she had had three of her own. Sometimes Barry worried that she might not want any more when he and she were married.

The Isadoros were having Jason for the whole weekend and maybe they would keep him over the Monday. Beatie Isadoro's youngest was about his age, a khaki-skinned fat boy with red, kinky hair. Beatie was an Irishwoman from County Mayo, but her husband was Jamaican, and they had produced some interesting color combinations among their seven children. Because she had plenty of room in her two adjacent houses, Beatie ran a kind of unofficial nursery and the older girls were expected to help when they weren't at school. Beatie wasn't registered with the council as a childminder or anything like that, but that was rather an advantage since it meant she didn't charge as much as a registered childminder would have. To Barry the houses seemed full of kids, twenty or thirty of them, though there probably were not so many as that. He paid up, six pounds for the two days, which he thought exorbitant but Carol said was cheap at the price.

Karen and Stephanie and Nathan Isadoro were watching a film on the video, *The Texas Chainsaw Massacre*. Barry was squeamish and didn't look. There was a little fair-haired boy strapped in a stroller and screaming his head off. No one took any notice of him and the video viewers didn't even turn their heads. The Isadoro's home always had a curious smell about it — a mixture of pimento, babies' diapers, and hot chocolate.

Barry collected Tanya and Ryan and took them back to Summerskill Road. Carol was ready by then, wearing the tweed culottes Mrs. Fylemon had given her, and a cream wool polo-neck sweater that showed off her figure. She had made up her face in a very clever way so that it looked luminous and glowing and not really made up at all. Her hair was in soft floppy curls and a true natural gold. Barry knew for a fact she didn't tint it. They all went shopping at Brent Cross and had lunch in a hamburger place and then went to the cinema to see a space fantasy film. Barry organized all that. Before he had come to live with her, Carol often hadn't bothered to take the kids out, she had told him. It had all got on top of her and she hadn't been able to cope. He had more or less taken charge of the children insofar as they needed to be taken charge of. He thought they liked him.

Waiting for the bus home, Barry hoped people would look at them and think Carol was his wife and the kids his. He was young enough to hope that. Carol would catch sight of herself in shop windows and make a face because Ryan came nearly up to her shoulder, and she would say to Barry: "I must have been off my nut having him so young. Do you realize I could be a bloody grandmother before I'm forty?"

It made Barry laugh to think of Carol being a grandmother. He put his arms round her and started kissing her there in the street and forgot about the kids watching them.

Next day they had to go back to Four Winds. Tanya never wanted to go. She always screamed and stamped and sometimes she clung to Carol and had to be pried off. It made Barry wonder why they had to be in care if they were so happy in their home and with their mother.

"You can *ask* the council to take your kids into care, you know," Carol said. "It doesn't have to be that they take them away from you. I couldn't cope after Dave died. I had to do something about the kids. I was desperate."

Less than two years after Dave's death, she had Jason. Barry had never asked her much about that; he didn't really want to know, he preferred to be in ignorance. He could probably even have convinced himself that Jason was Dave's child. Only one day, when Carol was telling him off and calling him a little bastard, Iris said: "You didn't ought to call him that, Carol. It'd be one thing if he wasn't one but he is, isn't he?"

When they were married, Barry thought, they could apply to take the kids out of care. Carol could give up work too, or at least she could give up working in the wine bar. Barry was ambitious. He had a good job as cabinet-maker and carpenter in a two-man business operating from Delphi Road. Or it would be a good job when this recession came to an end and things picked up a bit. They'd be able to move out of Summerskill Road then and maybe buy a place somewhere and be a real family. Sometimes Barry had a dream that was really a vision, it was so clear and solid, of a room in their house in the future, all of them sitting round the table eating Christmas dinner, all happy and wearing paper hats and laughing, and Carol in a sea-blue dress with their new baby on her lap.

Barry knew it couldn't all be roses. There were the children, for one thing, they weren't his and they never could be, and that wasn't just nothing, that wasn't something you could just dismiss. And there was Dave, always there, always smiling out of his plastic frame. Carol might look about seventeen but she wasn't, she was eight years older than him and that much more experienced and sophisticated. And there was one other thing that troubled him sometimes.

He was a gentle person, a bit too soft, he sometimes thought. He couldn't stand seeing a kid get hurt. You had to smack them if they went too far, he knew that, but not hard and always on the leg or the behind. So when he saw Carol strike Tanya with a back-handed blow across the little girl's face and head, using all the strength of her arm, strike her again and again after that, wielding her arm like a tennis player, he saw red and pulled Carol off and hit her himself to calm her down. That was the only reason he did it, to calm her down, like he'd been told you had to with hysterical people. There was no passion in it for him, no uncontrolled violence. He took her by the arm, and because he was young and strong, he held her hard, and struck her a sharp blow across the face.

It was her reaction that troubled him. She stopped screaming at the child, she was quiet, and that was all right. It wasn't that. She cringed a little, but she didn't put her hand up to her face, where his blow must have stung. He had the curious sensation — and he didn't know how he knew this then, he had no real evidence for it — that she was waiting for him to hit her again, that she *wanted* him to hit her again. She stood there in front of him, vulnerable, exposed, her hands hanging a little way from her body, breathing shallowly, her lips parted, sweat on her skin, waiting for more.

Of course he hadn't hit her again. He had told her he was sorry, he loved her, he wouldn't hurt her, but he had to do it to stop her when she was out of control like that.

"I didn't mind," she said and she gave him a curious sidelong look, a look that was sly and also faintly irritable.

That night, when they made love, she tried

to get him to strike her. It was a while before he realized, he didn't know what she was doing, provoking him with her teeth and nails, jumping from the bed to run across the room and stand pressed against the wall with her arms covering her body, then kicking him when he came near, hissing at him, darting her head like a snake. She had to tell him because he didn't understand.

"Hit me, lover, hit me as hard as you can."

He couldn't. He forced himself to pat her face, tap her shoulders a little harder with his fingers. That wasn't what she wanted. She wanted blows, she wanted pain. Why? How could she? You would have thought she had suffered enough of that from that father of hers. Barry struck her. He beat her hard but only with his open hands. He hated it. He had to tell himself it wasn't Carol, it was someone he hated, and he shut his eyes to do it.

She never asked him for anything like that again. He tried to forget it, to put the memory of it out of his mind, and he nearly succeeded. Sometimes he thought that perhaps he had only dreamed he was beating Carol just as he had dreamed of seeing her strike Tanya. Since then, though, their love-making had been more strenuous, more savage really. Barry didn't mind that. It was a change to find a woman who preferred it that way. But then Carol wasn't like other women. She was one in a million. . . .

After the children went back, they were alone. They went to bed. That was what they always did when they got the chance. When there were people there who were just going or when they were soon to be rid of the kids, Barry always had this sense of mounting excitement and, looking at Carol, he knew she had it too. It was all they could do to wait till the door closed. And yet such was the pleasure of anticipation that sometimes he hoped leave-takings would be prolonged or children's departure delayed so that he might be kept a little longer on this pinnacle of breathless expectancy.

Once they were alone they fell into each other's arms, desperate by then for love, kissing and licking and biting and holding, laughing for no reason unless it was at their own thralldom. In that big bed with Carol there was no one else in the world for him, no one and nothing beyond the invisible dome that seemed to enclose the bed. Carol told him that once or twice, she had watched them in the big mirror, it excited her more, but he never had. His love was here and now, not even at that small remove.

They slept. They awoke in darkness, still embraced, damp and cool with their own and each other's sweat. Carol got up first and washed and put on the black and white zig-zag dress. She painted her face with brushes, big ones for the foundation and the blusher and small fine ones for the eyelids and brows and out-lining her lips. She combed her hair and wound the little tendril curls round her fingers. They were going out for a drink with Iris and Iris's Jerry.

A big full moon was up, bright as a flood-light, competing with the harsh yellow that overhung Winterside Down. They went by way of the Chinese bridge, where Barry's graf-fiti still proclaimed his love and where it was light enough to see their own faces reflected in the calm glistening water of the canal. Their faces gazed back at them as from a mirror in a room which is dark but nevertheless faintly lit by light showing through an open door. Carol dropped her cigarette stub into the water. It was just heavy enough to fracture their images and, for a brief moment, distort them so hor-ribly that Barry stepped back, removing his own. He had seen Carol's beautiful face shud-der and collapse and melt until it became a rubber mask representing some cartoon charac-ter, voracious, lecherous, and coarse, while his own was a gargoyle with bloated lips and rolling, wobbly eyes.

He put his arm round her, rubbed her cheek with his, and kissed her lips. Carol put sealant on her lips so that you could kiss a hundred times without the lipstick coming off. They held hands walking down Winterside Down past Maureen's house with its curtains like fancy white lace aprons and the polished car outside. Iris and Jerry were already in the Old Bulldog; they had probably been there since it opened. Jerry was a smallish, fattish, pink-faced man, a heavy drinker but showing few signs of this. He was never drunk. His eyes looked as if they had been stewed in brine; they had a soggy yet shriveled look, and his clothes smelled as if they had been rinsed out in gin. His favorite pastime next to going to the Old Bulldog was watching television with a tumbler of gin and water beside him.

People said Iris had once been even prettier than Carol. Barry found that hard to believe. She was fifty, thin as a skeleton and with long bony legs. She wore her dyed yellow hair shoulder-length to make herself look younger, and she always had very high-heeled sandals on, summer and winter, to show off her high insteps and her thin ankles. Barry guessed she had had a hell of a life with the brutish Knapwell. Yet she was always cheerful, carefree, making the best of a bad job. She smoked forty or fifty cigarettes a day and had a cough which turned her face purple with the strain. Iris couldn't get down to anything without a cigarette.

"Let me just get a fag on," she would say, or "I'll have to have a cig first."

Since Knapwell went, there had been (according to Carol) a man called Bill and one called Nobby, but they hadn't lasted long and Jerry had been Iris's companion for years now. He was a mysterious man who seldom spoke, showed no emotion, seemed to have no family of his own, and preserved towards everything but gin and the television a sublime indifference. Even his real name was a mystery, for he had begun to call himself Knapwell within a year of moving in with Iris. He worked for Thames Water, which made Barry laugh, considering Jerry's tastes. Iris had a job in a small garment factory housed in what used to be the old Prado cinema.

Barry had a Foster's and Carol a gin and tonic. She and Iris talked about childminding arrangements for the coming week. Maybe Maureen could be roped in for one day.

"You have to be joking," said Iris. "Maureen's

doing up her lounge. She's been all day stripping."

"I'll have to take on another evening at Kostas's, that's all," said Carol. "It's costing me a fortune."

Jerry got up. "You going to have the other half?" he said to Barry as if his lager hadn't been the entire contents of a can but out of a bottle or jug. Knowing what they would want, he didn't waste words on the women.

"Let me get a fag on," said Iris. She smoked in thoughtful silence. Carol talked about taking on extra work. That troubled Barry, who had been feeling happy and contented. He longed to earn more, make a lot of money, so that instead of working longer hours Carol could give up altogether and stay at home with the kids. "There's always the council," Iris said suddenly. "You could try them, see what they come up with."

Barry didn't know what she meant for a minute but he could see Carol did. She took one of her mother's cigarettes, lit it from Iris's.

"It may come to that. It just may."

"I'd like to do more myself," said Iris. "You know I'd bend over backwards to give you a helping hand. But if it means giving in my notice, I have to draw the line. I couldn't let Mr. Karim down, I've been there seven years or it will be come New Year, and he, like, relies on me, doesn't he, Jerry?" She didn't even wait for the confirmation. She knew it wouldn't come. "You'll have to play it by ear, I reckon," she said cheerfully. "Just go on from day to day."

"I couldn't cope before, and if I can't again, they'll have to step in."

Barry understood then. "It's not going to come to that," he said. He felt that his voice was firm, authoritative, manly, the ruling voice the women were waiting for. "We'll manage. *I'll* manage."

Carol had been holding his hand. She put her other arm round him, over his chest, and held his shoulder. She leaned her head against chest. "You're lovely," she said. "You're so strong. Isn't he lovely, Mum? He reminds me of Dave. Doesn't he remind you of Dave?"

"He does a bit," said Iris.

Barry knew there could be no higher praise. Feeling Carol's soft warmth against him, a thread of excitement moved in his body. He began to look forward to the evening's end, to their parting from Iris and Jerry on the pavement under the white moon, for him and Carol once more to be alone together.

6

The days blended into one another without demarcation, without date, without weather, almost without light or dark. She lay, then sat, in her bedroom, the big room in the very top of the house in the Vale of Peace. Mopsa brought her food on trays, but when she saw Benet didn't want to eat, could not eat, the food was replaced without demur by cups of tea, of instant coffee, and, in the evenings, their coming preceded by no inquiries, tumblers of brandy and water.

Life had stopped. At first, because what had happened was unbelievable, it could not have happened, little children in the 1980s do not die — because of that, there was only shock which stunned and numbed. For a good deal of the stunned, numbed phase, Benet had been kept in hospital herself. In that same state, armed with sleeping pills and tranquilizers, she had been sent home to her chaotic house and Mopsa. There the shock began to wear off. It was like the anesthetic wearing off after you have been to the dentist and the pain starts. Only no physical pain Benet had ever known was like this. Even when she was giving birth to James and had shouted out, her cries had been part pleasurable, compounded of effort and intent and joy as well as pain. Now she found herself holding both hands tight over her mouth to keep herself from screaming out her suffering. She sat or paced the room because when she lay down she could not keep from twisting and turning and digging her nails into the soft parts of herself. One afternoon she stuck a pin into her arm to have a different focus of pain.

Because she had no idea of time or its passing, it seemed to her that she had been a year in that room at the top of the house, tended by Mopsa, with Mopsa coming every hour to the door. Perhaps it had been no more than two days. She took a lot of barbiturates and a lot of Valium. The sleeping pills she put down the lavatory and pulled the flush on them. The oblivion they brought was not worth the awfulness of waking up, appreciating the light of morning, listening for the first morning sounds from James next door — and realizing there would be no morning sounds from him, there never would be. Never never never never never.

The Valium stopped her wanting to scream or wanting to put her hands over her mouth to stop the scream. It made her, while sitting quiet and still, consider in a low muddled way methods of suicide. She threw those pills away too. She stood by the window, high above the Vale of Peace, looking at a large white moon like a radiant pearl. Two years before, James had not existed, yet she was the same person she had been then, not much older, unchanged in appearance. She looked into the mirror and saw the same familiar, regular features, almond-shaped dark eyes, high cheekbones, full, folded lips. The dark-brown, longish, implacably straight hair was the same, and the clear, sallow skin. Why then could she not be as she had been before he came into her life? It was such a short time ago. How could she have been so unimaginably affected, so transformed, in less than two years by another person, and that person scarcely able to speak?

She did not want to think of him as a person, as himself, of the things he had done and said. That was the worst. That way unbearable panic lay, the kind of panic that comes from knowing one more step in that direction and the mind will break. She went downstairs, all the way down the long flight that wound through the middle of the house, and came into the basement room and sat in the window looking up at the garden wall and the street. She felt she would never go out there again. It was impossible to imagine going into the open air, walking, confronting other human beings.

Mopsa was at the kitchen end of the room, apparently making a cake. What was the use of it? Who would eat it? Mopsa wore an apron Benet had never seen before, a pink-and-white check gingham apron with straps that crossed over at the back. She had cleared every trace of James out of that room. The doors of the toy cupboard were closed. The highchair was gone. Upstairs Benet had closed her eyes while passing James's bedroom door on her way to the bathroom. She had been afraid it might be open and its contents showing. Now she knew she need not have bothered to close her eyes. Mopsa would have seen to those things. Dimly, through that timeless time up there, she had perceived that Mopsa had been seeing to things, had seen to everything.

The things she could not name even in her own thoughts. The registration of death. The undertakers. The funeral. To herself she named them, shivering long and inwardly, with a euphemism she had once despised: the formalities. Poor mad Mopsa, who was mad no longer, who had taken up this terrible challenge better than the sanest of women, had seen to...the formalities. Vaguely, up in that high room, that dark tower, Benet had been aware of Mopsa going out, of the car starting, of doors closing and opening, of Mopsa returning, of Mopsa *bustling*, busy in her recording angel, amanuensis, indispensable role. And now, having turned to look at her daughter and give her a small, sad, pitiful smile, she was making a cake, beating eggs with a hand whisk into a creamy concoction in a glass bowl.

Mopsa had been — wonderful. That was the word one always used of someone who did what she had done in this situation — wonderful. Often Benet had heard the phone ringing. Mopsa had answered it, though Benet never heard what she said. It rang now. Mopsa rested the whisk against the side of the bowl and went to the phone and took up the receiver. She spoke to Antonia as if they were old friends, though to Benet's knowledge they had never met. Her tone was chatty, pleasant, in no way tragic. Benet would certainly phone Antonia, Mopsa said. As soon as she was up and about and fit again, she would phone her. Yes, Mopsa would pass on the message.

Benet addressed the first question to her mother she had put since she had come home from the hospital. Her voice, which had been silent for so long, sounded strange to her. She walked over to Mopsa, her legs feeling weak as if she were convalescent.

"Have there been many phone calls?"

Mopsa was sifting flour through a sieve. She worked neatly, without spilling. "Half a dozen. Quite a few. I didn't count them."

"What have you told people?"

"I've told them you're not well enough to speak to anyone. I've told them you're confined to your bed and can't be expected to talk."

It was the correct response, it was the pre-scribed, ideal, merciful way for anyone in Mopsa's position to behave. Benet felt, creeping into the immense wide cold sea of her misery, a trickle of unease. She ignored it. It was nothing. Unease was nothing anymore, of no importance, and never would be.

"Have you spoken to Dad?"

"He's phoned every evening nearly." The complacent look touched the corners of Mopsa's mouth. "He sent you his love."

Poor Mopsa who was unstable, ill really, not like other women, other people's mothers. A line came into Benet's mind — there's a part of my heart that's sorry yet for thee. . . . She said quietly, "It must have been very hard for you to tell him."

The thin, custardy stuff was poured into the tin. Mopsa had an air of frowning concentration. When it was done she expelled her breath with a puffing sound. She was like a schoolgirl making a cake for a home economics exam. She was like someone who had never made a cake before. Perhaps she hadn't. Benet couldn't remember cakes in Mopsa's crazy days. She put the cake into the oven and slammed the door as if slamming it on something she would never return to, the final closing of the door of a house she was quitting for ever.

She turned to Benet, wiping clean hands down the front of her apron.

"Oh, I didn't tell him, Brigitte. I couldn't *tell* him. He doesn't ask, you see. It's an embarrassing subject for him. He might have got over it if things had been different. But since he doesn't ask, there's no point in telling him, is there?"

"He will have to know sometime."

Mopsa didn't say anything. She looked levelly into Benet's eyes. At that moment, in her apron, a smudge of flour on one cheek, her hair silvery-gold with pins fastening it, she was exactly like other people's mothers.

"Have you told anyone?" Benet said.

A hand went up and touched the flour smudge; a finger rubbed and flicked at it. Mopsa's stare shifted from Benet's face to the light switch on the far wall.

"You haven't told anyone at all, have you?"

Mopsa began to mumble. "I couldn't, Brigitte. I didn't want to upset myself. It's bad for me to be upset."

Benet shouted at her: "Who do you suppose is going to eat that bloody cake?"

She ran out of the room and up the stairs. Behind her she could hear Mopsa starting to snuffle and cry. She didn't go back. She went on up the stairs, a feeling of pressure on the top of her head, a throbbing behind her eyes. She passed the open door to Mopsa's bedroom and the photograph on Mopsa's bedside table caught her eyes. It was a photograph of Edward. What was Mopsa doing with a photograph of Edward? Benet hadn't even known she possessed one. It was a head and shoulders shot, rather fuzzy, enlarged from a snap.

She went up the last flight and entered James's bedroom. The cot was still there, and the bare mattress. Apart from that there was nothing to show the room had ever been occupied by a child. From the window you could see the row of pines behind the pond, the green strip of the Heath, a large white empty sky. She shut herself in her own bedroom. Should she tell Edward about James? Was there any point? He had seen him only once, and that when he was two days old. He had come into the hospital and seen him and Benet and not known what to say.

"You have utterly humiliated me" was what at last he did say. He had glanced at the child and looked away.

"It would have been better if you hadn't come, Edward. You shouldn't have come."

She felt as bad about things as he did, in her own way. It *had* been wrong to use him, it *had* been wrong to set out to have a child by him when she had no intention of marrying him or even continuing to live with him. But it had not seemed like that at the time; it had seemed the obvious thing, even the moral thing. With that decision made, with the baby in her arms, even then she had not been able to ignore Edward's beauty, a beauty that inevitably moved her. She had thought, why can't that alone be enough for me, though I know there is nothing else, scarcely anything else to him at all? The world was full of men bound to women for no more reason than that those women were beautiful. Why couldn't it be the other way round and be so for her?

He sat on the side of her bed and once more

asked her to marry him. She said no, no, she couldn't, please not to ask her again, it was impossible, they would both be unhappy, all three of them would be unhappy. He had got up and gone and she had never seen him again.

From somewhere or other, Mopsa had acquired a photograph of him and had it framed and put it by her bed. As if he were her son. Did it matter why? Did it matter, come to that, that Mopsa had not told anyone of James's death? Did anything matter?

Strangely, she remembered dreams she had had which she had not known were dreams at the time but had believed, while she was living through them, to be real. Suppose she were dreaming now and due to wake and find it had been the most terrible nightmare of her life but still only a nightmare, find that it was morning and James was waking up in the room next door?

She went back in there and looked at the neat bareness Mopsa had made of it. Grief fills up the room of my absent child, lies in his bed, walks up and down with me. . . .

Next morning there was a note from Mopsa on the hall table. *I have gone to lunch with Constance Fenton,* it read. *Back about four.* Mopsa hadn't bothered to leave her notes on other days. Or had she? There was a small wastepaper basket under the table. It was full of screwed-up pieces of paper. Benet began flattening them out. They were all notes from Mopsa, daily notes. *I have gone to the hospital. I have gone to the registrar. I have gone to see Sims & Wainwright.* Benet did not want even to guess who Sims & Wainwright might be. She was touched, she felt guilty, that Mopsa had written all those notes and, seeing them ignored, had patiently retrieved each one and thrown it away before writing the next.

She opened the door of the room that was to be her place to work in, the room Mopsa inevitably called the study. What else, after all, could you call it? When last she had been in there, books had lain in heaps all over the floor. Mopsa had put them away. She had put them on the shelves, in no sort of order, some of them even upside down. And into the roller of the typewriter she had inserted a clean fresh sheet of paper as if inviting Benet to begin work. Benet wondered it she would ever work again. The idea seemed grotesque. How could she, in her own devastation, ever hope to render on to paper the emotions of others?

In the basement room she sat by the window. A woman went by, then a child with a dog on a lead. Benet made herself a cup of tea for something to do and drank it to pass the time. The time until what? She wondered about the rest of her life, how she could contemplate it, what she could possibly do with it. After a while she put a coat on and went out of the house and onto the Heath. It was a cold day with a cold wind blowing. The air was as clear as if this were some remote unspoiled place on the edge of the world where pollution and fog and fouled atmosphere never came. Acres of London roofs and spires and towers lay below her clear as a painting on glass, only faintly blurred with blue at the horizon. Clouds lay over Highgate and the north, piled, frothy, full of rain. She went back.

The phone rang three or four times. She didn't answer it. She ate a very small piece of bread and butter and half an apple, afraid she would be sick if she ate any more. After that she went back to the window and sat there, wishing she hadn't thrown Ian Raeburn's sleeping pills away. She sat and thought about James because there was nothing and no one else to think about. She had written a book and had a child and now the child was dead and she would never write again. It seemed like something that was happening to someone else because it was too bad, too terrible to be happening to her. Yet it was. The someone else was she herself and it was all for her alone. . . .

Above her, beyond the window, against the pavement, she heard her own car draw up. She knew the sound of that car; Mopsa was back. It was only just gone three.

She didn't look. It was only Mopsa. The front door closed and footsteps sounded along the passage above her head. A moment ago Benet would have said that she could never wish passionately for anything again, but she found herself wishing passionately that Mopsa was not with her, that Mopsa would go home, that she might be alone. It was kind of Mopsa, it was motherly, it was what mothers did — but it would be better if Mopsa were gone. At least, if not better, it would somehow be less intensely, grindingly, awful.

Mopsa came into the room. She was holding a child by the hand, a small boy. She said rather stupidly: "Were you asleep, Brigitte? Did we wake you up?"

Benet had eyes only for the child. Apart from the girl walking the dog, this was the first child she had seen since James's death.

"Who is that?" she said. It was her voice but it sounded to her like someone else's, coming from another part of the room.

"Don't you like him?" Mopsa said.

That seemed to Benet one of the most absurd

remarks she had ever heard. It was meaningless, not something you asked in connection
with a child. A dog perhaps. . . .

"Who is he?"

Mopsa had begun to look frightened. The
wary, alert animal look was on her face. The
little boy still held on to her hand in a docile
way. He seemed about two or a little younger,
James's age perhaps, but big and sturdy. Under
a dirty red quilted jacket with a dirty white
nylon fur lining, he wore blue denim dungarees,
green-and-brown striped socks, and sandals of
red molded plastic. His hair was fair, almost
white, a thick thatch of it. He had bright shiny
red cheeks and big coarse features. You could
already see the man he would become in those
features, in the strong nose and the rather
bloated sore-looking lips. Benet thought him
the ugliest child she had ever seen.

"He's Barbara Lloyd's little boy," Mopsa
faltered.

"I don't know any Barbara Lloyd."

"Yes, you do, Brigitte. You'll remember
when I tell you. She's Barbara Fenton that
was, Constance's girl. She married a man called
Lloyd who's something in computers. They're
living with Constance until their house is
ready."

Then Benet did remember. Not so much

Barbara Fenton, whom she must once have known by sight if not to talk to, but the phone conversation she had had with Constance a thousand years ago, when things were all right, when she was happy, when James was alive and she was stupid enough to be worrying over Mopsa. Constance had told her then that she had her daughter and son-in-law and grandson staying with her.

"What's he doing here with you?"

"I said I'd mind him for them for a little while. They were desperate."

The little boy had freed himself from Mopsa's grasp. He took a step forward in this strange place, looked about him, then up at Benet, back at Mopsa, his face beginning to work in that open, unrestrained way children's faces do. His mouth made a square shape and he started to cry.

"Oh dear, oh dear," said Mopsa. "Oh dear." She was saying it to herself, not to him. She bent to pick him up. In her arms he struggled and screamed.

Benet went upstairs to her bedroom.

It was dark when she came down again. She hadn't heard the car go. She looked and saw that the car was still there. The boy was still there too, and he was sitting in James's highchair. Mopsa had given him a scrambled egg and fingers of bread and he was using his fingers and a spoon to eat it. Mopsa herself sat up at the table beside him with a cup of tea in front of her.

"Isn't it time you took him home?" Benet said.

She could tell her mother was hiding something. Mopsa was tense with nervousness.

"Why did you have to have him anyway?"

"Someone had to. The lady he was going to stay with, she's his godmother, she fell over and broke her leg."

"He's got a mother and father and grandmother, hasn't he?"

"They were booked up for this vacation. They've been booked up for weeks."

Benet felt cold. "Mother, what vacation? What do you mean?" She recalled something Mopsa had said. "What did you mean 'going to stay with him'?"

Mopsa faltered. "He was going to stay with his godmother."

"Yes, you said. Do you mean he's come to *stay* here?"

Mopsa bit her lip. She was half-smiling while she did so, like a naughty child. She gave Benet a sly, sidelong look. The boy was eating his egg and bread, concentrating, apparently enjoying his meal.

"Where does one go on vacation in November?"

"The Canary Islands," said Mopsa.

Closing her eyes, Benet held on to the arms of the chair. She counted to ten. She opened her eyes and said to Mopsa: "You mean they are going to the Canary Islands and you've said you'll look after this child while they're away? You've actually offered to do that? For how long? A week? A fortnight?"

A very small, low voice whispered out from Mopsa's faintly tremulous lips: "A week."

Benet stared at Mopsa uncomprehendingly. It was not possible. How could anyone be like Mopsa? She would never get used to her, never accept her, never understand. How could Mopsa do what she had done, attend to everything, be caring and attentive and responsible, yet also be so brutally insensitive and thoughtless and cruel? To bring that child here where her own daughter had lost her child, a child of the same age and sex! How could she? How could anyone?

I must not hate my mother. . . .

Mopsa had tied a table napkin round the boy's neck for a bib. She was pouring milk into a mug for him and he put out his hands for it, making what Benet thought of as idiot sounds, not words. This was just the sort of child that hefty lump Barbara Fenton would have had. Benet thought she could even trace Barbara's big prominent features in his. Suddenly Mopsa began to talk, to recount in detail the plight of Constance Fenton and the Lloyds, how when she had arrived they had resigned themselves to having to forgo their holiday and lose the advance payment they had made for a reduced-cost flight. Barbara had been crying. It was to have been the first vacation she had had in five years. What could Mopsa do? She hadn't wanted to do it, she dreaded the thought, but she owed it to Constance, Constance had been so good to her in the past. And she hadn't been thoughtless, she had known how Benet would feel. But Benet was mostly up in her own room, wasn't she? It was a big house. Benet need hardly see him. She, Mopsa, would do it all on her own, have him to sleep in the same room with her, take him out....

Benet got up. She looked through the A-K phone directory. Mrs. Constance Fenton, 55 Harper Lane, NW9.

"What are you doing, Brigitte?"

"Phoning Mrs. Fenton to tell her we're sorry but we're not a nursery, we don't board kids, and we're returning her grandson to her in half an hour." Her finger in the dial, the first digit spinning.

"They won't be there; they'll have gone by now."

"I don't believe you, Mother."

She listened to the bell ringing. She was beginning to be angry. It was, at any rate, a change of emotion, it was different. The bell went on ringing. No one was going to answer it. Mopsa was right, they had gone.

The boy had got down from the highchair, his face still sticky with food. He was moving about the room, looking for something to do. There was nothing for him to do; there were no toys, no books, crayons, no television. He went into the kitchen area and opened a cupboard door. He paused, looked over his shoulder to see if anyone was going to stop him, and, when he saw they weren't, began removing from the cupboard on to the floor a saucepan, another saucepan, a sieve, a colander.

"I'm going out," said Benet. "I'm going for a walk on the Heath."

"It's pitch dark, Brigitte. I'm sure it isn't safe."

"That's all right. Maybe I'll get murdered."

Normally she would have regretted saying anything that made Mopsa's face change like that, quiver like that, made her hands go up to cover her wobbly mouth. Now she didn't care. She went out into the cold clear night under a moon that had just begun to wane from the full.

7

It wasn't until the following day that she asked his name. He was a child, he was in her house, none of it was his fault. She was going to have to see him and occasionally — though as seldom as possible — be with him. She had to know what he was called.

Mopsa looked foolish. This was not her witch or her frightened hare but her village idiot look. She smiled slyly.

"I don't know."

They had been out, Mopsa and the boy. She had taken him somewhere in the car. The thought came to Benet that he must have sat in the back, in James's baby seat. At least she hadn't seen it. She had decided she wouldn't go out in daylight again. After dark, yes, but not by day. They had been shopping and brought back their purchases, whatever those might be, in shopping bags from Mothercare and Marks & Spencers. The boy whose name Mopsa said she didn't know was taking off his dirty red coat and trying to undo the fastenings on his sandals.

"Yes, you do," Benet said. She thought her voice sounded like that of a psychiatric nurse. "Of course you know his name."

Mopsa squatted down to help him with his sandals. She looked up at Benet in a very shifty, sly, covert way. She held her head on one side as if assessing what Benet's reaction would be to the reply she intended to make. Benet wondered what sort of people Constance Fenton and her daughter could be to entrust this child to Mopsa's care. She was mad. Couldn't they see that? She was unfit to be in charge of a child. And Constance Fenton knew it, she knew Mopsa's past. In the circumstances, should she, Benet, allow Mopsa to be responsible for him? That thought with all its implications was something else she wasn't going to think about.

"Come on, Mother. What is his name?"

"It's James."

Benet said no more. She went upstairs. She didn't cry. She hadn't cried since they told her James was dead. Crying seemed an inadequate thing, not big enough for a great grief.

They had had to tell her twice. Ian Raeburn told her and she had fainted, and when she came round he was there with a sister and they both had to tell her again. James had stopped breathing before the anesthetist reached him. His airway had closed. If Dr. Drew had perhaps taken this emergency measure — this very rare emergency measure in the case of a child — half an hour before, if they could have foretold that the ventilation would cease to work, if. . . if. . .

"You ought to sue them for negligence," Mopsa had said.

But there had been no negligence, only mischance, only a human error of timing. And what was she supposed to achieve by an action? Compensation for the loss of James? She wasn't poor, she didn't want money or consolation or revenge. She wanted James again and no one could give him to her.

She lay down on her bed, thinking of what Mopsa had said, of the stream of insensitive, outrageous things that issued from Mopsa's slyly smiling, tremulous mouth, telling herself not to hate her mother, to bear with her, to try to understand. How can the sane understand madness? She wondered now how on that first day she could have thought Mopsa "cured" or even improved.

After a while she sat up and reached for the phone and dialed Constance Fenton's number. By now she knew it by heart, she had dialed it so many times. Much of what Mopsa told her she refused to believe. Mopsa lied if there was the slightest risk of anything unpleasant for herself, attaching to the telling of the truth. Lies made life smooth, so she told them as a matter of course. Benet knew that that whole tale of the Fentons going to the Canaries might be a fabrication. Instead of a week in the Canaries, they might be spending three days in Blackpool. They might never have gone away at all. The phone rang and rang. They might have gone away — and this would be the worst — not for a week but a fortnight. The phone went on ringing and Benet put the receiver back.

She began to think that it was perhaps wrong to leave that child in Mopsa's charge. When she had first understood that the boy was there to stay, that he was staying in her house for a week, she had considered going away to a hotel. It would be an irresponsible thing to do. She couldn't leave Mopsa and she dared not leave a child alone with Mopsa. As much as his presence distressed her, she couldn't leave Mopsa to him and him to Mopsa. The memory was strong and sharp of herself and her small cousin locked in that dining room, of the barricaded door and windows, of the knives.

Mopsa had dressed the boy in new clothes. Or at least in different ones. They looked new. It took Benet aback rather to see that at his age he was still incontinent. She could see the bulky outline of a diaper through his blue velvet jumpsuit. He sat in the small wicker chair which had been James's and which, like the highchair, had been hidden by Mopsa until yesterday. What would be next? Benet found herself briefly standing aside in an unexpected cold detachment. James's toys? His clothes even? What would be next?

"Jay," he said. "Jay. Jay wants drink."

So he could talk and he was called James. Well, it was a popular enough, even common, name. Mopsa came bustling in with apple juice in a feeding bottle. At least that wasn't James's, she must have bought it. A feeding bottle was something he had never used. The same snobbery which had caused Benet to recoil from the sight of the diaper now made her look askance at this big child, this very masculine-looking, hefty boy, sucking on a teat.

When he had finished the bottle, he returned to his favorite pastime of turning out the kitchen cabinets. He worked with an air of intense concentration, frowning and keeping his lips firmly compressed as he brought out pots and pans and bowls and dishes, examining them, fitting one into another. He came upon an egg beater, turned the handle and made the whisk blades spin, and looked up at Mopsa with a broad grin of satisfaction.

"May I have one of your sleeping pills?" Benet said to Mopsa. "I threw mine away."

Mopsa said they were in her bedroom on the bedside table and Benet was to help herself. Benet found the bottle of Soneryl between a container of Mogadon and the inevitable Valium behind Edward's photograph. She looked at Edward's face and he looked resolutely away into the distance. The face was intelligent and sensitive as well as handsome. It looked as if its possessor would say and think and feel wonderful things. An air of mystery hung about it as it does over all still and silent beauty. The extraordinary thing was that there was so little underneath and what there had been was so commonplace. It hurt her to think that and to remember that it had taken her three years to find it out.

She took the Soneryl quite early and had a long night's sleep. Where the boy was sleeping she didn't inquire. The house had five bedrooms, and in any case there was a second bed in Mopsa's room. Mopsa took him out, and of course they must have used James's stroller. Next day she had to go back to the Royal Eastern Hospital for further tests, and Mopsa asked would Benet look after him just for three hours? Benet said she had seen that coming. Sooner or later she had known that would happen.

"I haven't much choice, have I?" she said.

Mopsa was looking tired. She had dark bags under her eyes and hollows in her cheeks. Looking after a two-year-old was too much for her. Benet wondered if she had been up in the night with the boy, if he woke up in the nights and cried and wanted his mother and Mopsa had to deal with that. She didn't feel much sympathy; she had no room for pitying anyone but herself.

The boy was back in his denim dungarees today and his red plastic sandals. Benet thought she had seldom seen a nastier kind of footwear for a child. It made her wonder afresh about Barbara Lloyd. The boy clambered up and down the staircases. He seemed safe enough on them, climbing up on all-fours and down by sliding on his bottom. He spoke very little, never for the mere pleasure of making comprehensible sounds. When he wanted something, really wanted it, he expressed himself in the third person, calling himself Jay. Never

James or Jim or Jem but always Jay. He was extraordinarily self-contained and somehow self-sufficient. Benet, hunched up in her window chair in the basement, had to acknowledge that he was no trouble.

She hadn't seen him for half an hour so she bestirred herself unwillingly and went upstairs to look for him. He had got into the study room. There he had found a half-empty box of heavy-weight A4 typing paper, had helped himself to a dozen sheets, and was drawing on them with a blue ink felt-tipped pen. He sat on the floor with the paper spread out in front of him and resting on the stiff cover of Benet's book of days. Whether this was by accident or design it was impossible to tell, but it was obviously a sensible thing to do. And although he had got a lot of ink on his hands and arms and dungarees and the book of days, the drawings he had made were not scribbles; they were recognizable drawings of things, of a man, a woman, a house, of something that looked like a bridge.

Benet picked up one of the pictures and looked closely at it. She was astonished. It seemed to her more like something one would expect of a six-year-old, and she remembered children's drawings on the wall of the playroom where the tree of hands poster was. The memory of sitting in that playroom came back to her with a pain so sharp that she dropped the drawing and turned away, clenching her hands.

The boy said, "Jay wants drink." He was trying to put the cap back on the felt-tipped pen.

Benet did it for him. She picked him up to carry him upstairs, performing this action almost without thinking, automatically. Immediately she wanted to drop him again, she had such a sensation of recoil. But she couldn't do that. He was a person, he had his feelings, and none of it was his fault. She took him upstairs and filled a bottle with apple juice for him.

When Mopsa came back, Benet suggested they should rent a television set. The boy had obviously been used to watching television. When he had first come, he had gone about the room looking for it in much the same way as Mopsa had on her first day. "It would make things easier for you," Benet said.

Why wasn't Mopsa more enthusiastic? Benet had expected a delighted response, even a suggestion that they should all go out in the car now and see about it. But there had been a worn look about Mopsa since her return, something almost frightened or hagridden, rather as if, while she was away, she had seen or heard something to dismay her. Yet whatever processes had been gone through at the Royal Eastern, they had been routine and simple and not alarming. She told Benet that and Benet believed her. She screwed up her face, making a muzzle mouth.

"You don't like television."

"I shan't watch it. You and your little charge can have it upstairs in the living room."

Still there was no show of enthusiasm and Benet said no more about it, but Mopsa must have taken to heart what she had said, for a television set appeared, was brought over from a rental center in Kilburn and installed in the living room. Its big, gray, pupil-less eye gleamed out from the corner among the still unpacked crates. At half-past four Mopsa and the boy ensconced themselves on the settee in front of it, Mopsa with a cup of tea and the boy with apple juice, this time in a cup. Benet went past the open door and looked at them, but did not go inside.

Afterwards she dated what happened from the arrival of the rented television set. That seemed to mark the demarcation line between the wretched limbo she had lived in and what came after it, a time of discovery, of stupefaction, of fear. Yet for a day or two after the television came, nothing much did happen, and it would all have happened whether the television had come or not.

For a long time, petrified as a cameo in her mind remained that glimpse, that picture, of skinny, witch-like, galvanic Mopsa, sitting on the edge of the sofa – the way she always sat, poised, tense, as if ready to spring – and the little boy beside her, as snug in stretchy velour as a puppy in its skin, his thumb in his mouth, his other hand firmly holding on to a thick blue pottery mug. This image later seemed to her the last image in a cycle of despair or one that stood at the beginning of being afraid.

That night she did without the Soneryl. She dreamed of the tree of hands. James and she were walking on the Heath. She was pushing the empty stroller and James was walking beside her, holding her hand. In life they had never been on the Heath together, but this was a dream. They crossed a clearing by a sandy path and came into another piece of woodland, sunlit, high summer, the trees in fresh green leaf except for one in the center of the copse which grew hands instead of leaves, red-nailed hands, gloved hands, hands of bone and hands of mail.

James was enraptured by the tree. He went up to it and put his arms round its trunk. He put his own hands up to touch its lowest hands. And Benet was reaching up to pick a hand for him, a lady's white hand with a diamond ring on it, when his crying penetrated the dream, broke into it, so that the tree grew faint, the sunshine faded and she was awake, out of bed, going to James.

Before she saw the empty room, she remembered. Her body twisted and clenched itself. She closed her eyes for a moment, made the necessary effort, and went down the top flight to where the crying was coming from, the small bedroom next to Mopsa's. The room was in darkness. The boy stopped crying when she put the light on and picked him up. Had he been used to light in his room? Had light perhaps come into where he slept from a street lamp?

She switched on the beside light, covering the shade with a folded blanket. Sucking his thumb, he fell asleep while she stood and watched him. She found now that she was really looking at him properly for the first time and found, too, that his face reminded her of someone. Who that someone was she didn't know. But this boy was very very like some adult person she knew or used to know. Generally speaking, the "prettier" the child, the less he or she resembles an adult. Prettiness, loveliness in very young children is equated not with any individuality of looks but with a conformity to an ideal babyhood appearance, a kind of amalgam of a Raphael cherub, Peter Pan, and a Mabel Lucy Atwell infant. The sleeping boy looked quite unlike any of these. His nose was straight and bold, his chin long, his mouth full and symmetrically curved, his eyebrows already marked in sweeping lines. You could see exactly what he would look like when he was grown-up, a craggy-faced fair man, tall and big-built, ugly till he smiled. Some grown man she knew must be like that, or some woman with thick lips and blonde hair. Not Constance Fenton. Barbara Lloyd? She didn't think so. She had forgotten what Barbara Lloyd looked like, but now Barbara's face came clearly back to her, moon-like with low forehead and tip-tilted nose. He probably looked like his father, whom she had never seen. There was something faulty in that reasoning. He reminded her of someone she *had* seen, someone she knew.

She knew she would get no more sleep. In a dressing gown, wrapped in a blanket, she sat in the study room among the books, the boy's remarkable drawings on her lap, willing the morning to come, yet not much wanting the morning. At about five she made herself tea.

It didn't start to get light until after seven-thirty. A cold gray twilight seemed to flow out of the cloudy sky, the green Heath, the pond, into the Vale of Peace. There had been no sign of the sun for many days. A boy was delivering newspapers from a canvas bag on his cycle handlebars. Benet watched him. It came to her that she hadn't seen a newspaper for several weeks.

The boy was due to go home on Wednesday and it was Sunday now. Benet went out by herself. She walked down to South End Green. The world was green and gray and chilly, a feeling in the air of November hopelessness, but at the same time it seemed unreal, spaced away from her at a remove and she encased in a capsule of glass. She found a news-agent's open and bought a Sunday paper but she didn't read it. She took it home and put it on the table in the basement room, but still she didn't read it and later on she couldn't find it. Mopsa must have removed it to her bedroom.

Mopsa and the boy watched television. Benet sat with them. She looked for things to do that she had never done with James, walking on the Heath, sitting in the study, watching television. Mopsa seemed uneasy to have her there — perhaps she was troubled by Benet's inconsistency in saying she would never watch television and then doing so — but she became easier once the news headlines had been read.

Brezhnev, the Soviet leader, had died and there was a lot about his funeral. Benet watched for about ten minutes. The boy was holding on to a white rabbit toy Mopsa must have bought him. He sat with his knees slightly apart, holding the rabbit but having absent-mindedly taken it from his mouth like a man with a cigar. His lips were compressed, his eyes fixed on the screen. Benet got up and went upstairs to the boy's room. There was nothing in the room but the bed he had been sleeping in and a small chest of drawers. She looked in those drawers, but they were as empty as when she had bought that chest a year before. No suitcase had been sent with him, none of the inevitable carrier bags and holdalls of clothes and toys and paraphernalia that accompany small children whenever they travel. On top of the chest lay the Mothercare and Marks & Spencers bags Mopsa had brought home. The clothes in them had been new. Mopsa had bought them. In one of the bags an unworn garment still remained, a pair of brown velour pants.

His clothes might be in Mopsa's room. Benet looked in Mopsa's room, but there were no children's clothes anywhere. The *Sunday Times* that she had bought that morning lay curiously tucked between the two pillows on Mopsa's bed. She wouldn't have seen it if she hadn't opened the drawer in the bedside table and, in doing so, very slightly rucked up the bed cover.

Holding the newspaper, she began to go downstairs again. The boy's screams broke out of silence; they sounded as if they came from someone terribly injured. Benet ran down the stairs, seeing Mopsa's eyes, remembering the barricaded room and the knives. She opened the living-room door. The television had been switched off and the boy stood in front of it, screaming in distress, weeping bitter tears, be-laboring the screen with his fists.

"What on earth is the matter?"

"He didn't like me turning off the TV."

"Why did you?" Benet had to shout above his crying. She picked him up and tried to soothe him. He sobbed and beat her shoulder.

Mopsa didn't answer her. She was wearing her defiant, insouciant, nothing-really-matters face.

"What a silly noise," she said to the boy. She got up and turned the television on again, changing the channel, Benet noticed, before she did so. A picture came, a pair of shire horses pulling a plough across a meadow.

The boy struggled to get down. He went up to the set and did a curious thing. He put his fingers on the screen and then round the rim of the screen as if he were trying to open it, to get inside or find something that was inside. That was what it looked like to Benet. He gave up the attempt after a moment or two and his oddly mature face, his little man's face, looked sad, resigned. He sat down again, not on the settee beside Mopsa but on the floor quite near to the television, and he leaned forward, watching it intently.

Benet took the newspaper downstairs. There was a lot in it about Leonid Brezhnev. She was more interested in reading the home news but she couldn't find much of that and presently she saw why not. Pages three and four were missing. Someone — Mopsa — had cut them out.

If Benet were to ask her why, she would deny it. And although she knew Mopsa must have done it, she could not absolutely prove it. It might have happened in the news-agent's — there was the remote possibility of that. The phone began to ring. She thought she had better answer it, though it was nearly two weeks since she had answered the phone. She had to start answering the phone again sometime. She had to start doing the explaining that Mopsa had failed to do, been afraid to do.

The voice was her father's. How was she? Was she recovering from the flu? How was Mopsa?

"She's fine," Benet said and she added with a vindictiveness she almost at once regretted, "She'll be home very soon."

He hadn't asked about James. What would she have said if he had? She had felt vindictive towards him because he hadn't asked about James, though James was dead, though she could not have answered if he had asked. He should have asked, it was cruel of him not to, crueler than he knew. She went up to fetch Mopsa. The boy was still sitting on the floor, still staring at the screen, though the horses were long gone and replaced by a man in sequins tangoing with a microphone.

Benet heard her mother talking on the phone like a young girl in a bygone time, the Twenties perhaps, who had been rung up by some undergraduate or subaltern she had met at a tennis party. She sounded coy, petulant, flirtatious. To this man she had been married to for thirty years, she was coquettish, provocative. She giggled and gave a little scream of delight. Benet put on her coat and tied a scarf round her head and went out. She walked up the hill and down Heath Street and looked at a display of *The Marriage Knot* in paperback in the window of the High Hill Bookshop. There was a photograph of herself set in the midst of the arrangement. It had been taken when she was pregnant, though there was no sign of this through the folds of the dark loose dress she wore.

Go back two and a half years, she told herself, go back to the time before he was conceived. Go back to that. He was never conceived, it never happened. You didn't say to Edward, I'm going to have a baby but that makes no difference, it still won't work, it doesn't change things. You said a straight goodbye: Edward, it's over; we've come to the end. There was no baby, there never was. Hadn't Edward himself said there couldn't be?

"I don't believe you, Benet. You're lying. You wouldn't do that, even you wouldn't do that. . . ."

She bought herself a cup of coffee and a sandwich and sat alone in a corner watching the people, who were all in couples or in groups. It was strange, she thought, that you couldn't see she was pregnant in that photograph. James had been born three months later but you couldn't see she was pregnant. It was almost an omen.

They were both in bed asleep when she got back. She looked for the missing pages from the *Sunday Times* but she couldn't find it. Probably it also was in Mopsa's room, under the mattress perhaps.

Mopsa had two more visits to pay to the Royal Eastern, one on Monday morning and one on Friday. She left the boy with Benet and went off at nine-thirty. Benet sat him on the floor in the basement with some sheets of paper in front of him and three felt-tipped pens in different colors. He was wearing the brown velour pants and a yellow jersey, and his bright pale yellow hair, newly washed, stood out like a sunburst. After a while he asked for a drink, calling himself Jay, or something that sounded more like Jye. What words he did speak were uttered in unmistakable cockney. Barbara Lloyd herself probably talked cockney, she had left school at sixteen, Benet thought unfairly. Who knew what sort of background this husband of hers came from? Benet knew she was being mean-spirited and snobbish. She couldn't help it. Despair and desperation had returned to her in the night and clung to her like heavy, wet clothes.

When the phone rang, she considered letting it ring. It wouldn't be her father this time. It would be Antonia or Chloe or Mary or Amyas Ireland or someone she would have to tell the truth to.

The boy looked round and said, "Phone ring."

"I know. I can hear it."

"Ring ring," said the boy and he made *brrr-*

brrr sounds like a telephone bell.

Benet picked up the receiver, steeling herself.

"Is that you, Benet? This is Constance Fenton. Is your mother all right?"

"Yes. Yes, I think so. Quite all right. She's out at the moment."

"Only she did make a half-promise to come over yesterday, and when she didn't come and didn't phone, we rather wondered. There's usually someone here to answer the phone. I'm out at work, of course, but Barbara's been here with Christopher...."

Benet interrupted her. Her throat had dried and her voice sounded thin. "I thought your grandson was called James."

"No, dear. Christopher. Christopher John after his father."

"My mother hasn't been over at all then?"

"We talked on the phone, that's all. But we should so like to see her so if you could ask her just to give us a ring when she has a moment...."

Benet murmured the necessary things. She felt curiously weak and enfeebled. She could see the boy busily drawing away in red felt-tip. Even from this distance you could recognize a woman, a dog, a tree. She said goodbye to Mrs. Fenton, put the receiver down, sat there with closed eyes, pushing her fingers through her hair.

Presently she got up and went upstairs and searched Mopsa's room. The missing newspaper page was probably with her in her handbag. Benet found the boy's red coat in his bedroom. Mopsa had evidently washed it. When she was halfway downstairs a curious idea came to her, not at all a rational idea, that he shouldn't wear it, that it marked him out, that it made him immediately recognizable. Whoever he was. She went all the way up to the top again and made herself open the cupboard door in James's room, where all his clothes were. She had bought him a duffle coat in thick brown tweed for the winter but he had never worn it. It had been on the large side to allow for growth. She made herself not think, merely do. She took the coat off its hanger and carried it downstairs and dressed the boy in it. They were going out to buy a paper. She didn't know how it would be, walking out with a child in a stroller, a boy the same age as James. It wouldn't kill her though, that was for sure, it wouldn't kill her and she had to know.

They came home simultaneously, she and the boy and Mopsa. Walking up the hill, she had already read the few paragraphs on an inside page of the newspaper. It wouldn't have been a few paragraphs last Thursday, she thought, it would have been the front-page lead.

Mopsa saw the paper under Benet's arm. She came warily up the path and the steps, picking her way, almost wincing, as if it were hot sand that she walked on instead of cold concrete. Benet held the door open for her, closed it quickly. She hadn't yet tried calling the boy by his real name.

"Jason," she said, "let me take your coat off, Jason."

Mopsa made a little sharp sound and covered her mouth. The boy gave Benet a radiant smile. He was Jason; the smile seemed to say at last they had cottoned on, at last they knew.

Benet took him into the living room. She knew Mopsa would follow her. She opened the paper and read aloud:

"Six days after the disappearance of Jason Stratford, aged one year and eleven months, from a street in Tottenham, north London, a police spokesman said today that hopes of his being found alive are weakening. Jason was last seen in a street of houses scheduled for demolition near the North-eastern Canal at Winterside Down, where he lived with his mother, Mrs. Carol Stratford, 28, and Barry Mahon, 20, a carpenter.

"Mrs. Stratford made an appeal for Jason's return after the evening news on BBC1 yesterday. 'Jason would never have gone willingly with anyone,' she said. 'He wasn't used to strangers.' "

"The street was Rudyard Gardens," Benet said to Mopsa. It struck her sickeningly that it was she who had shown Mopsa the place. "When you came back from the hospital last Wednesday I suppose you took my route. Where did you find him? In a garden? Outside a shop?"

"He was sitting on a wall," said Mopsa. She made her voice throb with pathos. She thrust her face close to Benet's, the lips quivering. "All by himself. Left on a wall. No one wanted him. Then a dog came along, one of those big black Dobermans, and it sniffed him and he was frightened. He was so frightened, he fell off the wall and I picked him up. No one was looking, no one saw me."

"Evidently not."

Mopsa put her hands on Benet. She laid trembling hands on her arms.

"I did it for you, Brigitte. I said I'd do anything in the world for you. You lost your boy so I got you another one. I got you another boy to make up for losing James."

8

Jason had been gone for twenty-four hours, more than that, before they knew he was missing. That was almost the worst thing about it for Barry, that he could have been lost like that because one set of people thought he was with another set and the other set thought he was home with Carol. It was the hardest thing to explain to the police. Barry had just explained it for the umpteenth time. He sat in a room in the police station watching Detective Superintendent Treddick and Detective Inspector Leatham gather up their papers and get up from the table and leave him alone for yet another half-hour "to think things over, to think if there's anything you want to add to what you've said."

There were things he wanted to add, but he knew better than that. He knew what sort of construction they would put on it.

"Get on all right with the boy, do you?" they had asked him in an artless way, almost a light and casual way, only nothing they said was casual.

"Of course I do. Fine," he had said.

And that was true. But it was also true that he had wanted to be rid of him. Not for ever, not in *that* way, but just so that he could be alone with Carol. He recalled now what a relief it had been when Iris said to leave Jason with her overnight and how he had welcomed Beatie Isadoro's laconic acceptance of another child in the house, provided the money was there. To have Carol to himself with no one shouting out or crying in the next room, that had made him go along with Carol in all her complex baby-minding arrangements. Sometimes his conscience had given him a twinge, though not enough of one to make him do anything about it. That day, for instance, when Karen Isadoro or her mother or Iris or whoever it had been lost Jason, his conscience had been awake and active then, telling him to do something. He had bludgeoned it asleep. Did that mean it was really he who was responsible for Jason's disappearance? He hoped not, he didn't want to think like that. He remembered the day very clearly. Last Wednesday.

Ken Thompson and he were putting fitted furniture into the bedroom of a flat near Page Green. Considering the neighborhood and the dilapidated state of the house, it didn't seem worthwhile, but who were they to question it? The money was good. These days, jobs like that were getting fewer and farther between. Too many do-it-yourself shops flourished and there were too many do-it-yourself magazines about. Soon after one o'clock, they were finished but for the mirror, which was still in the shop at Crouch End being cut to this fancy shape. Ken said they might as well knock off and he'd come back himself and do the mirror around four.

Foreseeing they had no more than a morning's work there, Barry had made up his mind, while doing a final bit of glasspapering, that he would take Jason out somewhere for the afternoon. He got on to the Isadoros from a phone box. It was Dylan, the second or third boy, who answered. Jason was just going out with Mum and Karen in the stroller. Barry said OK, thanks, they'd pick him up around six. He had that familiar feeling, a mixture of guilt and relief, we all experience when prevented from doing a tedious duty. Of course he could have insisted, he could have said he was coming straightaway to take Jason to the park or to the swings or whatever, but he didn't say that. He told himself Jason was better off playing with kids than trailing about in the cold with him. It *was* cold. It was a gloomy, gray November day with leaves blowing about everywhere and wet leaves underfoot.

Barry's free afternoon stretched before him. Carol didn't go to the wine bar on Wednesdays. She worked all day for Mrs. Fylemon and knocked off at five. He decided he would go and pick her up, not exactly call at the house but wait for her at the top of Fitzroy Park. That was more than three hours off. He crossed Green Lanes into Delphi Road and made his way to Lordship Avenue by way of the passage between Rudyard Gardens and Zimber Road, coming out at the big junction where the ABC Cinema was. The ABC was showing *The Dark Crystal,* and the first program was about to start. Barry liked films that frightened him, horror films that made the audience gasp and jump. He considered for a moment, then went in, buying himself twenty Marlboros on the way and being shown to the smokers' side of the auditorium.

While he was in there, Karen Isadoro, sent by her mother to buy a large loaf, must have been pushing Jason in the stroller over the pedestrian crossing in Lordship Avenue towards

Rudyard Gardens, towards the only baker's open around there on a Wednesday afternoon. And when Barry had been in there half an hour, Karen had wheeled Jason back again, the loaf in a plastic bag over the stroller handles, and in Brownswood Common Lane rung Iris's doorbell in Griffin Villas and found no one at home. Karen had revealed all this later, too many hours later, when with Leatham and the sergeant they had gone round to her school. Barry had known nothing of it at the time; it hadn't crossed his mind to think of it while watching *The Dark Crystal.*

By the time the film was halfway through, Karen had encountered her friend Debbie in Lordship Avenue. That Wednesday was the last day of their half-term vacation. Debbie wanted Karen to go round the shops with her and buy a funny card for her mum's birthday. They didn't want Jason. Besides, Karen's mother had said Mrs. Knapwell would have him, Mrs. Knapwell had promised to take over, she'd got enough on her plate without Carol Stratford's kid day in and day out. They phoned Iris. Or rather they phoned the lady upstairs at Griffin Villas, a Mrs. Love, because Iris hadn't got a phone. Iris was still out.

They took Jason into a news-agent's. At this time, Barry calculated he must have been lighting his fourth cigarette. They took Jason into a sweetshop that also sold cards and he started to cry, wanting sweets, bawling when they said they had no money for sweets. Debbie said she was going to try down Halepike Lane, there was a shop down there that sold funny cards, and she was going *now*. Karen could come if she wanted but she was to get rid of Jason first.

Barry wasn't clear quite what happened next. Who was? Everyone told conflicting stories, saving their own faces, trying to present themselves in the best possible light. Karen said she took Jason out of his stroller and sat him on a wall in Rudyard Gardens while she went into the phone box there to phone Iris. She took him out of the stroller because the greengrocer's Doberman was sniffing around and Jason was frightened of the dog, which couldn't reach him up on the wall. The trouble was, kids had broken the phone box inside and it didn't work. So she'd left Jason on the wall and run round the corner, just a little way round the corner, and phoned Iris from the call box outside the greengrocer's. She'd only got 10p — well, two 5p pieces — and Mrs. Love took so long about the message. . . .

Iris had never got it. She'd got a message from Mrs. Love, yes. Oh, there was no doubt about that. It was that Karen Isadoro had got

Jason. She'd gone up with Mrs. Love to talk to Karen on the phone and Karen had gone; the line was making a dial tone.

"I left a message," Karen said to the inspector. "I said to the lady upstairs to tell Jason's nan Jason was sitting on the wall in Rudyard and to pop down for him."

"Did you really give that message?" said Leatham. "You really and honestly told the lady that?"

Karen stuck to it for a moment or two and then she started crying. "I meant to," she mumbled.

"You meant to, but what did you really do?"

"I hadn't got no more money and the beeps went..."

She was only eight. What did they expect? What had *he* expected? Barry hadn't thought much about it. He hadn't thought about it at all sitting in the cinema, watching extraterrestrial reptilian creatures, smoking his sixth cigarette.

Soon after four, the program was over. Barry got a bus to Muswell Hill and another down the Archway Road. By then it was five to five, so he walked as fast as he could, running part of the way, up the steep hill into Highgate Village and through Pond Square into the Georgian grandeur of the Grove. At the entrance to Fitzroy Park, in the gateway that marks the private road, he waited for Carol. He lit a cigarette. He knew that when she appeared, having turned the bend in the lane which stretched before him, walking towards him between the high hedges, under the over-hanging branches of trees, he would experience that movement of the heart and constriction of the throat that was almost a feeling of sickness, though a pleasurable discomfort, that he had each time he went to meet her or saw her coming from a distance or even, coming over the Chinese bridge, saw the lights on in her house. It was new to him, he had never had it before he met her, but he recognized it as a symptom of being in love, just as a man who has never had a heart attack knows the pain in his left arm and the iron grip on his chest for what they are.

He had been there about ten minutes when she showed herself to him at the end of the tunnel of trees. His heart moved, seemed to turn over and then right itself with a small deli-cate lurch. She saw him and waved. He began to walk towards her. When they met, he put his arms on her shoulders and stood looking at her, her porcelain doll face sullen and rather tired, the gold coin curls clinging to a forehead on which the make-up had clogged and smeared.

He took the holdall she carried from her. He didn't like to see her with it. His mother said you could always tell a woman who went out cleaning by her shopping bag with overall and rubber gloves inside.

"I'm knackered," Carol said. "The Prince of Wales'll be opening. I'm dying for a drink."

"Have to make it a quick one then. We've got to fetch Jason. Beatie was a bit funny with me this morning about leaving him there so much."

Carol always flared. She didn't like criticism. Well, she wasn't alone in that, Barry thought.

"She can get stuffed. She gets paid for it, doesn't she? And bloody good money too. Anyway you needn't worry about Jason. I phoned Madame Isadoro from Mrs. F's and Mum's got him, had him since three, so we can have ourselves a ball, my dear." She took his arm and snuggled up. "Mrs. F's off to Tunisia for three weeks and she gave me my money in advance, fifty quid and a bonus for keeping the houseplants watered. How about that?" She produced and waved at him a fifty-pound note, crisp, greenish-gold.

"I've got money," Barry said stiffly. "I don't want you spending your money."

"We had a turn-out of some of her stuff. There was this Zandra Rhodes dress she said I could have. I've got it in that bag. It's something else again, I tell you. Fancy a woman her age thinking she could wear Zandra Rhodes."

And no doubt Beatie Isadoro genuinely had thought Jason was with Iris, had been safe with Iris since three. Karen thought so too. It wasn't the first time she had left Jason in the street at an appointed place for his grandmother to find him. As for Iris, she had scarcely thought about it at all. Why should she? For all she knew she had been let off the hook for the afternoon. Jason was with Karen, with Karen's family, in the security of the two overcrowded houses, and she had an unexpected free afternoon to unsqueeze her feet out of her high-heeled sandals, get a fag on, watch the TV, wait in peace for Jerry to come home and take her down to the Bulldog.

Barry and Carol had a drink in the Prince of Wales and then another, and then they went over to the Flask. Carol said Dennis Gordon had said something about this new club at Camden Lock called the Tenerife, a drinking club with a disco, you just paid a two-pound membership fee at the door, and she wouldn't mind trying it. They had something to eat in a steak house first, and Carol went into the Ladies' and changed into the dress, which was yellow and red and gold with a short skirt and huge balloon sleeves and a gold sash. She had her red boots on, so it looked good, it looked marvelous.

"You look great," said Barry. "I wish I'd thought to change, I feel a bit of a mess."

"You're OK," Carol said indifferently. With overt narcissism, she gazed into a mirror on the wall of the restaurant at her glittering image.

Barry had suggested they gave the lady upstairs at Iris's a ring and say where they were and they would be late back. He was glad now he'd suggested that, though sorry he hadn't pressed the point. Carol had dissuaded him, and dissuaded him easily. He was already anticipating dancing with her, their bodies pressed close among the other hot young bodies, the blue and violet and red lights winking and spotting, the music a hot, throbbing, heavy sound.

If he had got through to Iris, talked to Iris, what good would it have done? Jason was gone by then, gone three hours and more. And Iris would probably have been out anyway and he would have thought she was doing what he always suspected her of doing but had never probed into too deeply — putting Jason to bed with a drop of whisky in his bottle and leaving him to go down the pub with Jerry.

As it happened, it was nearly two before he and Carol got back. They had to have a taxi. Winterside Down was dead at that hour, though the yellow lamps on their stilts were still on, casting over the straight streets, the U-shaped streets, the single lonely tower and the sluggish strip of canal a phosphorescence that bleached everything to moonscape brown. The taxi wound through the chilly, yellowish-brown, treeless place. They had attempted to grow trees on Winterside Down, but somehow they had quickly died natural deaths or kids had destroyed them. Overhead the sky was a reddish, smoky ocher, uniform and starless. There had been a moon when they had been down at Camden Lock, but the moon had gone now. Two of the motorbike boys without their machines loitered on the corner of Summerskill and Dalton. Barry wondered if they ever went to bed; sometimes he wondered if they were real. The colors of their plumage were drained by the lamps, but he could tell from the shape and stance of them that they were Blue Hair and Hoopoe. They stared at the taxi. Their stillness and their silence, their apparently purposeless biding of time, gave them an air at once threatening and sinister.

Carol had had a lot to drink. She didn't want to wait to get upstairs. In the half-dark, streetlamp-lighted living room, without drawing the curtains, she pulled off the Zandra Rhodes dress and her tights and bra. Her body, which was very white, gleamed like marble. She lay on the settee and pulled Barry onto her and into her, her thighs and hips no longer marble-like but soft and moist as cream. There was sweat in pearls on her upper lip. Carol had a way of making little moans alternating with giggles when she made love. Barry held his mouth over hers to stop the rippling, gurgling laughter.

She fell asleep. He had lit cigarettes for them, but she was asleep. He picked her up and carried her to bed, and then he went down again to fetch the dress and put it on a hanger.

The first time the police really questioned him — the first time they had him down here at the station — they had wanted to know why, next morning, the Thursday morning, Barry hadn't gone straight round to Iris's to fetch Jason. Carol didn't work on Thursday mornings till she started at the wine bar at eleven. Why hadn't he fetched Jason — why, rather, hadn't he *tried* to fetch Jason — from Iris's and taken him home to his mother before he went to work? It was something he had often done in the past. The first time Inspector Leatham asked him, he simply said he didn't know why, he was late, he left it to Carol. This time, half an hour ago, he had admitted to having had the worst hangover of his life that Thursday morning. With hammering going on in his head, with a dry mouth, hardly able to walk upright, he had staggered downstairs, drunk water out of the cold tap. If he was going to make it to the house in Alexandra Park where Ken and he were due by nine sharp to start fitting bookshelves, he had to be out of Winterside Down by eight-twenty, and out he was, grimly walking with hunched shoulders, his aching eyes screwed up against the cold. The last thing that concerned him was where Jason was or who was going to look after him that day. He didn't think of Jason; he had forgotten him.

Coming home, he remembered. He remembered because, as a matter of course, he called in on Iris or Beatie's to collect him. On Thursdays Carol did a split shift at the wine bar, eleven-till-three and five-till-eleven — long, awful hours that Barry hated to think of her having to work.

"You hadn't seen the boy," Superintendent Treddick said to him, "for what? A day and a night and half a day? You hadn't seen him since about eight on the Wednesday morning?"

"We knew where he was." Barry realized what a stupid answer this was as soon as he had made it.

"That's just what you didn't know."

Iris lived in the bottom third of a very down-at-heel yellow brick Victorian house. There were three rooms and a kitchen with a bath in it, concealed most of the time by a wooden cover that doubled as a counter. Carol and Maureen had been born and brought up there. There they had been punched and kicked and scarred with belt buckles, and Maureen, who cried a lot, had had her arm broken. Barry had occasionally wondered what Iris had been doing while all this went on. Watching TV, probably, smoking, calculating that it couldn't go on forever, and thankful at least that it wasn't her taking the brunt of Knapwell's violence.

It was Jerry who had come to the door.

"Jason?" he said as if he had never heard the name before, as if it were a foreign name he might not be pronouncing properly.

Iris screeched from inside somewhere: "Who's that at the door, Jerry?" She came out, wiping her hands on a dishcloth. "Oh, no, Barry, you've made a mistake here. Come to the wrong shop. Those blackies have got him. I haven't had sight nor sound of him since — when was it? — Monday. Don't know ourselves, do we, Jerry, we've been so quiet."

Before he got to the Isadoros, Barry remembered being up in Highgate the night before and Carol saying she had phoned Beatie and

Beatie saying Jason was with Iris. But he went to the double house just the same. Carol could have made that up to keep him quiet. She wasn't untruthful but she wasn't above telling a while lie so as not to spoil his evening. He thought of her fondly, of those small human weaknesses that made her more lovable.

"Jason's with his nan, Barry." Beatie herself had come heavily to the door, the baby Kelly settled on her flabby hip as in a beanbag chair. "Karen handed him over to his nan like half-three yesterday."

That was when Barry had his first sensation of alarm. "She hasn't got him; I've just been there."

"Then he'll be with his auntie Maureen. Maybe that's what Karen did say, that he went to his auntie Maureen."

Jason had never stayed a night at Maureen's. Maureen didn't like children. She liked her home and presumably her husband, Ivan, to whom, though only twenty-six, she had been married for nine years. In those nine years, she had turned her three-story terrace house in Winterside Road into a little palace. She and Carol didn't look alike but you could see they were sisters. There was something similar in the roundness of face and the way their hair grew at their temples. But Maureen's hair was straight mouse and she was dowdy and flat-chested. She reminded Barry of a gerbil he had once seen in a children's zoo while taking Tanya and Ryan out one weekend.

"Carol shouldn't bloody have kids if she can't keep tabs on where they are," she said. She had been ironing and the place smelled of spray-on starch, breath-catching, too scented. "It's kids like hers get murdered; you see it on TV all the time."

"For God's sake..."

"Someone's got him, that's for sure. He's not taken a room somewhere on his own."

After that he had phoned Carol at the wine bar.

"I can't tell the fuzz I haven't seen him since yesterday morning. I can't do that, Barry. What'll they say to me? You know what a bunch of shits they are. I can't stick my neck out like that. What'll they do to me?"

"I don't know," said Barry, feeling young and useless.

"Oh, Dave, Dave," Carol shouted. "What did you have to die for? Why did you leave me all alone? Why aren't you here to look after me?"

Barry put his arms round her. "I'll look after you."

Dennis Gordon, the man who drove trucks

across Europe, had brought her home. When he wasn't in Turkey or Yugoslavia or somewhere or in the big house he had out Mill Hill way, he was generally to be found in the wine bar. Barry caught a glimpse of his car, a metallic-finish blue Rolls, an amazing car; but he hadn't come in. Carol had gone very pale. She kept licking her lips until most of the lipstick had come off. It took him a while to persuade her to go to the police — they *had* to go, what else? — but in the end she agreed, making a face, clenching her fists. She went upstairs to change and came down dressed in a gray flannel skirt and black sweater with a fawn-colored mac Barry hadn't seen before. It made her look older and, at the same time, more like Maureen's sister.

He hoped she would tell the police he was her fiancé but instead she said what she said to the neighbors at Winterside Down, that he rented her spare room. Barry didn't let himself be hurt by it. It was natural that Carol, who had had a hard life and a struggle, should want to appear respectable. No one believed her anyway, Barry thought tenderly. What man, looking at Carol, would believe she hadn't got a lover?

The search for Jason had begun that night. He had gone out with the search party himself.

The police had questioned them all – him, Carol, Iris, Beatie, Karen, and all the kids, everyone on the estate for all he knew. And sometime on the Friday morning, around eleven, Carol and he and Inspector Leatham and a young constable, a whole party of them, had stood in Rudyard Gardens at the Lordship Avenue end and been shown something lying among the rubble and rubbish and litter that filled a narrow strip of front garden behind a low wall. Barry recognized it at once. He had washed it himself the previous week after Maureen had said, looking at it in Jason's hand: "It's a disgrace, Carol, that animal, whatever it is. I reckon you ought to have that painlessly destroyed."

A woolly lamb but made of nylon. A Christmas present from Kostas' wife, Alkmini. Carol looked at the gray, shapeless object and started screaming.

"His lamb! That's Jason's lamb! He'd never have gone off on his own without his lamb!"

So they had known then, they had known for sure.

Superintendent Treddick didn't come back, nor did Inspector Leatham. They sent a sergeant in. The sergeant told Barry he could go now if he liked, and Barry walked home. Neither he nor Carol had been back to work yet. They had hardly been alone either. Iris and Jerry had been there most of the weekend and then there had been Maureen and Ivan and one neighbor after another. Carol had never got on with the Spicers next door, the people who kept the Old English rabbits Jason liked to look at through the fence, but Kath Spicer had been in and Carol had cried on her shoulder.

When he turned into Summerskill Road, he saw Dennis Gordon's Rolls parked outside the house, half-a-dozen children round it, and one of them, a Kupar, not an Isadoro, with a sharp-pointed nail at the ready. They looked at Barry in silence, as if Barry might tell them off, but he didn't say anything; it was no business of his if Dennis Gordon was daft enough to leave his flashy car unattended on council estates.

Dennis Gordon was in the house with Carol, and Kostas with them. Gordon had brought Carol an armful of red roses tied up in cellophane and silver ribbon. Kostas had brought her two bottles of Riesling. Though no more than forty, Kostas had a face like an old brown leather bag. His hair was jet-black, he had a brigand-like mustache, and he always wore very pale-colored suits. Today he was wearing a pale-yellow one with a black shirt. Dennis Gordon, whom Barry had often heard about

154

but never seen before, was a big, dark man with a very long chin and hooded eyes. He wore a signet ring that looked as if hewn out of a nugget of silver — though more probably a nugget of platinum or white gold. It was a knuckleduster of a ring, an ever-ready weapon, and Barry remembered Carol talking admiringly of his violent ways. He had the look of a thug, a gangster. There was some story that he had shot his first wife, only luckily for him she hadn't died of it but just divorced him.

When he saw Barry, Kostas acknowledged him by raising his dirty-looking hand an inch or two off his knee. Dennis Gordon looked round and away again. He was asking Carol if there was anything he could do for her, anything that was in his power he'd do; she only had to name it. It broke his heart thinking of her all alone.

Carol had probably told him that tale about having a lodger. "She's not alone," Barry said. "She's got me."

Dennis Gordon put his fist up to his mouth and bit on the great platinum lump. He ground his teeth on it for a bit. "I saw you on the TV," he said to Carol. "You were a real little cracker."

"D'you reckon?" Carol said, looking pleased.

"You've got what it takes, you're photogenic. They ought to give you a job at the studios."

Barry went out into the kitchen, looking for something to eat. He made himself a cup of tea but he didn't take it into the living room. Somehow you couldn't imagine those two drinking tea in a million years. Dennis Gordon looked the sort who'd subsist on undiluted brandy. When he went back in, they had gone and Iris had arrived. Iris never drank tea either. They opened the Riesling.

"They've started dragging the canal, I see," said Iris.

Carol looked at her wide-eyed. She clapped a hand up over her mouth. Barry could have killed Iris.

"It's routine," he said. "They told me it was just routine."

Iris lit a cigarette. Her fingers were yellow with nicotine; her eyebrows and the front bit of her hair were yellow with it. She showed her yellowed teeth when she stuck out her tongue to take a shred of tobacco off it. "There's swans sometimes on that canal. He was a little monkey; he used to want to get down to them swans."

She spoke as if Jason were dead. Barry sometimes wondered if she had any feelings, any affection or interest even or sorrow or anxiety. Perhaps all that sort of thing had been wrung out of her years ago in her married life. Carol took one of her cigarettes and lit it, and a little color came into her face. She hadn't bothered to put any make-up on, and Barry knew that was a sign of how she must be feeling. Her anxiety for Jason had distanced her from him, he felt, and they hadn't made love since that Wednesday night. She sat hunched up in the armchair in jeans and the gray sweater he didn't like, her arms wrapped round her knees. She looked about fifteen. They hadn't had a single photograph of Jason for the police. Carol had looked Leatham straight in the eye and said, "I haven't got money to spend on cameras," but the newspapers had made up for that by printing pictures they took of her. She had been on the front page of a couple of papers, looking like she looked now, young and unhappy and beautiful. Barry had kept those two front pages for the sake of the photos; he thought he would keep them forever.

Perhaps it would sound unfeeling. The truth was he was upset about Jason, of course he was, but his anxiety was for Carol. He couldn't honestly say he *loved* Jason; he wasn't gutworried like he would have been if he was Jason's own father. It was for Carol's sake he wanted him back. Looking from Iris to Carol and then at smiling Dave in his frame on the radiator shelf, Barry thought for the first time about Jason's father. He had to have a father, somebody had to be his father, he hadn't been made in a test tube by some anonymous donor and planted in Carol.

While Jason was with them, he had never thought about who his father might be, but now he was gone, it had begun to weigh on his mind. Somehow the identity of his father mattered more now. Sooner or later, and probably sooner, that man, whoever he was, would re-enter Carol's life because Jason was lost and Jason was his son as well as Carol's.

Barry made up his mind that he would ask Carol straight out who Jason's father was. He longed for Iris to go so that he could be alone with her.

9

Mopsa was proud of herself. "I took his stroller too. I folded it up and put it in the trunk of the car."

"Where is it now?"

"My goodness, it must still be there!"

"You really thought any child would do for me. I'd lost mine so any child would do for a substitute. Just get a new one. Like when your dog dies and you go out and buy a puppy."

"It wasn't any child," Mopsa protested. "I found you a little boy. I found you a fair-haired boy."

Benet said in a stifled, faint voice, "A puppy of the same breed. . . ."

Jason came over to her for her to take his coat off. James's coat. They were almost the same size as well as the same sex, the same type. Two Anglo-Saxon boys. She thought of Gregory's dictum — not Angles but angels. Mopsa, driving by, had found him on a wall. . . .

She took Jason's hand and went downstairs. Mopsa crept down after them. She really did creep, treading stealthily, as if to make one false move, one jarring noise, would bring Benet's wrath down upon her. She tip-toed across the kitchen, watching Benet out of the corner of her eye. Her face had a lopsided look today as if she had Bell's palsy or were purposely holding the cheek nearest to Benet rigid. Jason found his drawing things and a clean sheet of paper. Police over the whole country are searching for him, Benet thought; they suspect the worst; they think he's been assaulted, injured, murdered. And all the time he's been quietly here, drawing pictures, going for walks, watching television — watching his own mother on television and trying desperately to make the set disgorge her!

A timid hand was laid on her arm. Mopsa twisted her head round until it was touching her shoulder and looked up into Benet's face. It was a grotesque parody of a small child's appealing attitude. Mopsa's eyes were blurred and absolutely out of focus.

"I did it for you, Brigitte."

"I know. You said so." Benet tried to keep her voice gentle and even. I must not hate my mother.... "The question is whether I ring up the police and ask them to come and fetch him or whether I put him in the car and drive him down to the police station in Rosslyn Hill. The latter, I suppose. Explaining on the phone will be difficult, to say the least."

"You mustn't do that," Mopsa said. "You won't do that, will you?"

"Which? Not phone them or not take him?"

"You mustn't go to them at all. You know what they'll say, Brigitte." A look of ineffable foxy cunning spread over Mopsa's face. When she strained her face into these expressions, the tensed nostrils went white. She made her way over to Jason, who was sitting on the floor drawing, and pounced on him. She snatched him up in her arms, drawing paper and pen and all. He flinched as if he expected a blow. Mopsa clutched him, sitting him on her knee and holding him as if he were some sort of prop she needed for her act. "You know what they'll say, don't you? They'll say you stole him to make up for losing your own boy. It's a well-known thing, it's what bereaved women do. I've often seen about it in the papers. And you're famous – well, you're well known, people have heard of you. It'll be all over the papers that you kidnapped him."

Jason struggled off her lap. He made his

escape, first to the door and then he started up the stairs. Back to make another attempt on the television, Benet guessed.

"Yes, but I didn't," she said. "You did."

"They won't believe that."

"Of course they will. I shall tell them. I'm sorry but I haven't any choice. I shall have to tell them you have a — a history of mental illness and you took him."

What happened next made Benet glad Jason wasn't in the room to see it. Though he must have heard Mopsa's screams, he wasn't present. Mopsa simply opened her mouth as wide as it would go and let out screams of terrific volume. She stood there screaming into Benet's face. Benet had never seen or heard anything like it, and for a moment, beyond putting her hands up ineffectually to cover her ears, she couldn't move. She knew the prescribed thing was to strike a hysterical person in the face, but she couldn't bring herself to do this; her arm felt as weak as when one attempts to strike a blow in a dream.

"Mother, stop. Please stop. . . ."

Mopsa went on screaming. She fell on her knees and put her arms round Benet's legs, hugging her legs and screaming, breathily and hoarsely now as she exhausted herself. She crouched on the floor, scrabbling at Benet's shoes.

"Mother, I can't stand this. Please stop."

For a moment she had been afraid. The skin on the back of her neck had crept and she had felt the hairs standing erect on gooseflesh. She had been frightened of pathetic, crazed Mopsa. She bent down and got hold of Mopsa's shoulders and shook her, though without much result. Mopsa slithered out of her grasp and drummed her fists on the floor and shouted: "They'll commit me, they'll make you commit me, I'll be certified, I'll never come out, I'll die in there!"

"Of course they won't. I won't let them."

"You can't stop them if you tell. The court will do it. I'll be up in court and the court will make an order to put me away and I'll never come out again!"

Her voice rose once more to a scream. It was true, too. She knew all about it. What fool was it had said the mad don't know they're mad? She knew all right, and she knew what could happen. If she were convicted of abducting Jason Stratford, the court might well make a hospital order that she be detained for treatment and then restrict her later discharge.

"Please stop shouting, Mother."

Benet again tried to lift her up. Jason opened the door and stood there, looking in warily. It suddenly seemed to her unforgivable that they should detain him here and then subject him to this sort of thing. She picked him up and told him it was all right, there was nothing to be frightened of, though she was by no means sure if this were true. She wasn't sure if locking Mopsa up where she couldn't do any more damage and cause any more chaos might not be the best thing for everyone. Mopsa was sobbing now, crawling and groping to hoist herself up on a chair. She's my *mother*, Benet thought, I can't send my own mother into a madhouse. A feeling of helplessness took hold of her, a sense that she was inadequate to handle the situation Mopsa had got her into. And holding Jason like this, snuggled up against her, the way she had been used to holding her own child, was suddenly so repugnant she could have opened her arms with a violent rejecting gesture and dropped him.

Of course she didn't do that. She set him down as gently as she could. The urge that had come to her when Mopsa first brought him home now returned. Why shouldn't she leave, go off to a hotel somewhere, go abroad even, and leave them here together to sort out Mopsa's mess? Phone the police from an airport and tell them where Jason Stratford was?

Sitting on an upright chair, Mopsa wound her feet round its legs. She wrung her hands, pulling at her thumbs with her fingers.

"I haven't got a driving license."

"What does that mean?"

"It ran out before we went to live in Spain. I never got another one. Your father said it wasn't safe to let me drive." Mopsa's manner had become a spiteful little girl's. "They'll know I haven't got a license. I'll tell them I can't drive. They can see I'm not strong enough to lift a big boy like that." Because Benet wasn't answering she began to drum with her heels. "Why would I take him? I don't like children. I didn't take him, I didn't and you can't make me say I did! How dare you say I took him!"

Now, too late, Benet saw she should have said nothing to Mopsa about going to the police. She should simply have gone. Put Jason in the stroller, said she was going shopping, and gone. Speaking firmly to Mopsa, speaking one firm sentence to her, had this terrible effect. She had been told it had, though she had never actually seen it happen before.

"I didn't take him, Brigitte. I didn't."

"No, you didn't take him."

"You took him and tried to put the blame on me."

"All right," Benet said. "As you like, anything you say."

I must not hate my mother....

She fetched two Valium for Mopsa and made her a cup of coffee. Jason would be hungry even if she and Mopsa were not; he would want his lunch. She opened the oven door. There was a cake tin inside. A tide of hysteria welled up inside her when she saw it. Mopsa had put that cake in the oven last week but she had never turned the oven on. Little circles of pale-green mold grew on the uncooked but dry crust of the cake mixture. Benet ran the cold tap and threw water over her face. It kept the hysteria down; it left her with a slight headache. She had no idea what she was going to do, and she pushed it out of her mind, concentrating on lunch, on keeping Mopsa calm and the boy contented.

Jason had a sleep and then they all went out for a walk on the Heath. Benet realized that ever since she had known who Jason was she had been hourly expecting the police to phone or call, that while she was out she expected policemen to come out from behind bushes. The doorbell rang after they had been back about ten minutes and she knew it was going to be two policemen in plain clothes, an older one and a young one, one of whom would produce a warrant card and put a foot in the door. She braced herself, hesitating for a second before she opened the door. It was a Jehovah's

Witness, an ingratiating young woman with a child not much older than Jason.

Mopsa's day had exhausted her. She fell asleep on the settee watching television. The last item on the news was of police dragging the canal at Winterside Down. In the background Benet recognized the rears of the houses in Winterside Road where she and Mary and Antonia had lived and where Tom Woodhouse had lived next door. It seemed to mean nothing to Jason. If he recognized the Chinese bridge and the green lawns and the tower he gave no sign of it. He seemed more interested in Mopsa's sleep behavior. Her mouth was slightly open and every so often she gave a tiny, light snore. Jason was listening for the next snore, and when it came, he turned to Benet and laughed.

It was his bedtime. She supposed she would have to bathe him. Why not? Tomorrow morning she would take him to the police without telling Mopsa. She would take him to the police and explain about Mopsa as sensibly and rationally as she could, and whatever the consequences might be, they must both face them. As it was, she had probably done a dreadful thing in keeping Jason from his mother a day longer than was necessary. She thought of James and of how she would have felt.

Jason sat on her lap in the bathroom and she

took off his clothes. He was impatient to get into the water. She stripped off his vest. She caught her breath and made a little sharp sound.

Old bruises, yellowish now, covered the left side of his back, the side of his body, and the underside of his left arm. There was also on the arm an abraded area which had scabbed. Besides this, on his back, a little to the right of the spine, was a big scar not yet whitened, that looked as if made by some metal object with sharp edges, and above it, almost at the shoulder, reachable if the collar of a shirt or jumper were pulled down, the deep scar of a small circular burn. Once while living in the Winterside Road attic, Benet had seen a man, reputed to be on hard drugs, unaware of what he was doing, stub out a cigarette on the back of his own hand. It had made a mark like that.

She lifted him into the water. Unable to bear the sight of his back, she turned her face away. To her own astonishment, because what she had seen first shocked her, then filled her with undirected anger, tears came into her eyes and began to fall. A violent emotion of quite a different kind from grief had triggered off the crying that had to come. At last she was crying for James. She laid her arms on the edge of the washbasin and her head on her arms and cried.

Jason stood up, banging the water and shouting, "No, no, no, no!"

He hated her crying. She rubbed her face with a towel and took deep breaths. Watching her carefully, he waited until she was done with all that, until she was calm again, and then he picked the soap out of the soapdish and handed it gravely to her, indicating she was to wash him. His very mature face was intensely serious.

Up in the other bathroom were all James's bath toys. Washing Jason, going carefully over the bruised places, she supposed he would have enjoyed playing with them. But she would not have enjoyed seeing him play with them, to say the least, the very least. In spite of the bruises, the scarred back, her dislike of him returned. He had caused her so much trouble, it would be a relief to be rid of him, whatever the consequences of handing him over.

Early in the morning, before Jason and Mopsa were even awake for all she knew, she was down at Hampstead station buying a newspaper. The missing boy story rated three paragraphs on an inside page. Jason's mother was mentioned as having two other children, both in the care of the local authority. She had been a widow for nearly four years and for the past six months had been living with a man eight years her junior. There was nothing in the story about the possibility of murder or anyone being charged or even that it was expected someone would be charged.

She found a café open and sat in there drinking coffee and reading the paper and trying to eat toast. It reminded her of those distant days when she had lived in Winterside Road, had been trying to make it as a freelance journalist, before she met Edward, before James was dreamt of. Dropping into cafés had been a feature of her routineless life then, of her days in which time and its pressures were of minor significances. Yet she was not back in that time; she could not by any effort of the imagination unmake James.

When the High Hill Bookshop opened, she went in, found the sociology section, and bought two paperbacks called *The Battered Child Syndrome* and *The Endless Chain: Some Aspects of Child Abuse.* The feeling that the police were waiting for her, watching her, tailing her even, had gone. She felt quite different from the way she had yesterday; the world looked different. She had had a hideous dream she wanted to forget of Mopsa being made to confess by sadistic policemen who were torturing her with lighted cigarettes.

Back in the Vale of Peace, Jason was sitting on the floor of the basement room drawing something that might have been a woman with curly hair. Mopsa was working over the room with spray polish and a cloth, humming to herself Herbert's hymn about who sweeps a room but for Thy laws makes it and the action fine. She broke off to say, though quite calmly, that she and Jason had wondered where Benet was, they had been worried, they hadn't been able to think where she had got to.

What am I going to do? Benet thought. I need time to think. Am I going to see my mother in court — and incidentally the fact that she is *my* mother all over the papers? Am I going to see her *committed?* I don't think I can face the beginning of it, let alone see it through. She sat in the chair by the window and started reading *The Battered Child Syndrome.* The case histories were painful to read about and ultimately depressing. One of the longest and most detailed was one of a boy to whom the author, to conceal his true identity, had given the after all common name of James. Mopsa put her blue raincoat on and tied her head up in a scarf and took Jason out for a walk.

The phone rang twice, but Benet didn't answer it. It was impossible to imagine at the moment speaking to anyone in that world outside, to anyone not involved with Mopsa and Jason. Or to anyone — and that was everyone — who did not know about James.

"When were you thinking of going home?"

Mopsa looked injured. "I suppose you want to get rid of me."

"Do you have to go to the hospital again?"

"On Friday morning."

"Then if you went home on Saturday it might be the best thing. I don't want to be unkind, Mother; it isn't that I want to be rid of you. But we have to do something about this child. I thought, for your sake, I'd wait till you were on the plane and then I'd hand him over to the police. I'll wait until you've gone. And if it's any comfort to you, I'm pretty sure we don't have an extradition treaty with Spain. They couldn't get you back."

"But I've got a return ticket and it's for next Wednesday week."

"I'll buy you a seat on a plane for Saturday."

"Fancy having so much money you can just buy plane tickets like other people go on a bus," said Mopsa.

Benet made no answer to this. She was already marveling at her own behavior. How had it come about that yesterday morning there had been no doubt in her mind that Jason must immediately be returned to his family, while now she was calmly resolved on keeping him for a further four days? For Mopsa's sake? Yes, partly. To expose Mopsa to the humiliation, the terrors and indignities, of appearing in court would serve no useful purpose, social or moral. All it could ensure — and there was a good deal of doubt about this — was that Mopsa would receive treatment. But she was receiving treatment already, or plans were afoot for her to receive treatment. That was what those tests at the Royal Eastern were about. But there was another reason for not handing Jason back in haste.

All day yesterday, while reasoning with Mopsa, while trying to keep Mopsa calm and on an even keel, she had been thinking about Jason's mother, about that woman of precisely her own age who had appealed on television for the return of her son. It was wrong of her, monstrously cruel, to keep that woman in suspense an hour, a moment, longer. And then she had bathed Jason and seen his scars. Since then she had read those books. Was she going to send him back to that?

It was not so much Carol Stratford she had in mind when she thought along these lines as the twenty-year-old boyfriend. Barry Mahon. There were young stepfathers or mothers' young boyfriends in a good many of those case histories. Benet had a picture in her mind of Barry Mahon, a big, good-looking, probably illiterate hulk. Impatient with children. Given to violence. Maybe a drinker. She told herself she had no grounds for thinking this way — but didn't she have? Hadn't she seen the scar of a cigarette burn and the scar made by some metal tool?

She needed time to think. Those four days she had would give her time to think how she would handle Jason's return. Someone was going to have to be alerted about the violence that was being meted out to Jason. She wouldn't be in a very strong position to press this home, but somehow she was going to have to, so that he was never sent back to that.

Against Carol Stratford she hardened her heart. Mopsa was her concern, and she herself was her concern, and Jason, who had been a defenceless victim, but not Carol Stratford, whose other two children had already been taken away from her legally and justly. . . .

10

Jason had been missing for a week. Wednesday had come round again and he had been gone a whole week. Barry had to go back to work. It might have been different if Jason had been his own child or if he had been married to Carol. As it was, he had no real excuse for leaving Ken to carry on on his own. Jobs were hard to come by too. It wasn't that he thought Ken would replace him but rather that he might just decide he didn't need a partner at all.

He asked Carol to marry him. It wasn't the first time, more like the fourth or fifth. They weren't as close as they had been; he felt that, he felt as if she had slipped a little away from him since Jason went. For one thing, they hadn't made love. He didn't like to touch her; it seemed wrong unless she made it plain she wanted him. The doctor had given her sleep-

175

ing pills and she was asleep sometimes before he got into bed. Often he just sat there looking at her while she slept; for a whole hour he sat watching her and wondering what experiences were chronicled inside that sleeping brain under the soft, blonde baby curls. Thinking like that made him feel distanced from her, a stranger, as if she might wake up and ask him who he was and what he was doing in her bed-room.

That first evening he got home, he found her dressed up again and with make-up on. She looked like the Carol he had always known. There was nothing now to stop them going out in the evening. He thought that, but he didn't say it aloud; he was shocked that he might have said it. They had the take-out Turkish he had brought in with him and the wine he had bought on the way.

"Let's get married, Carol," he said. "If we make up our minds now we could be married in three weeks."

She didn't answer him. Slowly she lifted her shoulders in a shrug.

"If I was your husband, I could look after you better. I could shoulder some of this."

"I don't see what difference it makes," she said.

He tried to persuade her. After a bit she said

176

illogically, unfairly, "It's not your kid that's missing, that's probably got himself murdered."

She had hurt him. She could hurt him more easily than anyone. But he stood up to it. "As good as," he said. "It'd be as good as mine if we were married."

She made him a devastating reply that silenced him.

"A baby's part his mother and part his father and that's all there is to it. You can't alter that."

He quoted that back to her next day. It was early evening and they were on their way back from the doctor's. The doctor had said to come back and see him next week, and Carol had and got tranquilizers. She held on to his arm as they came into Winterside Down. It was the first time for a week she had touched him of her own volition and he was ashamed of feeling so happy.

"Do you really feel that, what you said, about the kids being part of their father? I mean, I expect you feel that about Dave, I can understand that. You'd sort of *see* Dave in Ryan and Tanya...."

"I could see Jason's father in him then, couldn't I?"

Why had he asked? Why had he mentioned it? Until he met Carol, Barry had not known how serenity and contentment and peace can be cut off by a dozen indifferently uttered words. But I've no right to be happy, he thought, and it's only fair she's punishing me for it. He felt her hand tighten on his arm and he thought she was reassuring him, even saying she was sorry. He turned his face to hers. She was looking ahead of her at Beatie Isadoro walking towards them with Kelly in the carriage and Karen and Dylan walking alongside.

Carol hadn't seen Beatie since Jason's disappearance. Beatie's vast shape in a pink slicker over a green smock over a brown striped dress or skirt took up most of the pavement.

"Get out of my way, you fat cow," said Carol.

Beatie stared at her. "The police come up to me today," she said. "I told them a thing or two about the marks I seen on that poor little baby you neglected."

Barry didn't know what she meant. His parents had almost pulled themselves up into the middle class, and among the middle-class attitudes he had grown up with was dread of a scene in public. But before he could get Carol away, she had thrown herself on Beatie, punching and scratching. Karen screamed. Barry got hold of Carol and pulled her away, but not before she had drawn blood on one of Beatie's slab-like cheeks and Beatie had kicked her on the shin. Carol sobbed in Barry's arms. People in front gardens and on doorsteps watched them, silent, impassive, curious. Most of them had not been born in England, but they had absorbed, sponge-like and as unconsciously as sponges, English ways of reacting. They watched with vague cold curiosity. Barry took Carol home, holding his arm round her as if she had been taken ill. On the corner of Shinwell Close, the motorbike boys stood, Hoopoe, Blue Hair, and the Jamaican that Barry had heard someone call Black Beauty. He felt their eyes following him and Carol, though he wouldn't look back.

It was lucky they had the tranquilizers. They calmed Carol down. She was talking on the phone to Alkmini at the wine bar when Iris called in with Maureen. They had brought the evening paper with an article in it about all the children in the London area who had gone missing and never been found in the past five years. Jason's disappearance had sparked it off. Jason's name was the first to be mentioned.

Maureen was comfortable only in her own home. She always looked uneasy in other people's houses. She didn't take off her coat. It was the same straight, up-and-down fawn raincoat she nearly always wore. She had flat brown shoes on and the hem of the raincoat came halfway down her thin calves. Her hair looked, Barry thought, as if she put her head under the tap, dragged the hair back as tight as it would go with a rubber band and let it dry that way. Although she wasn't a speedy person but rather slow and deliberate in her movements, she seemed unable to relax and wandered about the room picking things up as if looking for dust under them. She picked up Dave's photograph and studied it. You would have thought she had never seen it before.

Her voice had no rise and fall in it. It was low and lifeless.

"Why didn't you have an abortion?" she said to Carol.

Carol looked at her and asked her what she meant, her tone the slow, dangerous one Barry knew he would hate if it were ever directed against himself.

"You told me when Dave was alive you didn't want any more kids. You could have had an abortion."

"She was scared," said Iris with the air of someone giving what seems the most reasonable explanation while knowing it is not the true one. "You don't want to have those anesthetics if you can avoid it."

It was the tranquilizers, Barry thought, that stopped Carol flaring at Maureen. She had been looking at the paper in a listless way and now she laid it down.

"I'm going back to work tomorrow," she said. "I've got to go back sometime. It's no good hanging about here moping."

"That's true," Iris said. "That won't bring Jason back." Barry, in the recesses of his mind, feared Jason was dead and he knew Carol felt the same, but Iris spoke as if he were dead beyond a doubt. She even looked cheerfully matter-of-fact about it. She lit a cigarette.

"Work will take my mind off things," said Carol.

It came as a shock to Barry. Somehow he had thought of her never going back. They would find Jason, dead or alive, and she would have to either stay home getting over it or stay home to look after him. An awful, groundless, quite irrational thought came to him that perhaps they would never find Jason at all.

He didn't want Carol back in that wine bar with those men. But he wasn't her husband, he had no rights, he hadn't even a right to an opinion. How did those other, older, men deal with this kind of thing, how did they handle jealousy? How had Dave handled it? He liked her better made up and with her nails painted and wearing the stolen black-and-white dress, but so would those others like her better. She was safer, more securely his, in the old gray sweater.

They watched television after Iris and Maureen had gone, sitting side by side on the settee. He took her hand and she let him hold it. The program wasn't very compelling and his thoughts drifted away to Jason. He thought a lot about Jason, where he might be and what could have happened to him. Maureen's question had shocked him, though it was one he had sometimes dared to think about himself. Why hadn't Carol had an abortion? Was it because she had *loved* Jason's father?

He and Ken were working in the new office block just off Finchley High Road. It was a piece of luck that they wanted the managing director's office paneled out in sappele wood and an even greater piece of luck that Ken had got the job. It was no more than half an hour after they started that the police came for him. Not Treddick this time but Detective Inspector Leatham and another man called Sergeant Dowson. Ken didn't say anything when they said they'd come to take Barry away for a bit to help them with a line of investigation, but he looked incredulous.

In the car, no one said anything. Barry noticed that the driver took a route to the police station by way of Delphi Road and Rudyard Gardens, though it would have been easier and quicker to go straight down Lordship Avenue. Barry never used Rudyard Gardens. It was a depressing place, row after row of houses with their windows and doors sealed off under corrugated metal — a quite reasonable method of ensuring that squatters and meths drinkers and glue sniffers didn't get in, but sinister to look at for all that. And there was no chance of Jason or Jason's body being inside one of them. The previous weekend each one had been opened, the metal removed from back doors like lids from cans, and the squat, damp, mold-smelling room searched. The street had been cordoned off section by section for the search to be carried out, and Barry, who had been shopping in Lordship Avenue for Carol, joined the crowd that was watching.

"What would you say, Barry," Dowson said when they were in one of the interview rooms, "if I told you a young chap answering your description was seen in Rudyard Gardens last Wednesday afternoon?"

It was the first time they had called him by his first name. It was possible, though, that this was just Dowson's technique. Barry was astonished by the question. Who had seen him?

"It wasn't me. I never go down Rudyard

Gardens. In the car just now was the first time since I started living here."

Leatham pounced on that.

"You know where it is all right, then?"

Of course he did. Didn't it turn out of Lordship Avenue directly opposite Winterside Down? Hadn't he been there with Carol and the police and found Jason's lamb?

"What's wrong with it then that you don't use it? Rudyard Gardens would be your shortest way through to Green Lanes."

Barry knew why he didn't use it: because those boarded-up houses depressed him. Delphi Road or the canal bank, even though that passed nothing much but factories and warehouses and dumps, were more cheerful, but he didn't know how you explained that to men like Leatham and Dowson. They were both looking at him with impassive, interested eyes. How to tell them Rudyard Gardens was a dead street, lined with the corpses of houses, all with blinded eyes? They'll think I've been watching too many horror films, thought Barry, too much TV.

"It's depressing," he said. "No one about, nothing to look at. I like a bit of life."

"A bit of life?" Leatham made the phrase sound extreme and distasteful. Barry shrank awkwardly under his gaze, though he had nothing to feel awkward or guilty about.

"A bit of excitement, then," he said and had the feeling he had made matters worse.

They wouldn't leave it. They refused to understand. Barry's mother had labeled him "too sensitive" years ago and he knew he had a lot of imagination, a lot of sensitivity to atmosphere. He knew too that an ordinary working man isn't supposed to be sensitive. That was for the middle class or for women. They kept on asking him about Rudyard Gardens. How did he know it was depressing if he never went down it? Had he ever tried? Just once or twice maybe? It got to lunchtime, and he thought they would let him go, but they only took him into another interview room, where they left him with another detective constable who didn't speak a work to him but sat behind a desk filling in forms. After about half an hour, someone came in with lunch for him on a tray — a Cornish pasty, some biscuits and a bit of cheese in a packet, and a plastic cup of coffee.

Leatham returned with Dowson just when Barry was plucking up courage to tell the DC he was going, he couldn't hang about there all day.

"You were saying how you liked a bit of excitement," Leatham said as if there had been no break in the talk, as if a couple of hours hadn't passed by. "There can't have been much excitement living with Mrs. Stratford with a little kid about."

"He's a good kid," Barry said. They had been on this tack before. "He wasn't much trouble."

"Come on, Barry. A kid of under two not much trouble? I've got one of my own that age and I know just what trouble they are. And I'm used to it."

Barry said, "We couldn't have gone out in the evenings anyway. My — Carol — Mrs. Stratford works evenings."

"Thought she'd got herself a nice little unpaid nursemaid when she picked you, didn't she?"

Barry felt his face color. It was one of those blushes you feel rising in a tide, turning your face brick red. He touched his burning cheek. Leatham didn't seem to expect an answer. He was satisfied with Barry's blush. He sat back and folded his arms.

Dowson said, "I'll put my cards on the table, Barry. We're not trying to trick you. Honesty is the best policy, don't you think?"

It was at this point, Barry always remembered, that the penny dropped. At this moment, for the first time, he understood that they thought he had murdered Jason. All these questions, these and the questions they had asked him on previous occasions, were not to establish Jason's movements or learn where he might have gone or what he might have done, but to make him, Barry Mahon, confess to the murder of Carol's child. A sweat broke out on his body and turned cold on his skin. He was not afraid, only horribly shaken and indignant. He found he was gripping the table edge in front of him in the way a man might when he intends to overturn it.

They thought he had murdered Jason. He stared at the policemen in dazed silence.

"We haven't found Jason's body," Dowson was saying. "Maybe we never shall. Maybe when we do find it it'll be too — well, let's just say it'll be too late in the day for us to see what we know is on that body. Marks, Barry, bruises, scars."

Beatie Isadoro. Was that what she had meant when he and Carol met her in the street?

"Now Mr. Leatham just called you a nursemaid and I'm not going to press that, I'm not in this game to make you look a fool, but just for the convenience of the word, let's say you were a nurse to young Jason over the past five or six months. Nurses get aggravated sometimes, don't they? It gets too much for them like it does for anyone else and that's when they have to lash out."

"I never laid a finger on him," said Barry. "I never touched him." And nor had anyone else. He thought of Carol's sufferings at the hands of Knapwell. As if, after that, she would dream... "He used to fall about and hurt himself," he said. "He was always falling over and he fell off things. He gave himself a black eye back in the summer walking into a key sticking out of a door lock." Carol had told him that. He could remember the circumstances clearly, a heatwave it had been, and he and Carol going swimming up the council pool. He'd gone up the road to get milk and burgers and buns to make their lunch and when he'd got back Jason had had this swollen eye starting to go black even by then.

"Funny how some kids are accident-prone and some aren't," said Leatham. "Very funny. It's always the kids that get taken into care, they're the accident-prone ones, they're the ones that are a mess of cuts and bruises, not to mention broken limbs. Now I don't think either of my boys has ever had even a minor accident. Funny, isn't it? It makes you think."

It didn't make Barry think. He hadn't the faintest idea what Leatham was on about. He was smarting, burning, at the unspoken accusation against him. Dowson began asking again about his movements on the Wednesday afternoon and, truculently now, Barry told him all over again how he had been to the movies to see *The Dark Crystal*. He was prepared to tell them the plot of *The Dark Crystal* but they didn't want to know, they said he could have got that from seeing it the day before or the day after. Had he kept the half of his ticket?

"I didn't keep it. Why would I?"

"You tell us, Barry. It'd make a difference if you'd kept it."

Barry didn't answer.

"The way things are," said Leatham, "it looks a lot more likely you never went near the movies. You walked home down Rudyard Gardens and found Jason sitting on that wall. It wasn't the first time he'd been dumped in the street, was it? Dumped in the street waiting for some hit-or-miss arrangement for picking him up. It looks like you found him and put him in that chariot of his and wheeled him off somewhere. Home maybe. Or maybe you took him into Lordship Park or out on the Marshes. What did he do, Barry? Go too far? Rile you too far? Start screaming and wouldn't stop? Did you stop him, Barry, and did you go too far?"

He hadn't been afraid of them — ever. In his total innocence, he knew they couldn't touch him. But he was insulted. He felt himself withdraw into a bitter offended silence they perhaps interpreted as guilt. At five-thirty, they let him go. By that time, no doubt they too had had enough and wanted to get home themselves. He would have liked to have walked back to Winterside Down, but they insisted on taking him by car. Hoopoe and Black Beauty and the boy with the nose ring were in Bevan Square, bikes at rest round the *Advance of Man* sculpture. They watched the police car go by with Barry in it. Spicer was going in at his gate with a sack of rabbit food, weeds he'd pulled up out on the Marshes. In her widow-white sari, Lila Kupar, who no one ever spoke to and who never spoke to anyone, looked up from washing window sills and stared. It was never dark at Winterside Down; the overhead lamps brought it an endless unearthly daylight.

They could have put two and two together from the next day's papers anyway. There was a bit on the front page about a man being all day with the police helping them with their inquiries. That in itself wouldn't have been sufficient, but those reporters had made it follow quite a long account of how Mrs. Carol Stratford waited in suspense day after day in the home she shared with twenty-year-old Barry Mahon. Then it said the man helping with inquiries was twenty and local and in the building trade. Barry winced. He bought the paper at the news-agent's in Bevan Square and he sensed Mr. Mahmud, the news-agent, and his pretty daughter with her long black pigtail looking at him with more than usual interest.

The police came for him again next day. It was Saturday so he was at home. Down at the station they hammered at him again. Had the movie been crowded? Half-empty? Fewer people than that? How many people? Had he smoked? Which side of the theater had he sat on to smoke? Barry answered calmly; he didn't have to invent anything, and when he couldn't remember, he said he couldn't.

They asked him if he had a bad temper. What did he think about corporal punishment? Did he think it possible to discipline a child without smacking it? Barry answered mechanically. He was wondering why he should be the only man to suffer this inquisition. Perhaps he wasn't. Perhaps they had had Ivan, Maureen's husband, down here for questioning. Perhaps they had questioned Jerry and Louis Isadoro. They hadn't got into the papers, though, as helping police with their inquiries. . . .

There was another man in Jason's life. Had they asked about him? Had *they* asked Carol who he was? Barry wanted to shout at them:

Jason's got a father! He nearly did. In the end he couldn't bring himself to do it. Loyalty to Carol, respect for her, stopped him. He suffered their questions, answering yes or no, sometimes not answering at all. In a curious way he had lost interest, just as on the previous day he had lost fear.

This time he walked home. Carol had gone out. There was a note from her though, with two crosses on it for kisses, so he had to not mind. He tried to watch the Ipswich-Arsenal match on television but he couldn't concentrate, he could think of only one thing. A fellow-feeling for Dave – something he had never experienced before – made him pick up the framed photograph and study it closely. Dave looked so happy, smiling and carefree. Within a month of that picture being taken, he was dead, his body mashed in the wreckage of his truck on a Croatian mountainside. Barry found it hard to imagine him and Carol and Tanya and Ryan as one happy ordinary family. He didn't know why, but he couldn't imagine it, he couldn't see Carol as part of it. Yet Carol said that was how it had been. And afterwards? How had she handled her life afterwards?

The children had been taken into care and she had been on her own. Only Carol was too beautiful ever to be on her own for long. Who had taken Dave's place? Barry hardly knew what he would prefer, a hundred or just one. He found himself wondering what went on in her mind when she was alone, what thoughts were passing through her head now, for instance, as she walked somewhere window-shopping or sat in the pub having a drink with Iris and Jerry. If he thought of Jason so much, her mind must dwell on him all the time, on Jason himself as he had been last week and also on how he had been as a baby, at his birth, and in the months before his birth. It must be so. Barry knew that if he were a woman, if he were Carol, he would think like that. And how could he judge others' ways of thinking except from his own way? She must think of when she first knew she was going to have Jason and about the love-making that had led to that. Perhaps it was because she thought of those things that they were less close than they had been.

On an impulse, he wanted to make a good evening for them. He wanted to get her thoughts back for himself. Wine, he decided, and a chicken to roast, he could do that all right, he could make them a real meal for a change. Going out of Winterside Down by the main exit he saw no one he knew. It started to get dark very early, especially when the sky was overcast as it had been all day. People were coming back from the last shopping of the week, laden with heavy bags. By the time he came back with his own bags, the yellow lights had started to come on.

A half-formed idea of going to talk to Maureen brought him back this way, along Winterside Road to the canal and the Chinese bridge. He passed Maureen's house; he didn't even pause at the gate. She wouldn't tell him, she probably didn't know, and anyway it was Saturday and Ivan would be home. On the bridge a fresh sample of graffiti had appeared – *Chicken Rules* – done in red aerosol. Barry thought he ought to know what it meant, he was young enough, but for all that, he had grown too old to know. The canal water was very clear today. You could see the pebbles on the bottom, the cans and broken bottles.

The motorbike boys had assembled on the Winterside Down side of the bridge. They weren't supposed to take bikes on to the path, still less across the lawns, but who was going to stop them? There were deep tire marks in the green turf. Hoopoe was wearing new leathers of kingfisher blue.

One of them – he thought it was Nose Ring – called out something as he passed by. That was all. He came over the bridge and they didn't try to stop him, they didn't molest him in any way, but as he passed, Nose Ring called out something he couldn't catch. It was the first time that had happened. He knew they called out dirty things to girls and other sorts of things to pensioners. He had heard Blue Hair say to Mrs. Spicer when she wore her right trousers: "For an old woman you've got some good arse."

But that they should pick on him, who was of their own sex and generation – that narked him almost as much as the police getting at him. He hadn't caught what Nose Ring had said and he didn't want to know. But he felt their eyes on him as he walked the path between the green lawns. Their eyes, which in the past had glanced indifferently at him or even with tolerance, with acceptance, he now felt gazing with the same contempt he had noticed they had for others. Hard words and hard looks did you no harm, he thought. There were lights showing in the backs of the houses in Summerskill Road. He counted the houses from the end and in the eighth house, Carol's house, he saw the lights were on. She was home. He began to hurry.

The bikes revved up behind him and then, one by one, they coasted slowly past him, six of them, heavy, powerful bikes, all gliding with deliberate slowness past him along the path.

There were a lot of mirrors in the house. Carol was standing in front of the one in the hall doing something to her hair with what Barry thought of as a "kind of hairdresser's thing" she had plugged into the socket above the skirting board.

"What's that?" said Barry, standing behind her with his hands on her waist.

"A hot brush. It's for styling hair. I nicked it from one of those rip-off places up Brent Cross."

She smiled at him in the mirror. She was back to normal; she was as she used to be. From the feel of her, a softness yet somehow also a return to electric springiness, he knew they would make love that night, perhaps before tonight. Curling her hair, smiling, she let her body rest in his hands.

"I got a chicken," he said. "I got a couple of bottles of wine. You didn't want to go out, did you?"

She spoke dreamily, "Whatever you say, lover."

He took his bag of groceries into the kitchen. It made him smile to see how she hadn't been able to wait to try out her new gadget, all the more precious because she hadn't paid for it. That was typical of Carol, the old Carol, to rush in and drop her coat on the floor because she couldn't wait. He picked up the coat and her handbag and her gloves and a bag the hot brush had been in and took them upstairs. Out of the bundle of Carol's things, whether from coat pocket of half-open bag or carrier he didn't know, had fallen a slip of paper. It was a receipt for purchases from Boots and on the back of it was written: Terry, 5 Spring Close, Hampstead. The writing wasn't Carol's, it was a man's. While she was out, she had met a man she used to know and he had changed his address since last they saw one another. It was all quite clear to Barry. He knew now why she seemed excited and loving and the way she used to be.

This man wouldn't have written down his address and Carol wouldn't have accepted it if she didn't intend to see him again. Barry made up his mind to ask her about it, just as he would ask her who Jason's father was. An idea that was very unpleasant came to him — that they might be the same person.

He would ask her all this later, after they had made love. He put the slip of paper into her bag and closed the clasp.

BOOK II

11

Up until the last moment he hadn't believed Freda would go without him. All the odds and his own experience were against it. A woman of fifty-four lucky enough to get hold of a man of thirty-two doesn't go off on her own for an indefinite time to the Caribbean when she could easily afford to take him with her. She wasn't even a well-preserved fifty-four and she could never have been much to look at. It was humiliating to remember it now, but that last day, the day before she went, he had been waiting for her to surprise him with an air ticket.

They had been out to eat and were back in the house in Spring Close and Freda was packing her hand case.

"I suppose I'd better pack," he had said. He had never quite got used to taking and using things in this house as if they were his own.

"Can I have one of the brown cases?"

She had smiled. Something was making her happy. "Lambkins, we had all that out last week. I'm going alone and you're going to stay here and look after the house for me. I know you think I like surprising you, and I've fixed a few surprises in the past, but not this time. I'm sorry, lambkins."

"Don't call me that."

"I'm sorry, Terence. A month ago I said I was going to Martinique and would you stay here and look after the house for me, and you said you would. Did you really think I was playing games?"

"You needn't look so bloody happy about it."

"I'm looking forward to the sun and the sea, Terence. I'm looking forward to seeing old friends. Why shouldn't I be happy?"

The prospect of staying here on his own, a sort of caretaker, depressed him already. When she came downstairs, he had another go at persuading her. She wouldn't listen. It was as if she had gone already. Her body might be here but her heart and soul were up there in that Boeing 747, heading west.

They slept in different rooms that night, he on the futon on the lower level of the first floor. The house was an architect's extravaganza of split levels, teak wood, slate floors,

Italian ceramics, smoked glass. The windows had blinds instead of curtains, the carpets were shaggy black and the furniture purple leather and chrome. The two baths were the sunken kind, one in a marble grotto. A black marble woman with a hole instead of a head stood on the pillar at the foot of the stairs and a man with one leg throwing a sort of plate was poised on the edge of the stone houseplant garden in the hall.

Five more houses, the work of the same architect, were set at angles to each other, in this enclave off Christchurch Hill. The only pleasing thing about it as far as Terence (whose taste ran to eighteenth-century cottages) could see was the view from the penthouse "game room." Much of Hampstead Village could be seen from there and all the East Heath, the ponds and the woods and the Vale of Peace.

In the view, Terence saw not its beauty nor the wonder that so many ancient buildings and so much open space had been preserved, but the affluence it evinced. He saw it as a "rich" view, possibly the richest in the British Isles. Looking down on it, he could tell himself not that he had arrived but that he was well on his way to going places. It was all a far cry from his mother's council flat in Brownswood Common Lane, his room in Holloway, the furnished frame house he had shared with four other guys in Rockhampton working for the Queensland railways. It spoke of money, it was full of money.

"You're salivating," Freda had said to him not long ago.

"*What?*"

"You know what salivating means, lambkins. Your mouth waters. Whenever I talk about money, a little bead of saliva pops out of the corner of your mouth. Truly. I'm not kidding."

Was that why she had refused to marry him? Because he couldn't conceal his fondness for money? He couldn't help it; he'd been deprived all his life. What did she know, a widow who had never had to work, whose husband had given her every little thing she wanted?

In the morning when she left for Heathrow, he had gone down into the street with her, as far as Heath Street actually, to get her a taxi. There was no point in quarreling at this stage of the game. He had that horrible house to live in and he'd have to make the best of it. He even kissed her, not quite on the mouth though because she had painted her lips very glossily a fuchsia color to match her suit.

Just as last night, up till the last moment, he'd expected the presentation of that air ticket, so now, up till the last moment, he had awaited the wherewithal to carry him through till she came back. It couldn't be a power of attorney, he'd have had to sign something for that, gone with her to her bank maybe. But an open check or cash in notes. . . .

"Are you still on the dole, lambkins?"

"Don't call me that, Freda. Dole's stopped. I get the SS. Twenty-three pounds fifty a week if you want to know."

"Really?" she said. "As much as that? Benefit for the unemployed is really wonderful in this country, isn't it? I don't think people appreciate it."

He looked at her, at her puce-pink lips flapping. It was incredible, that sort of talk. It floored you.

"I asked about the dole," she said, "because I'm not going to give you any money. The rates are paid six months in advance, and the gas and electricity and phone I've fixed to get paid on a banker's order. Use the phone all you like, Terence, and don't be cold, will you?"

Empty-handed he made his way back to the house. He had made a mistake in taking it for granted she would marry him just because he was twenty-two years younger. Hangdog about it because the prospect didn't thrill him though the money did, he had said something, when next year came under discussion, about supposing they would be married by then. She had given him such a strange, long look and he could have sworn he saw tears come into her eyes. He had expected her to throw herself into his arms. And when she didn't but had slowly shook her head, he anticipated one of those wisecracks of hers he always found hard to take. But all she said was: "No, lambkins, I don't think so. I don't think that's ever going to be possible."

He felt ditched. Landed like a foolish fish and left gasping. Stuck with the house but without the means to make anything of it. He couldn't even afford to have a party. She was punishing him, he was well aware of that, punishing him in that light, half-laughing way of hers for the way he had enjoyed it when people took her for his mother, for the times he had left her to give some girl the runaround, for his impatience when she couldn't stand the pace of staying up till three, for his raised eyebrows when she had a hot flush.

Alone in the house, he resolved to waste no time. Whatever she had left around in the house he was going to have, whatever money there might be and whatever objects were salable. He began by making off across the black carpet — it was shiny and curly like the coat of a cocker spaniel — towards the bookshelves that filled the wall at the end of the upper-level bit. Here a picture window gave on to a paved court with raised flowerbeds and urns round which the six houses were built. Terence twisted the acorn-shaped knob on the bottom of the blind cord, dimmed the room, and made it impossible to see in.

Freda bought every new novel that made any sort of stir. Between *The Marriage Knot* by Benet Archdale and the latest Dick Francis was a Morris West in a striking cover. Terence knew that inside that cover was, in fact, a French dictionary with a cuboid hole cut out of the center of its pages, roughly from *devoir* to *mille.* Freda kept it as a spare cash store. Once when she didn't know he was watching her, he had seen her abstract a fifty-pound note. But now when he opened the book the cache was empty. He shook the pages in vain.

He went down the step and over the carpet and up the other side into the bit where there were red-painted girders in the peaked ceiling, three thin windows like the slits they shot arrows through in castles, and an indoor flower-bed built up with red bricks and full of castor oil plants and maidenhair fern. Against the wall opposite the windows was Freda's writing desk.

It would be locked and the key hidden somewhere. He looked around for the key, inside shiny, black, rhomboid vases, in the earth round the castor oil plants, under the carpet where it stopped at the polished wood steps. For once in his life, while he was living with Freda's predecessor, rehearsing for Freda so to speak, he had possessed a credit card. It had probably expired by now. Freda wouldn't settle his accounts for him so it had never been renewed. He had kept it because he had read that you can make yourself a gadget for opening simple locks with a piece of credit card. Eventually it was an old one of Freda's he found in her bedroom.

He had a look through the wardrobe and dressing table and vanitory drawers before he went down again. There was no money and she had put her jewelry in safe deposit somewhere. Would he dare to sell those silver-and-tortoise-shell-backed brushes, the property no doubt of the late John Howard Phipps? That was something to be thought about after he had been through the writing desk.

It took some opening. Whatever you were supposed to do with the credit card, he couldn't do it. In the end he used a cold chisel and a hammer and banged away until he heard the lock split. The front of the writing desk flopped down with a rattle. From the first he was sure he wasn't going to find any money. He went through the four small drawers and the two pigeon-holes. All the cash he found was an envelope with coins in it, two American quarters and a nickel, three hundred and fifty lire, and ten Swiss francs. Also in the drawer was a building society passbook which had once shown five thousand pounds in credit. The account had been closed a year before he met Freda and while her husband was still alive.

Underneath it lay a green cardboard National Savings Certificate book, the holder's name being that of Freda's late husband. There were two certificates of a hundred units inside, each purchased five years before for £500 and now worth, according to the small print on them, a total of £1400. The holder's name was on the back, along with the holder's card, which bore his signature.

Terence had never in his life done anything really criminal. He wouldn't have had the nerve to try shoplifting, for instance. Watching Carol Stratford nick that Pifco brush thing up at Brent Cross the other day, he had marveled at her courage, her cool confidence. She had slipped it off the shelf and into her carrier and tripped jauntily out of the shop to the corridor where he had preceded her. He was tempted to put his hand on her shoulder and say, "Excuse me, madam, but..." only he hadn't the heart. He had always been fond of Carol and she was having her share of trouble anyway with that business of her kid Jason.

So they had only had a bit of a natter over a coffee because the pubs weren't due to open for an hour. He had written down his address for her, though he didn't think he'd be there much longer. That was when he still thought Freda would take him with her. Carol was quite cheerful. She said she had been down at first but now she had a feeling Jason was all right and would come back.

"He'll turn up like a bad penny," she said.

It was Carol who, two or three years before, had suggested the Golders Green beat to him. She was a widow herself, though only about twenty-five. Her husband had been killed in a road accident a few weeks before Terence had met her and had left her with two children.

Carol had done quite a lot of mildly criminal things. She was a good shoplifter and had never been caught. At one point she had somehow managed to collect dole in her maiden name while having two jobs in her married one. She was always full of ideas for making money without working or for getting things on the fiddle, and most of them were too fantastic to be taken seriously. But this one was different. She said she would do it herself, only she was the wrong sex.

What he was to do was hang around Golders Green Crematorium every day and keep an eye on the funeral parties that came in. It would be best to have a dark suit on and then no one would know he wasn't just another mourner. He was to look out for the widows until he spotted a likely one. She must be well-off — well-left, in fact — not too old, preferably childless. He would soon get the hang of it, Carol said, and she was right. Terence hung around ten funerals, all men's, and then he found his prey. Again Carol had been right when she had said all the younger ones that died would be men. He was a chance bystander at two women's funerals but in each case the woman had been over eighty.

Quite skillful by this time at diagnosing wealth and a measure of solitude, Terence latched on to Jessica Mason. She attended her husband's funeral in a sable coat. Terence introduced himself to her afterwards while they were admiring the floral tributes. He said her husband and his father had once been close friends. There were only four other people there, the late Roy Mason not having apparently been a popular man. Terence found out where

Jessica lived, was impressed by the address, and phoned her a week later. By the time Roy Mason had been dead a month Terence was living with her in her neo-Tudor detached house on the Cricklewood-Golders Green border.

There was nothing wrong with Jessica. She was only forty-five. She had no children. She had even more money than he had guessed at — but she was the most possessive, demanding person he had ever known. When she found out he was still sometimes seeing Carol, she threatened him with a kitchen knife. She was going to kill him and then herself. Terence stopped seeing Carol and stayed on for a few months more, spending freely on the Barclay-card Jessica had got for him and practicing forging her signature. He became expert at this but just the same never quite got up the courage to use it as a means, for instance, of drawing a check on Jessica's account.

One afternoon while she was out visiting a friend's mother in hospital, Terence left. He simply walked out, taking with him all the clothes she had bought him in one of her suit-cases. On the doorstep he hesitated and thought of going back and helping himself to some pieces of her jewelry and a knick-knack or two. Again his nerve failed him. He wasn't very brave and he knew it. Whenever he did anything of that sort — such as the time he took Jessica's wallet out of her handbag and persuaded her that the loss had occurred in the crowds at Oxford Circus tube station — he was liable to feel deathly sick and wake in the night in a cold sweat. Terence knew all about the native hue of resolution being sicklied o'er by the pale cast of thought. He left the jewelry and the knick-knacks behind and went off to his new home in Spring Close. By that time, as a result of further reconnaissance at Golders Green, he had met, ingratiated himself with, and already made love to Freda Phipps.

Looking now at her late husband's National Savings book, Terence reflected that Freda could have cashed those certificates as soon as John Howard's will was proved. Sooner, probably. She had been his sole heir. She just hadn't bothered; she had enough without that £1400. Terence still couldn't help feeling bitter about things like that.

He thought he might as well have a look through the stack of papers on the two shelves of the writing desk. Nothing but reports of company meetings on the top one. What had she kept that lot for? Underneath was a copy of John Howard's will, and one each of his birth certificate and death certificate. Freda's birth certificate and her marriage certificate were there too, along with some car and house insurance stuff and other documents. Useless. About as much use to him as those company meeting reports.

Terence found himself a sheet of writing paper and began to practice copying John Howard Phipps's signature. He wrote John H. Phipps a dozen times and then tried doing it faster and with a fine flourish. The trouble would be when he had to do it under the eye of some post office clerk.

Much later in the day, when he had been up to the King of Bohemia for a drink and had cooked himself baked beans and a fried egg for lunch and thought about trying the Golders Green circuit again, he sat down once more at the desk, pen in hand. After all, cashing those fourteen hundred pounds' worth of savings certificates was his only hope, any idea of ringing up and returning to Jessica not being realistic.

How old had John Phipps been? Her late husband's age was not a subject Freda had ever brought up. There was nothing as far as he could see on or in the green book to indicate the holder's age, unless there was some coded mark somewhere. It wouldn't do to present this in the post office and then find out the holder was supposed to be sixty-five. He knew he was experiencing one of his failures of nerve.

"The trouble with you, Terence Wand," Carol had once said to him, "is that you've got a well-known stomach complaint. No guts."

Anyway, the man's birth certificate was in among that lot somewhere. He pulled out the brown envelope in which he thought the certificates were contained and saw he had got the wrong one. This one was labeled: *Title Deeds of 5 Spring Close, Hampstead.*

Terence looked at the envelope. He slid the documents out. The deeds, on thick, lined, parchment-like paper, listed only one owner of this house, which had been purchased five years previously. Ownership might have been in the joint names of John Howard Phipps and Freda Phipps or Freda might have had the title altered when she inherited, but neither of these contingencies were so. John Howard, though deceased, still appeared as the sole owner.

The magnitude of the idea which came into Terence's mind and exploded there, the sheer daring of criminality of it, made him feel sick with fear. He felt the sweat start in pinhead drops on his forehead. Cashing someone else's National Savings would be nothing to this. It was impossible, he couldn't dream of doing it — or could he?

12

Jason sat in James's seat in the back of the car holding the white rabbit Mopsa had bought him. Benet put Mopsa's suitcases in the trunk along with Jason's old stroller, which had been there ever since Mopsa stole him. He was looking fit and well, she thought, his color less high, his expression more alert. Is it my imagination, she thought, or is he actually a bit better-looking? When Mopsa was gone, when in an hour or two Mopsa was gone and she had to face the music, or at least seriously contemplate and plan facing the music, nobody was going to be able to say Jason had suffered in her care. They could only congratulate her on the improvement in him.

"This is going to be a red letter day for Daddy," said Mopsa. "Do you know we've never been separated so long in all our married life?"

She had forgotten the long periods spent in psychiatric wards. This morning she was the epitome of sanity in her gray suit, a red chiffon scarf round her neck and lipstick to match but carefully blotted and powdered so as not to look too bold. As to her father's reaction to this homecoming, Benet doubted if he faced the day with the enthusiasm Mopsa predicted. On the phone the other night he had been reproachful.

"Surely you could have kept your mother with you for the month we planned on?"

And Mopsa herself had not helped when she took the receiver and said in a plaintive voice that there was nothing really to keep her in London now all the tests had proved negative. She didn't want to outstay her welcome.

John Archdale's voice was pregnant with unspoken miseries. You had her for three weeks, it implied; I have her for life. I don't complain, I shoulder it, but all I asked was for four short weeks. It wouldn't have hurt Mopsa in the circumstances, Benet thought, to tell the poor man that she was looking forward to coming home.

Now, of course, in the car, it was evident she was. The climate for one thing. The temperature would be twenty degrees higher than in England. And there would be the sunshine and her own cosy little home that Benet had only seen once and showed no sign of wanting to see again. She chattered on about the amenities of southern Spain in the winter, when most of the tourists were gone, the expatriate couple from High Wycombe they played bridge with, the beach. Jason, it seemed, she had forgotten. For days she had virtually ignored him, leaving him to Benet's care. Once she had referred to him as James.

"Isn't it time James was in bed?"

The knife that was always poised, ready to rend Benet with reminders, struck home. But Mopsa had spoken unconsciously. She had never been much interested in James, still less in Jason, as a person. It seemed that, to her, they had blended and become one, little boys who were no more than tribal creatures sharing a group soul. Once only had Benet made another attempt to explain to Mopsa what she intended to do about Jason, but Mopsa her merely shrugged.

"I shan't be here. Why tell me?"

At Heathrow, at the news-agent's within the check-in area, a pyramid of *The Marriage Knot* was on display. The sight of that familiar glossy cream paperback with the drawing of a woman in a jeweled headdress reminded Benet of what she was going to have to face when she handed

Jason over. Mopsa was nobody; for Mopsa there would have been only a brief blaze of publicity, a day of notoriety. But she was Benet Archdale, a best-selling author, a famous name if not a famous face, already a personality. And she would never live it down. Whatever she might write, do, achieve, that she had once kidnapped a child would be forever remembered. If someone one day wrote her biography, it would be there. A chapter would be devoted to it. Her mother's mental instability would be brought up, the fact that she had had a child and he had died. There was no need to wait for some biography in the distant future. All that would be in the newspapers at the end of the week.

She bought a paper. The Jason affair was back on the front page, down near the bottom across two colums, another interview with Carol Stratford. . . .

"It's your birthday!" she exclaimed to Jason. "Oh, Jay, it's your second birthday!"

Jay was what she had taken to calling him. It was what he called himself. She picked him up and looked into his face.

"How awful that it's your birthday and we aren't doing anything about it."

"He doesn't know, does he?" said Mopsa. "He's too young to know what birthday means."

"Many, many happy returns of the day, Jay!"

"It's *my* birthday next week. I don't notice you making a song and dance about that."

Mopsa had become cross and sulky. She was apprehensive about her flight now, swallowing Valium with black coffee. Jason had ice cream because it was his birthday. Watching him, Benet marveled how her dislike of him had faded. How could she have disliked a little child anyway, scarcely more than a baby? If she could make them understand, if they didn't deal too harshly with her, was it conceivable she might occasionally be allowed to visit him, to see how he was getting on?

The flight to Malaga was called. Reluctant as Mopsa might be to get into an aircraft, she was nevertheless raring to go at the first call. The plane might leave without her. She might get into trouble for being late. After all, her ticket had been purchased only four days ago.

Benet went as far with her as she could. They made their farewells at passport control. Mopsa, who had been cold and carping these past days, flung her arms round Benet's neck, kissing her fervently.

"You don't know how I miss you, Brigitte. I only had the one and it's a bitter fate to be separated by so many hundreds of miles."

Benet said she would phone, she would write.

She didn't remind Mopsa that it was she who had created the separation, who had chosen to live in Spain. Mopsa didn't say goodbye to Jason. She took no notice of him. Benet was surprised how much she resented this, how deeply it embittered their parting. It's because I know she would have been the same with James, she thought.

I must not hate my mother. . . .

Mopsa went through the doorway. The last Benet saw of her, she was dropping her handbag onto the conveyor belt of the baggage scrutiny.

Now that she knew it was Jason's birthday — the newspaper had quoted Carol Stratford as saying so and lamenting the party she wouldn't be able to give him — Benet felt bound to buy him a present. Even thought this might be his last day with her, he should have a birthday present. They would let him keep it afterwards. Why not?

Jason didn't make a choice. He would have chosen everything in the toyshop. The place recalled to Benet forcefully the playroom at the hospital. You could see where some of the toys in that playroom had come from. She remembered now how she had sat in that room, waiting for the phone to be free so that she could phone Mopsa, and how she had looked at the tree of hands. James had still been alive then. All the upraised hands had seemed to be pleading, but for what? For what?

A rocking horse was what she bought. It was big and beautiful and dappled gray. The shop would deliver it to the Vale of Peace first thing in the morning, but Benet didn't want Jason to have to wait so long for it. The car was parked only a short way away. They took it with them, they set off to cross the road, Benet with her arms full of brown paper-wrapped rocking horse, and they were halfway over the pedestrian crossing when she saw Ian Raeburn on the other side.

Benet had a curious feeling when she saw him. It was as if she had always known him — no, more than that, as if he were a close friend or member of her family whom to see here unexpectedly was a delightful surprise. She felt as if he belonged to that small group of persons who loved her, so that in a moment he would turn his head and see her and his whole face would light up with the pleasure of it. This feeling lasted no more than a few seconds. It came over her in a vivid spontaneous flash: an instant of pure happiness, the first she had had since James's death. And it was immediately succeeded, or even overlapped, by apprehensiveness. The only thing was to hurry on past, to hope he hadn't seen her. An appalled regret took hold of her. She stepped onto the curb, the hand that held Jason's tightening.

Ian Raeburn was buying fruit, two kiwi fruit and a bag of small, loose-skinned oranges. He took his change and turned to meet her eyes, to smile with instant recognition. He must wonder at me, she thought, standing here holding a child's hand, I who lost my child. The explanation that had been Mopsa's, that had been believable for a while, was ready and waiting.

"I'm looking after him for a friend. I said I'd look after him while she went away."

"Let me carry that for you," he said.

He took the rocking horse from her. Its painted hoofs were breaking through the paper.

"Do you find it a help?" he asked gently.

He meant having Jason to care for, he meant having a child of the same sex and comparable age to James.

"I don't know." She surprised herself with this entirely truthful reply. "I honestly don't know." A week ago she could only have shouted, "No, no, never!"

"I phoned you a couple of times. Just to see how you were. I expect your mother told you."

Mopsa hadn't. But what difference would it

223

have made if she had?

"My mother's gone home now."

"Are you going to be all right alone?"

She nodded. He lifted the trunk lid and put the rocking horse inside beside the stolen stroller. In a moment he would suggest they meet, he would ask to see her again; she knew that, she could sense it in the charged air between them. But that was impossible; she had no future, nothing, after she had given Jason up. Ian Raeburn wouldn't want to know her. She would be a lost woman, many would think her mad, mad as Mopsa.

She bent down and picked up Jason. He enjoyed farewells and had begun to wave his hand and say goodbye.

"A generous present for a friend's child." Ian closed the boot lid. "Is he your godchild?"

"It's not for Christmas. Today's his birthday."

Saying that was something she immediately regretted. It had slipped out. But suppose he too had read those paragraphs on the front page?

His eyes were on her, gentle with understanding. And yet he didn't understand at all. How could he? He only thought he did. We despise those who claim to understand us when in fact their comprehension is wide of the mark. She didn't despise Ian but she wanted to get away from him. She said goodbye abruptly and got into the car.

The phone was ringing as she came into the house. It was Antonia, inviting her to dinner. Did she find it easy getting babysitters for James in the new place?

For a moment she couldn't speak. Because of Mopsa's lies, people were going to speak to her as if James were alive. Yet she found herself unable to tell Antonia the truth. Her voice sounded in her own ears remote, bemused, as she said no, she couldn't go out, she knew no one here yet, had no idea what sitters might be available. Jason came to her and pulled at her sleeve, asking for the horse to be unwrapped. She rang off.

He climbed onto the horse and rocked back and forth. The expression on his face made her smile, there was so much in it of delight, of wonder, of a sort of glee. She began to imagine the conversation that would take place between her and a policeman or policewoman when she took him back. Any explanation she might give of Mopsa's behavior and then of her own subsequent behavior now sounded insane to her, unreal, above all, unbelievable. Why hadn't she brought Jason back as soon as she knew who he was? They would ask that. That would be one of the questions they would hammer over and over at her. And she would only be able to say it had been to stop Mopsa screaming. Looking back now, she couldn't understand herself. Perhaps it was not only Mopsa whose mind had been unbalanced. . . .

There was no dialogue she could construct between herself and the police that did not end in their charging her with abducting Jason. The facts, the evidence, were all against her. The Winterside area was known to her; she had once lived there. The car used was her car. She had recently lost her own child. And more than that. She had concealed − or so it would seem − her child's death from all her friends.

Benet gave Jason his tea, a rather special one because it was his birthday. She set him on her lap and read Beatrix Potter to him, *The Tale of the Pie and the Patty-pan*, although it was too old for him. He liked the pictures. He seemed to like them more and with a more intense enthusiasm than she thought most children of his age would. If I were his mother, she found herself thinking, I should imagine him growing up to be a painter.

His mother. . . . That pretty little blonde woman, that living doll. And the thuggish boy just out of his teens she lived with. They had to have him back. There was no doubt about that. It was not for her, Benet, to judge them and pronounce sentence. All she could do was try to ensure that once the relief of having him back was past, they didn't begin beating him again.

The bruises were almost gone, she noticed as she lifted Jason into the bath. Only a faint yellowish staining remained at the base of his firm-fleshed rib cage. The burn hole would always be there, of course. It would be there when he was an old man. But she couldn't prove it had been made by a cigarette. And the police wouldn't want to believe it, she thought; they would rather not have the additional trouble of believing it.

She put Jason to bed and tucked him in. The white rabbit had disappeared. They had both hunted all over the house for it and now Benet began to wonder if Mopsa had inadvertently taken it back to Spain with her. She thought, she braced herself, and then she opened the toy cupboard and got James's tiger cub out and gave it to Jason. Seeing him with it hurt but not agonizingly. He accepted it happily as a substitute for the rabbit and fell asleep with one of its round golden ears stuffed in his mouth.

By this time she should have handed Jason back. Yesterday she had made a firm decision to take him to the police station by three o'clock this afternoon. She had even told herself she was *looking forward* to it. It was going to be a relief getting it over, being free of him, being alone again and responsible only for herself. She must have convinced herself then that they would accept her story of Mopsa's part in it, of Mopsa's almost total guilt. Another night must now pass before she could return him, and that in itself, the fact that she had not handed him back immediately after Mopsa's departure, must further militate against her innocence.

Wandering downstairs again, walking about the basement room, alone for the first time since James had died, she knew quite suddenly that she was not going to take Jason to the police. The idea of it – realistically faced, fair and square – made her feel sick and horribly frightened. It was no good imagining conversations, anticipating ways of bringing the police round to her point of view. They weren't like that; it wouldn't be like that. Two minutes inside that police station and she would be turned into an insane criminal. And next day the newspapers would have everything. She would have to see in print the fact of James's death.

She wouldn't do it.

It was a relief to have decided. She felt quite

limp and weak with relief. Jason would not be taken to the police; there would be no excuses, confessions, explanations, for her to make. Poor mad Mopsa would not be implicated.

That did not mean Jason wasn't to be returned. Of course he must be returned to his mother, his family, his home, and as soon as possible. Benet did something rare with her. She went upstairs to the drink cupboard and poured herself a stiff double measure of whisky. Not since the days with Edward had she drunk whisky. She sat down in the window chair with her drink and began to think out ways of returning Jason, foolproof ways that were both safe and secret.

13

The photographs in the estate agents' windows were of all kinds of houses, from listed Grade One Georgian to 1980s studio open-plan. Terence looked at the pictures and the specifications underneath them, noting prices. He hadn't known quite how costly houses in Hampstead were and his investigation was starting to make him feel slightly, though not disagreeably, sick.

One more agent in Heath Street remained to be examined. Terence made his way down as far as the corner of Church Row and stood with his face close up to the glass. He didn't intend to go in. It was better to do these things by phone. It had been an educational morning, but as he walked back up the winding hill, he wondered if he hadn't undertaken these researches less because they were necessary than to put off still further the first fateful step.

Nearly a week had passed since he had found the deeds for 5 Spring Close. Since then he had thought of very little else but his plan, and short of Freda coming home suddenly or some agent or solicitor personally knowing John Phipps (or knowing he was dead) or the neighbors getting wise (how could they?), he didn't see how it could go wrong. But he was scared stiff. What scared him was that it seemed so simple, a real walkover once things got moving, that it couldn't happen, there must be a flaw somewhere. It couldn't be that easy to get hold of — what? A hundred thousand pounds? A hundred and fifty?

Both Jessica and Freda were regular users of Valium. Jessica took one every morning to start the day. Terence had removed a hundred in a container when he left.

"It's cheaper than drink," frugal Freda used to say. She had left him nearly two hundred. He was amply supplied and they didn't seem to go off, in spite of what doctors and chemists said. He took two with half a glass of water and on second thought added some of Freda's Chivas Regal. It made him shudder; he had never been much of a drinker.

The estate agent he had chosen answered the phone promptly. He was put on to a Mr.

Sawyer. Mr. Sawyer's accent was very much like his own, north London born and schooled, overlaid (when the speaker remembered) with some mimicry of television announcers' diction. Terence had rehearsed his opening line over and over. He had found himself muttering it in his sleep. Now he uttered it aloud into the phone:

"I should like to put my house on the market."

The sum Sawyer named as the asking price was a hundred and forty thousand pounds, or, in estate agent's parlance, a hundred and thirty-nine thousand, nine hundred and ninety-five.

"When would it be convenient to come and measure up, Mr. Phipps?"

"Measure up?"

"We like to take measurements of the rooms for our specifications. And perhaps a photograph. Of course I'm familiar with the property. A very nice property indeed."

"How about this afternoon?"

"Wonderful. Three? Three-thirty?"

Three o'clock was fixed. Get it over with, thought Terence. He had never thought much about the neighbors before. When, for instance, he used to bring Freda's car in at two in the morning, give the accelerator a final flip, get out, and bang the door, the neighbors might not have existed for him. He looked out of the middle one of the three narrow windows. A thin, worn-looking woman with white hair was planting something, bulbs probably, round the trunk of the catalpa tree which grew in the middle of the courtyard. She looked the nosy kind but there was nothing he could do about her. Suppose she or any of them saw Sawyer taking a photograph? Even if they knew who Sawyer was, they would only think Freda was selling her house. They might not even know she had gone away.

The only danger would be in someone hearing Sawyer call him Phipps. Terence made up his mind not to let this happen. Now that he had taken the first step, he felt less nervous. What had he done, after all? He had committed himself to nothing, he could always withdraw, change his mind. As for being called Phipps, he might easily be a cousin of the late John Howard. A young cousin. John Howard had died at the age of fifty-one, Terence had noted from his death certificate.

Sawyer turned up on time, in fact two minutes early. Before he could make too much of a song and dance on the doorstep about how lovely and tasteful this little enclave was, Terence got him inside by saying to shut the front door, he thought he had a cold coming.

"The market," said Sawyer, on his knees with the tape measure, "is, so to speak, moribund."

It sounded like a word he had just learned. Terence supposed it meant "improving" or some such thing. The afternoon's proceedings had an unreal feel to them.

"Townhouses," said Sawyer, "are by no means easy to sell at this moment in time, but these, of course, are in a class of their own. Describing this as a townhouse at all might give a false impression. Careful handling will be in order. I shall have to put my thinking cap on. May I ask if you've found somewhere else?"

"Pardon?"

"I mean are you in the process of purchasing a new property?"

"You needn't worry about that. I'm going abroad. And I want a quick sale. I don't want to hang about."

He asked Sawyer if he'd mind seeing himself out and then he ran upstairs and watched the photograph being taken. As far as he could tell, no one else was watching. Sawyer put his camera away and strolled off under the archway that led into older, cobbled regions of Hampstead.

Terence didn't expect any developments for a week or two, but two days later, as he was plucking up courage to go up to Heath Street and see if the photograph was in Steiner & Wildwood's window and how he felt about that if it was, Sawyer phoned to say a Mr. and Mrs. Pym would like to see over the house. Would in an hour's time suit him?

Freda had done her own housework. She said it gave her something to occupy herself and she didn't like cleaners in the place. In a way Terence was glad of that. A cleaner would have taken a keen interest in everything he was doing, would have gossiped, might even have written letters to Martinique. But he had also rather taken it for granted that the house was clean and stayed that way by magic. No one had laid a duster on it for nearly a fortnight and it wasn't looking its best. Still it was too late to worry about that. He took two Valium and was feeling quite serene by the time the Pyms arrived.

They didn't stay long. When they found the garden was approximately the same size as the smallest bedroom, they lost interest. But it was a start. Terence got out the vacuum cleaner, found some dusters, and cleaned up. He hooked a cobweb off one of the red girders and polished the discus thrower. It was the first time in his life he had attempted house cleaning but he didn't find it difficult. It would even be a way of making a living if all else failed, he thought.

The photograph Sawyer had taken wasn't in Steiner & Wildwood's window. They must have used it only to stick on the forms with measurements and whatnot that they gave prospective buyers. This comforted him. He would have felt very exposed if that photograph had been there staring at everyone who went past.

Ever since Freda went away, he had been living a hermit's existence, so that evening he broke out and went to an old haunt of his, Smithy's at Camden Lock, where he had sometimes gone with Jessica and where you could drink all night. In Smithy's he picked up a girl called Teresa and told her his name was John Phipps. She went home with him in a taxi and was deeply impressed by the house. In fact she was overwhelmed and kept on saying he hadn't seemed that sort of fella. They were still in bed next morning when Sawyer phoned. A Mrs. Goldschmidt would like to come and see the house at 2:00 P.M.

That gave him time to get rid of Teresa. He caught her making a note of Freda's phone number from the disc in the middle of the dial, but it didn't seem important. He swallowed two Valium once she was out of the way and another at one-thirty. Mrs. Goldschmidt was late, and by the time the doorbell rang, he had almost given her up. He made himself go slowly to the door, keep her waiting for a change.

She was an extremely good-looking woman, of the same type as Carol Stratford, but there was as much difference in class and style between her and Carol as Sawyer had said there was between 5 Spring Close and your average townhouse. She had very short, back-swept blonde hair, a pale, gleaming tan, and her mouth was like a cross-section of a ripe strawberry. She wore a pale gray suede coat, primrose leather boots, and a long primrose scarf. Such as she, Terence thought, were never to be found being assisted out of Daimlers at crematorium steps.

He had no experience of buying or selling houses but he knew by instinct or telepathy that she would want to buy this one. It wasn't that she said much as he led her from room to room, she hardly spoke at all; but she took a long time, she was thorough, sometimes she nodded to herself in a satisfied way. It was three-thirty by the time she had finished, the worst time of day to offer anyone a drink, and he didn't feel like making her a cup of tea. Tea-making hardly fitted in with his 5 Spring Close image. In a way it was a pity she so obviously liked the house. It put paid to any ideas he had about using that image to get to know her better.

She had a monotonous, zombie-like voice which Terence found rather attractive. "I'd like my husband to see it."

"Fine. Any time."

"I'll fix it through Steiner's."

Terence's nerves needed calming, in spite of the Valium. He got out the vacuum cleaner and did a bit more to the spaniel fur carpets so that he wouldn't have to worry when Goldschmidt came. After that he put in an hour's practice on John Howard's signature. His hand was steady, he breathed deeply. He went through the desk again and found two old books of check stubs, one with a single unused check remaining in it. John Howard had died suddenly of an unforeseen heart attack. Funny to think he couldn't have had a clue that check no. 655400 would never be used or that 655399 (to North Thames Gas for £95.43) would be the last he would ever draw. Six days later he had an appointment at Golders Green....

Such fatalistic musings were not really Terence's style and he soon dismissed them. Freda's husband's bank account had been with Barclay's in Hampstead High Street, which was what he wanted to know. He wanted to know which branch of which bank to avoid.

Goldschmidt himself came along next day

and again on the following day. He was fat and dark and bald, with thick-lensed, thick-rimmed glasses. His wife was in a black leather suit with a kind of scarf thing made of mink wound round her.

"It's my dream house," she said in the voice of one coming out of a coma.

"Would you be open to an offer?"

Terence said what Sawyer had instructed him to say. "You'll have to do anything like that through Steiner & Wildwood."

Within the hour Sawyer was on the phone. Terence found himself nearly voiceless, a common enough symptom of nerves with him.

"Still got that cold of yours, Mr. Phipps?"

Terence croaked out some sort of assent.

"Mr. Goldschmidt would like to make you an offer of one hundred and thirty thousand pounds."

That would have been acceptable. He wouldn't have argued. It was Sawyer who suggested haggling. Twenty-four hours went by during which Terence was afraid to go out in case Sawyer phoned. Besides, he felt continually nauseous and he had an idea that the cold – it had turned bitterly cold – would attack him and make him actually throw up. He was in Freda's *en suite* bath when the phone went and he jumped out and rushed for it, not even waiting to grab a towel. The receiver slithered in his wet hand.

"That seems to be a compromise satisfactory to both parties, don't you think, Mr. Phipps?"

Terence nodded. Realizing Sawyer couldn't see him, he translated the nod into a staccato fusillade of "Yes. Sure. Fine. Right. Yes."

It looked as if he had sold, or was well on the way to selling, Freda Phipps's house for one hundred and thirty-two thousand, nine hundred and fifty pounds.

14

It was rain falling, though it was cold enough for snow. An icy wind blowing down the side street caught you at the corners. Barry, doing the Saturday shopping, saw Maureen coming down the steps of the public library with a thin, flat book under her arm. Maureen had black wellies on and her long mud-colored slicker. She stopped on the steps to put up a big black umbrella that was probably Ivan's.

He had wanted to catch her alone. He followed her into the International. She had laid her umbrella and the library book (*Advanced DIY for the Home Expert*) in her shopping trolley. Her face showed no more reaction at the sight of Barry than it did when confronted by a pyramid of dog food in cans.

"I heard about you helping the police with their inquiries," she said, and in the same tone,

"Pass me one of them packets of Flash. I can't reach."

"Have you got time for a coffee, Maureen, or a drink?"

She scratched the side of her nose. "What for?"

"I want to ask you something. I mean I thought if we were sitting down somewhere..."

"I'm washing the paint in our lounge. I only came out for a sponge."

"It doesn't matter," said Barry.

They walked side by side towards the check-out. Like a couple with prams going to the baby clinic, thought Barry. He remembered what Carol had said about Maureen not being human. In a way that made it easier to talk to her of things that were only too human. He brought it out quickly.

"Maureen, do you know who Jason's father is?"

"Is what?"

He said it again, he explained, and had to stop because the check-out girl could hear. Maureen trudged along the pavement reading the print on the Flash packet. She let him hold the umbrella over both of them. He tried again.

"It made me think, you see. I mean she might still be fond of Jason's father. She might have a sort of special feeling for him on account of that."

Maureen didn't lift her eyes from the green print. "There was a lot of fellas. There was a fella that drove about in a beach buggy and that garage fella three or four doors down from me and there was a black bloke. Me and Ivan were disgusted. There was a fella called something Wand, Terry Wand. Mum used to know his mum down Brownswood Common." She looked at Barry for the first time since they had left the shop. Talking about herself aroused a small spark of interest in her. "I've never been with any fella except Ivan," she said. "I wouldn't. I don't see what people want to for. It just goes to show the difference between sisters. Can I have that bag you've got your butter in? If this stuff gets wet, it'll be a right old mess."

He left her at the bridge. It struck him that she was very happy. She had got what she wanted. She and Ivan hardly ever spoke to each other. All the time he wasn't at work or she wasn't doing things to the house they sat in front of the TV holding hands. They would never have children, split up, move, go away on holiday, make a friend, feel jealousy, suffer. One day they'd wake up and find they were sixty and things were just the same. He could almost envy them.

Terence Wand's name had been the only one Maureen could remember. It sounded from what she said as if he and Carol had been friends since childhood. The other men — well, Maureen hadn't any *proof,* she and Ivan had just been guessing. No doubt they had been after Carol. Men would always be after Carol. Terence Wand was different — somehow Barry intuited he was Jason's father. Being a father gave you a sort of dignity, a sort of *weight*. It made you memorable. It was Jason's father's name that Maureen had remembered.

Carol had started working Saturdays. All across the lunchtime and throughout the evening. She had never done that before, but as soon as she went back, Kostas had asked her if she would work Saturdays and she had agreed. The house smelled of the perfume she had taken to wearing, a musky French cologne Barry knew — because he had priced it in the chemist's — cost twelve pounds a bottle. It was her money, she worked for it, she had a right to spend it as she liked. Barry wouldn't even have thought about it if only he could have been sure it was Carol herself who had bought that perfume.

Unpacking the shopping, putting things in the fridge, he began to think along lines he often did when he was alone in the house. He would fancy then that Jason was still there, that the events of the past weeks had never happened, and that he would turn round and see him standing in the doorway. The little boy's face he could easily conjure up, he had no difficulty in remembering what he looked like. Jason had an *unusual* face, not babyish at all, not in the least like Carol's. It was a funny thing, an ironical thing, that Carol, who had a baby face at twenty-eight, had produced a boy who at two had, if not a grown-up's face, at least a mature one for his age.

That meant he must look like his father. He bore no resemblance to any Knapwell Barry knew, nor was he like his half-brother and sister. Barry was suddenly absolutely sure he would recognize Jason's father if he saw him, just from having known Jason. This wouldn't be a case for blood tests but something you could see at a glance. Barry imagined a tall, biggish man, fair-haired and sharp-featured, with white skin that got sunburned red, and eyes darker than Carol's and with more green in them.

He wandered into the living room, wondering what he was going to do with himself for the rest of the day. He could go down to Kostas's himself for the evening, of course. An evening spent with Dennis Gordon, who had two topics of conversation, money and his own aggressive exploits, wasn't an attractive prospect. Dennis Gordon treated Barry as if he really believed he was Carol's lodger or a boy she let stay with her in exchange for doing odd jobs. He was crazy about Carol, you could see that, but he wasn't jealous of Barry. He didn't take him seriously enough for that, Barry thought.

A police car had stopped outside. The Spicers were coming in with two bags of washing from the laundrette just as Leatham got out of the car. Barry closed his eyes momentarily. He realized he need not have wondered about how he was going to pass the rest of the day.

They had found Jason's body. They told him that as if it were true, positive, beyond a doubt. But all the same they wanted him to identify the thing that had been dug up in a garden in Finchley.

First he was taken to the police station. Chief Superintendent Treddick was there, talking in knowing tones as if to say Barry was being very clever and he understood all about that and even rather admired it, only Barry must realize the police were cleverer still. He talked as if Barry were a murderer beyond a doubt and insinuated that if he would only admit everything – take his time and admit every single thing – the police would be very kind and lenient with him. Leatham was more brusque and offhand. His beefy red face and hooked nose and corrugated yellow hair brought to Barry's mind what he had been thinking of earlier. Leatham was the Jason's father type, though not handsome enough.

The Finchley householder had been digging a hole to plant a tree. Two to three feet down he had unearthed a rotting bundle. He had been living just a week in the house, which before that had been empty for six months. The house and garden were about a hundred yards — a stone's throw, Treddick said — from where Barry and Ken Thompson were paneling the office.

"We've only been working there a week," Barry said.

"It was six weeks ago you went over there to have a look at the place for an estimate," said Treddick.

But Barry hadn't been there. It was always Ken who did the estimates. He tried to explain this but it seemed to have no effect on them. The fact that he had some little hearsay knowledge of the area was enough for them.

"I'd never been there," he protested. "I never talked about it with Ken. You might as well say because I've got a street plan I might have looked it up."

"Maybe you did," said Leatham.

They were illogical, they didn't reason things out. This made him much more uneasy than any evidence they might fancy they had against him. They asked him about the street in which the dead child had been found, about where he and Ken went for their lunches, about how he got to Finchley, by what method of transport, and then they took him to the mortuary.

Until then he hadn't known this building was the mortuary. He had known it all his life as a red brick wall with windows high up through which you could see white tiles. They took him in through a door that had a very highly polished brass handle. The image of that shiny brass sphere remained in Barry's mind, making him flinch whenever he saw well-polished brass. There was a very powerful smell — not of death or decay but of disinfectant, yet ever afterwards when Barry smelt it or had a whiff of something like it, he associated it at once with death.

In the mortuary he behaved, he thought, as he might have done if he had really murdered Jason. They uncovered the face. Barry's throat rose up, closed, strangled him. He covered his face and staggered back. Someone must have caught him. He didn't remember any more till he was sitting in a chair with his head down on his knees.

If they had tried to get Carol there to identify the awful thing under the cover, he thought he would have fought them all, killed them all. That would have made a murderer of him. But they didn't attempt that. They got Maureen. He saw her brought in, blank-faced, head tied up in a scarf, and come out again, no less steady and calm. They drove him back to Summerskill Road, where two reporters were with Carol, who had been fetched from the wine bar. But before that, they put him through the grueling process again. How well did he know that part of Finchley? How many times had he been there? For several months an estate agent's board had stood in the front garden of the house where the child's body had been found. The side gate had been off its hinges and had stood propped against a fence. On the day of Jason's disappearance Barry had been working in Wood Green, hadn't he? It was easy to get by bus from Wood Green to Finchley. He could have picked up Jason in Rudyard Gardens, taken him to Finchley, killed him and buried his body, and still been in Highgate by five....

He and Carol slept that night because they were both drunk. They didn't bother with wine. They had a bottle of gin between them. He woke up with a cracking headache and a mouth that felt as if it were filled with dry fur. Carol's face on the pillow was young, china pink and white, beaded with sweat. He left her sleeping and went off to buy the Sunday papers. He wanted to see what they said about him and if they had yet established who the dead child was.

Mr. Mahmud at the paper shop was always a bit distant and his daughter off somewhere in a world of her own, so Barry hardly noticed that he didn't get a thank-you for producing the right money for the *Sunday Mirror* and the *Express*. This Pakistani family were known for conducting a lot of their business in silence. But as he came out of the shop and into Bevan Square, he encountered two girls who hadn't that reputation at all. Stephanie Isadoro and a girl Barry thought was called Diane Fowler, Blue Hair's sister, were coming across the square, mackintoshed, wearing high-heeled sandals, arm-in-arm. He had been reading headlines, so relieved that there was nothing new that he could even distract his mind enough to admire the big, beautiful photograph of Carol on the *Mirror's* front page, but now he looked up to say hello to them.

These girls were usually giggling, usually pleased with themselves. Karen had once told him that Stephanie fancied him. If it had ever been true, she had got over it now, for she pointedly turned her head the other way and so did Diana. It was a funny thing, he'd often thought most of this lot couldn't read but they had read the papers all right, they had read the bits about him helping the police with their inquiries.

Carol didn't get up till lunchtime. The phone rang a couple of times before that but they must have been wrong numbers, for each time Barry picked up the receiver, he got silence and then the dial tone. Unless, he thought, it was someone trying to get Carol who didn't want to speak to him, who didn't even want him to know they wanted to speak to Carol — "they" being a man, of course. He cleared up in the kitchen, washed their glasses from the night before and the cups and saucers the reporters had used when Iris had made tea for them, and carried the rubbish bag out from the waste bin to the dustbin that stood by the back door.

It was cold today but dry, colder than it had been when he went out for the papers. He noticed how green Winterside Down was, all the little rectangles of garden, all the lawns and banks and slopes, a brilliant, hard, acid, treeless green. It was a green to hurt the eyes. Mrs. Spicer was putting bowls of some sort of steaming mash stuff into her rabbits' hutches.

She turned round and smiled at Barry and said good morning to him and it was better today, wasn't it, at least it was dry. He felt unreasoningly grateful to her for speaking to him, for greeting him with warmth. He could have kissed her.

Carol said she couldn't stand another evening on their own, she'd go off her rocker. She had a long, leisurely bath with avocado and peach-nut essence in the water and an herbal pack on her face. In the black-and-white dress with, over it, Mrs. Fylemon's cast-off, beauty-without-cruelty synthetic fox coat, she was the old Carol again, his love, his child-mother of three children. They hadn't seen Tanya and Ryan since before Jason went. Barry didn't want to think about that; he pushed it away, he had enough without that. He and Carol were going to meet Iris and Jerry in the Bulldog, but just as they were leaving, the phone rang again. Carol answered it this time and she was a long while talking. Barry was already in the hall, waiting for her by the front door. She had gone back into the living room to answer the phone, and when she'd said, "Hello," and a less impersonal "Oh, hi," he saw the door pulled shut. She had shut herself in with the phone, leaving him alone in the hall. He felt the sudden swift descent of the worst loneliness he had ever known in his life. It made him cold. He shivered with the cold. She was on the phone only a few minutes, three at most. She came out and took his arm and said it had been Alkmini.

Iris and Jerry were sitting at a corner table with a couple Iris said lived down the road from them. Barry immediately thought of Terence Wand's mother. Could this possibly be her? Iris never introduced anyone to anyone. You were supposed to know who people were without being told. Carol knew all right. She called the woman Dorothy. Barry found himself studying the sixty-year-old, raddled, sagging face, the bravely painted mouth, the hennaed gray hair, looking for a likeness to Jason. In the nose perhaps, in the eyes, which were faded now but once might have been as blue as cornflowers. He was working out ways of finding out what he wanted to know when the Dorothy woman and her husband or boyfriend or whatever he was got up quite abruptly and said they must be going. Barry was rather disappointed. It was only afterwards that he realized that, just before they left, just before a glance passed between them and they got up, Iris had spoken to him and had called him for the first time that evening by his Christian name.

Carol looked rovingly round the saloon bar, twining a curl round one of her fingers. A great cavernous place, it was, of Edwardian etched glass and red plush and a ceiling whose scroll-work was chestnut-brown with nicotine. Jerry sat silent, dumb with gin, his face a dull blue. Her claw of a hand on Barry's arm, Iris cocked her head in the direction of the departing neighbours.

"Don't take no notice, Barry. There's some get very funny about folks what have contact with the police."

Her habitual placid half-smile lay on her mouth. It was a fat woman's smile on a thin woman's face. Iris pushed two cigarettes into the smile, lit them, and handed one to Carol.

On the way home with Carol, taking her arm and putting it into his, he asked her if Dorothy's surname was Wand. She was preoccupied. He didn't wonder at that. He asked her again, look-ing into her face this time, though he never much liked doing that after dark in Winterside Down. The khaki, color-draining light was unkind to even the prettiest face. It made skulls out of faces and gave them empty eye sockets.

"You what?" she said.

"I thought she might be a Mrs. Wand."

"Well, she's not, she's a Mrs. Bailey. What's made you so nosy all of a sudden?"

The tall single tower block dominated the estate, lights on all over it. It was like a chimney full of holes which the fire inside showed through. They went across Bevan Square where Hoopoe and Black Beauty and Nose Ring and a couple of girls with black lips and fingernails – or lips and fingernails that looked black in this light – stood outside the Turkish take-out, eating chips. Hoopoe said something as they passed, but he didn't say it loudly and all Barry caught was the word "woman."

"They're just ignorant," said Carol loud enough for them to hear. "That's what you have to put up with living round here, ignorant scum and scrubbers like those two." Her body trembled against his side and he was filled with a fierce pride that she should be angry for him. Then she said, speaking softly, to him alone: "I'd do anything to get away from here. I hate this dump. Sometimes I think I'll be in this dump till I'm old, till I die."

"Carol," he said. "Carol – a year or two, just give me a year or two. I'll make money. I'll get the down payment on a house for us."

She looked away from him. Her words were rough but she didn't speak them unkindly. "It'll just be piddling little bits of money, won't it? I want real money, I'm sick of struggling. I had a chance of that with my husband and he had to go and die."

"I'm young. I can make as much as Dave ever

could. Let's get married, Carol. I want it to be me you mean when you say 'my husband.' "

"How can I get married?" she said. "I can't get married when we don't know if Jason's alive or dead."

Her voice sounded sincere, yet he had a feeling it was something entirely different she was saying, some far more genuine excuse she was really making.

The police came in the morning and told Carol they had established beyond a doubt that the dead child wasn't Jason. Carol didn't say anything; she lifted her shoulders in an indifferent little shurg. They had caught her as she was leaving for Mrs. Fylemon's, her first day back since Mrs. Fylemon's return from Tunisia. The detective sergeant told her that the boy whose body they found had been nearer three than two, and from the shape of his skull was shown not to have been Caucasian. In any case he had been dead for at least six weeks, a fact which didn't surprise Barry, remembering that face.

He had an unreasonable urge – unreasonable only because he knew they wouldn't dream of doing it – to ask the police to put posters and banners up all over Winterside Down saying, *Barry Mahon Is Innocent*, or something like that. Maybe have a car going round and a man with a loudspeaker like they did before elections, shouting that he hadn't done it, that he was in the clear. His imagination was running wild, he knew that. He watched the sergeant go, having said not a word.

What did it matter anyway? Sticks and stones may break my bones but hard words cannot hurt me. His mother had taught him that when he was a little kid and had been subjected to verbal bullying in the school playground. He had always remembered. It wasn't important that an old bag with dyed hair didn't want to sit in a pub with him or that Hoopoe called after him that some folks wouldn't dare show their faces outside — for he was certain now that this was what had been said — without a woman to protect them.

But it was in the forefront of his mind as he and Carol walked together to the bus stop. Not that there was anyone for her to "protect" him from this morning. Going along the path to the Chinese bridge, they met no one but the old boy in the Sherlock Holmes hat who sat there fishing in the canal most wet mornings under a green umbrella. Barry's bus came first. He didn't want to go to Finchley, he never wanted to go there again. He was hours late anyway.

One bus to Wood Green and then change

onto another. What curious trick of chance brought that double-decker bus with an L plate rather slowly and steadily past the stop? No buses to Hampstead or through Hampstead came this way, but this bus, out on a practice run, had Hampstead on its front. The address on the paper that had fallen from Carol's coat came back to him. 5 Spring Close, Hampstead. Terence Wand. It had said Terry on the paper but Barry didn't want to think of him like that, it sounded too close to his own name, it put it in the same *class* of name. Terence. Terence Wand, who lived in Hampstead at a classy address that was a far cry from what Carol called "this dump," from Winterside Down.

Getting on the next bus that came, climbing up to the top deck, Barry found himself looking at all the men about, looking for the kind of man he sought. He sat in the front, looking at the men in the street. It seemed to him that there were more of them about at this time of day than there had used to be a few years back. That was all the unemployment, of course. Barry didn't want to think about unemployment, it made him go cold down his back.

A lot of men were black or Indian or men he instinctively knew to be of Irish descent like himself, dark and wild of face with a light in their eyes. Some were fair and sharp-nosed but none he could see really looked like Jason grown-up. The idea formed and grew solid in Barry's mind that for his own peace of mind — or if not for peace, for the easing of his mind — he would have to go up to Hampstead and find Spring Close and take a look at Terence Wand.

15

It gave Benet a curious feeling when she read in the newspaper about the discovery of the child's body in Finchley. If they decided it was Jason she wouldn't have to give Jason back. There were two major faults in this hypothesis: one that the child's body couldn't be Jason's since Jason himself was standing a yard or two from her feeding his rocking horse with sugar lumps, and secondly, that nothing could be more disastrous for her, nothing so militate against her work and her life as feeling herself obliged to hang on to Jason. Yet the discovery of the body had strangely pleased her. For that she castigated herself. It was dreadful and wrong to feel that way, for whoever this wretched little corpse might have been, it had once been a child, some child, murdered or killed by a violence that went too far, and buried in squalid suburban earth.

Just as she had been almost pleased by the unearthing of the corpse so she was vaguely and irrationally disappointed when it was identified as that of Martin M'Boa, a Nigerian child who had been missing for more than three months. It brought her back to something she had shelved or suspended while there was doubt about the child's identity; it brought her back to decision-making. She still had to fix on a way of returning Jason, though it was a week now since she had decided to return him clandestinely. Jason had taken to waking up in the night, waking just once and calling for her. The first time he called "Mummy" she felt a sort of horror because, momentarily, as she woke to that cry, he had been James. She hadn't wanted to go in to him, to see him instead of James, but she had gone. It wasn't his fault, he was responsible for none of it, and he called her what he would have called any young woman who had the care of him. After she had quieted him, she lay awake for a long time wondering at herself and what had happened to her. Mopsa, of course, was mad. But hadn't she too been a little mad from shock and grief in that she had kept Jason so long after she knew who he was? She wasn't mad now. She was sane and level-headed — she was even writing again, working well in the study room after Jason had been put to bed — but it was *too late now*. A rational mind had been recovered too late. That mind looked askance at Mopsa-type ideas for taking Jason back, restoring him to the wall where he had been when Mopsa found him, taking him into a store crowded with Christmas shoppers and giving him into the care of the management as a lost child, placing him in the arms of a policeman in the street and then running like a hare. Mopsa ideas all of them, if Mopsa could ever have been persuaded Jason must be returned home.

She hadn't spoken to Benet since her return to Marbella. It was Benet's father who had phoned to say her mother had arrived safely, had a good journey, been in good spirits and talking constantly of her visit. It made Benet wonder what story she had told to account for Jason's presence. If she had told any. She must have said something, for John Archdale asked just before he rang off: "How's the boy?"

It wasn't until an hour or two afterwards that Benet understood he had meant James.

She needed someone to confide in. Curiously enough, in an unsatisfactory and inadequate sort of way, Mopsa had filled that role. In the middle of this populous place, Benet was aware of her isolation, a solitude she had created for herself and must maintain until Jason was gone. Since Antonia's, there had been only one phone call and that had been from Ian Raeburn. He asked her to come out for a meal with him.

Benet longed to go. Her abruptness to him, her coldness, when she met him in the street with Jason and the rocking horse had troubled and nagged at her ever since. Without Jason, in some restaurant and later on their own, she could get to know him better. It surprised her how very much she wanted to do this. But Jason couldn't be left and there was no one she could ask to sit with him. All the people she could think of as possibilities had, in the past, sat for her with James. This was an excuse she couldn't make to Ian. She had to tell him she was busy every evening.

"Some other time?" he said. "How about next week?"

She found herself saying "Yes, *please*," like a child promised a treat, a way she had never before spoken to a man.

Now next week had come and she was waiting for him to phone. If he would phone, that would make her do something about Jason. Lying in bed thinking like that at three in the morning seemed perfectly rational, to arrange to have dinner with Ian on, say, Thursday night and therefore be impelled to get rid of

Jason by Wednesday. Dressing Jason next morning, giving him his breakfast, talking to him about the day ahead, one felt quite different. Her sense of responsibility returned, her care for Jason's welfare and for his status as a human being worthy of respect. But she waited for Ian's phone call like a teenager with a first boyfriend. She kept on thinking she heard the phone when it hadn't rung. And when one day she found the receiver had been off for hours because Jason had been playing with it, she had to make an effort not to show her anger.

It was that afternoon when, to divert him from the phone, she broke down another barrier and unlocked James's toy cupboard.

He fetched the toys out in a methodical, adult manner, examining each one. A paintbox James had never used, had been far too young to use, interested him deeply. He couldn't possibly have known what the paints in their small square troughs were or what they were for. Perhaps he simply liked the colors. It brought Benet enormous entertainment to observe how manually dextrous he was. He hardly ever dropped anything. He was a clean and tidy eater. Now he took out a paintbrush and tested the soft camel hair on the pad of his left forefinger. The feel of it made him look up at her and give her one of his broad, radiant smiles.

After a while he found the xylophone with its rainbow octave. It was the colors, the spectrum and the gold, that held his attention. James, she remembered with a catch of pain, had wanted the notes of the scale, that was what had pleased him. But Jason, after a time, did pick up the wooden mallet and slowly and speculatively produce a *do-re-mi-fa-so-la-ti-do*....

Up above them the front doorbell rang. She heard the gate close, footsteps on the short paved path, then the bell. She jumped up and went to the window. No one ever came to the door, no one ever had. The police would come, she thought, and her mouth went dry.

At six o'clock it was dark, the Vale of Peace lamplit in its cosy, antique Hampstead sort of way. She looked out through the slats of the blind. No police car, no stranger's car at all. What cars there were were her own and those of her neighbors habitually parked in this corner of the Vale of Peace. The thought came then that her caller might be Ian. Perhaps he didn't live far away. That the Vale was not exactly on the way to anything except the dark uninhabited Heath itself did occur to her. And wouldn't he have phoned first? Well, Jason had had the phone off the hook for hours.

The bell rang again, a long, insistent peal this time. She ran upstairs. All the time she was thinking, let it be him, let it. To sit and talk to him over a cup of tea down here in the warm basement with Jason was the nicest thing she could think of doing. Yes, please let it be him. . . .

She put on the hall light and opened the front door. It wasn't the police and it wasn't Ian.

It was Edward.

The firm of solicitors Terence found to act for him was in Cricklewood. He saw the name in gilt letters on a row of windows over the premises of a building society. Cricklewood was safer than Hampstead. He took the deeds with him. By now he was getting used to being addressed as Mr. Phipps and he felt fairly confident about signing as Phipps, having practiced John Howard's signature every day.

Terence expected a lot of questions, but the solicitor wanted nothing more than the name of the estate agents. He seemed surprised to be offered the deeds of the house.

"We'll press for an early exchange of contracts and ten percent of the purchase price on that date," he said.

Going down the stairs, Terence worked that one out. Thirteen thousand, two hundred and ninety-five pounds. If he lost his nerve, if the strain of it all got too much for him, he could pull out once he got that money. He could simply walk out and go. The thought comforted him and his churning stomach quieted. When he got home he found a letter waiting for him on the mat. It was one of the few letters he had ever received while living in Spring Close, the first since Freda went away.

He recognized Freda's writing on the envelope.

"Dear Terry" – he would have expected "Dearest lambkins," though he had never had a letter from her before. The opening seemed ominous. He read quickly, fearful she might be coming back. There was no risk of that, though. Not much was said about what she was doing, yet somehow the two sheets reeked of happiness, and all through them were references to someone called Anthony. A brief explanation of who Anthony was – "an old friend I knew before I was married, we lost touch over the years. He has a house here...." – came near the end. Terence saw it all. That was why she had gone: she had had a letter from, perhaps even been invited by, this Anthony. Some old rich man. Money calls to money, he thought. Very likely she would marry Anthony.

The letter annoyed him. She was obviously indifferent to his welfare. The tone was rather as if she were writing to a caretaker. "The heating system should be overhauled before Christmas. Would you like to ring them and arrange a date? It is on contract so there is no need for you to worry about payment. . . ." It also pleased him. She wasn't coming back, she wouldn't poke her nose in where she wasn't wanted. If he could only hold on to his nerve, keep cool; why do a moonlight flit with thirteen thousand when he had only to wait in perfect safety for ten times that?

He phoned Steiner & Wildwood to give Sawyer the name of his solicitor. In the course of conversation it came out that they would be taking three percent commission. Terence had been told this when he first put the house in their hands, but it was irritating to be reminded of it. A pleasanter piece of news was that Mr. and Mrs. Goldschmidt were not dependent on the sale of their own house to buy 5 Spring Close.

"There won't be any question of a chain," said Sawyer.

"A chain?"

"I mean there won't be any question of Mr. and Mrs. Goldschmidt waiting to sell their property to a purchaser who is waiting for someone to buy his property. And so on."

"I see. Great. That's fine."

There seemed cause for celebration. Terence

seriously contemplated selling those National Savings certificates of John Howard's. He was confident of his ability to forge the signature perfectly. And he would only have to forge the signature on a withdrawal form. He had found out there would be no need to present himself for scrutiny at a post office. But was it worth even that small risk for £1400? How would he feel forever afterwards if he threw up his chances of £130,000 for not much more than a hundredth of that?

For the time being, he had to be content with the benefit he got from the DHSS. He phoned Teresa and took her to the cinema. They went to the Screen on the Hill so they were back at Spring Close soon after ten. For the first time Terence had used Freda's car, noting it was high time it had some exercise. The battery needed a good deal of stirring into life. Because he put the car away in the garage again, they entered the house by the back way.

Teresa said could she have a bath? Freda's *en suite* bathroom reminded her of a photograph of one she had seen in *Homes and Gardens* while waiting to have her teeth scaled. Terence went to the bedroom window to pull down the blind, which was made of black silk with a Chinese painting on it. It was not modesty or prudishness that stopped him putting the light on before doing this but rather an unwillingness to draw any sort of attention to himself on the part of the neighbors. Seeing a naked man and a girl in Freda's bedroom wouldn't, of course, have the effect of making a neighbor ring up Steiner & Wildwood and spill the beans, but it would make him conspicuous and even talked about in a way he felt — at this moment in time, to quote Sawyer — undesirable.

A man was standing under the archway that was the entrance to Spring Close. Terence could see him quite clearly in the light from the fancy carriage lamps that were secured on each side to the uprights of the arch. He was a young man, very young, perhaps no more than what newspapers and television called a youth. The lamplight showed Terence that he was dark, handsome in an Irish sort of way, very lanky, and narrow-hipped. He had jeans on and a leather jacket, a sweater with a high polo neck. Exactly the way a young detective constable would dress getting himself up to be taken for a yobbo.

Terence's heart thudded as if it were kicking him. There was no doubt the man was watching this house. A non-confronter and one who could readily convince himself black was white and things almost anything but what they seemed, Terence nevertheless couldn't be persuaded that the man under the arch was interested in any other house or was there for any other purpose but to keep his eye on 5 Spring Close. Their eyes met, only Terence knew the man couldn't actually see him, having sometimes himself looked back at this window from the arch after dark.

What was he doing there? Had the police somehow got wise to what he was doing? That solicitor, he thought, and he broke out into a sweat. Probably the solicitor had been a personal friend of John Phipps. Terence padded over to the bedside table and swallowed two Valium. He could hear Teresa splashing about in the bath. Why would the police watch the house? Why wouldn't they just come and arrest him?

It occurred to him that the man might be waiting to do just that, only he thought he was still out. He'd soon know, he *had* to know. What had he done, anyway? Nothing. He had signed nothing. He would say that he was Freda's cousin and that she'd asked him to sell her house for her in her absence. And if they asked her at this stage, she wouldn't betray him. She might hate him, never speak to him again, but she wouldn't betray him to the police. He took a deep breath, snapped on the overhead light, and immediately pulled down the blind.

Teresa came dancing out of the bathroom in wafts of Freda's *Opium* bath essence. Her scented nakedness had not the slightest effect on Terence, who hoped to God things would improve later. It was his turn for the bathroom. He cleaned his teeth. Then he stood on the rim of Freda's bidet and looked out of the window.

The close was empty but for a white cat sitting under the catalpa tree. The man had gone.

In the light of her porch he looked pale and rather thinner than three years before. He walked in without a word, as if he were expected. And suddenly, as he was unwinding his long scarf and hanging up his jacket, she understood that he *was* expected. At least as far as he knew. He had been among those anonymous phone callers, one of the many Mopsa alone had spoken to and given God knows what replies. Of course Mopsa had invited him. It would be one of Mopsa's dearest wishes to see her and Edward married, irrespective of their feelings for each other, for the sake of a weird, specious propriety, for the sake of James, who was dead.

"I suppose my mother asked you?"

"Your mother said *you* asked me."

"Edward, what on earth do you mean?"

"You were ill in bed when I phoned. She

said she knew you'd like to see me, you were always saying so, but to leave it a week or two till you were better. She said you'd call me back if Wednesday turned out not to be convenient."

Had his tone always been so sulky? It was a voice, she thought, full of paranoia.

"I didn't invite you. It's the first I've heard of any of this."

"I had an extraordinary feeling as I was coming along this dank enclave," said Edward, "that when I got here I wouldn't be greeted with open arms."

He hadn't changed in his ways or his appearance. He was dressed as he always had been, with all the eccentricity of an athletic teenager: jeans, open-necked, thin white shirt, leather jacket, and striped scarf that hung to his knees. The boyish look was still there, the lock of yellow hair dipping over the forehead, the chiseled mouth with its tilted corners, but it was growing strained, the process of desiccation was beginning. Edward's nose looked sharper and more aquiline. The wonderful blue of his eyes was as intense as ever.

"Come and have a drink," she said.

She had been going to take him into the living room where the drinks were, but she remembered Jason. Jason was down in the basement on his own and the kitchen was full of dangerous gadgets, the electric kettle, the gas taps, knives. She went towards the basement stairs, Edward following. He always walked softly and springily, in a catlike way, as if on his toes. He is like a cat, she thought. We always think, when we make that comparison, of dark people, dark-haired people, and Edward is fair. Yet he is like a cat, a long, lean ginger tomcat. . . .

The same explanation of Jason's presence must be given to him as had been given to Ian Raeburn. Why not? He wouldn't be interested anyway. In the past he had often said he disliked children.

"I read your book," he said. "I liked it. It's a great book; it deserved to win that prize."

She was astonished and touched. She turned her head to him. "Why, Edward, how very nice of you!"

"One of the things that gratified me was how much of it you owed to me."

There was nothing to say. He had taken her breath away.

"The fact that you went to India at all, for one thing. That you had the entry to places you'd never have set foot in but for me. Not to mention what you learned about writing from me. You might have given me a credit; a single line of acknowledgement would have been less

274

ungracious – 'For Edward Greenwood, without whose help, et cetera.' "

"The gratification you felt wasn't an adequate recompense then? You'd have liked a fee?"

She ran down the last half dozen stairs, her heart pounding with anger. Jason, who had abandoned the xylophone for the time being and was filling James's wheelbarrow with James's bricks, looked up and smiled when he saw her. His pleasure at her return lit up his whole face. He had waited, he hadn't cried, but he was relieved to the point of delight that she had come back. He came to her and put up his arms. She picked him up, calmed by him, her anger cooling.

Edward was looking at them both. A flush had come up into his face. He said in his sullen way:

"So that's my son?"

She hadn't expected that. Bringing Edward down here she hadn't foreseen it, though obviously she should have. It would be easy to say yes, the easiest way out. After all, she would seldom see Edward again, she was going to make sure of that. In no possible way were they going to become "friends." If James had lived, if this were James he was looking at in Benet's arms, that would still be true. There was nothing to make a link between them now that James was dead.

She had only to nod. A shrug, simple silence, would do it. To put an end to questions, inquiries, suspicions, she had only to nod her head, take a step forward, and present this handsome, fair-haired, blue-eyed child to this handsome, fair-haired, blue-eyed man. She couldn't. It seemed an outrage. So Edward did mean something to her still? Or what there had been between herself and Edward meant something? Enough anyway to make it impossible for her to look him in the face and tell him this was his child.

"No. He's a friend's child I'm looking after."

He didn't believe her. "Don't give me that, Benet. You've kept yourself from me and your book and your success; you must be the meanest-spirited woman living. And now you'd even deny me the identity of my son."

"I'm not denying anything, Edward. This isn't James."

She set Jason on the rocking horse and set it swinging. But Jason had had enough of rocking horses and xylophones and wheelbarrows. He rubbed his fists into his eyes.

"Jay wants juice."

It was what he always said when he was tired. She carried him with her to the fridge, took out the feeding bottle of apple juice, held it under the hot tap to take the chill off, Jason seated on her hip. Edward followed her. He was standing very close to them.

"If it's not James, where *is* James?"

To gain courage, to have the strength to say the words, she found herself doing a curious thing. She tightened her grasp on Jason and held him close to her, feeling his warmth.

"James is dead, Edward."

"*What?*"

"I did say that. You did hear me. James is dead. He died in hospital about six weeks ago."

"Children don't die these days," he said. "Children don't die."

"That's what I thought. I was wrong. They do."

Jason liked best to feed himself with the juice. She sat him in the big Windsor chair, propped with cushions. Edward was staring at him.

"I don't believe you, Benet. It would be typical of you to invent some stratagem to keep me totally from my son. I've no legal claim anyway, but the fact that he's my son and you know it and I know it would be enough to bother you. You'd even cut that."

She lifted her shoulders. She said stonily, "I'll show you the death certificate."

When Mopsa had come home in the late

afternoon of that first day Benet left the hospital, she had seen her tuck a long buff-colored envelope into one of the pigeonholes of the desk. They had not talked about it but she knew what was inside. She took out the certificate, and, without looking at it, handed it to Edward. He read it and looked up at her with haggard eyes.

"How did you let that happen to him? How could you allow him to — to asphyxiate?"

So that was what it said. She didn't want to see. She felt a cold, contemptuous anger against Edward. What did he know? What did he *care?* He put his head into his hands and covered his face. Jason leaned against her, then climbed into her lap. She hoped and prayed Edward would go now, that he would have his little show of grief he couldn't possibly feel for a child he had never known and then — doubtless uttering threats, abusing and accusing her — he would go. He took away his hands and looked at her, red-eyed.

"You offered me a drink about half an hour ago. I should have thought the least you could have done was fetch it when you went upstairs just now. After what you've told me, I rather *need* a drink."

She knew who he reminded her of. Of Mopsa. Had it always been so? Was there something in her own personality that needed a Mopsa, a parasite creature to batten on her and insult her and amaze her with its own gross selfishness? It made her laugh, not ironically but with pure amusement.

"Three years ago," he said, "I thought you couldn't be harder, but I was wrong. I hoped you'd changed. Don't you want to know why I came here? I thought we might get together again. I even thought we might marry."

"But now you're disillusioned?" Jason had fallen asleep. She took the bottle gently from him. "If you want that drink, Edward, you'll have to fetch it yourself. Room above this one, cupboard by the window. I have to put this boy to bed."

Barry went down the hill towards Hampstead tube station. He felt shaken. There had been very little warning of what had happened. All evening the house had been in darkness and then, just as he was giving up hope of seeing Terence Wand that evening, a faint light had come on, not in one of the front rooms but a light somewhere in the back of the house seen from where he stood through an arch or an open doorway. Terence Wand had come in the back way. It hadn't occurred to Barry that there *was* a back way, but after he moved away from the arch and before he left for the station, he had investigated and found the garages, the one numbered five with the small blue Volvo tucked inside.

But after that light came on, he had for a while been given new hope of seeing and identifying Terence Wand. He counted on his showing himself at a window, and this was what had eventually happened, but in a shocking and almost horrible way. Barry wondered how long Terence Wand had known he was there and, come to that, known who he was and where he stood in relation to Carol. For that Terence Wand must have known this, his subsequent behavior clearly showed.

If Barry had had any doubts about Terence Wand, they were gone now. About who Wand was to Jason and had been to Carol and would be again if he could. Wand had mocked him with it in a single moment's *macho* display. The house had been dark but for that glimmer of light in the back regions. Somehow its darkness seemed permanent, still, enduring. He had let his attention wander and watched a white cat jump one of the low walls and stroll towards the tree in the center of the courtyard. What had made him look up again towards the blank, black, shiny windows? Certainly not any change in the unchanging aspect of the house. A sixth sense perhaps, a spark of electricity transmitted from this man to him with whom he had something strong in common.

He lifted his head and looked up. The light came on in an explosive flood and a naked man stood there for an instant of mocking exposure. The light made a gold gleam on his hair; he looked tall as a statue. Then the blind went down in a black cascade and shut him out.

Barry came home over the Chinese bridge. He counted the houses from where the footpath met Summerskill Road but there were no lights on in Carol's. It was only just gone eleven; the wine bar didn't close till eleven.

Winterside Down seemed unusually empty. Even the motorbike boys weren't about. Lila Kupar, who never drew her curtains, whose curtains were perhaps not ample enough to draw, could be seen in her scarcely furnished front room ironing a white sari. A naked light bulb, rather too powerful, hung just above her head. Barry let himself into the house. The Spicers had their television on loudly and you could hear the meaningless prompted laughter in Carol's hall. In the dark, Barry saw Terence Wand's face. In reality he had glimpsed it for no more than five seconds but he was sure it had imprinted itself on his mind. It was Jason's face thirty years on that he conjured up.

Barry didn't possess a pair of gloves. He put on Carol's rubber ones, which hung over the rim of the kitchen sink. Wearing the gloves, he found himself the ballpoint pen he and Carol used for writing messages to each other and the milkman, and the notebook Tanya had for school and had once left behind in the house. He would have to buy an envelope tomorrow. He began to write his letter, carefully printing the words.

16

The anonymous letter came into the hands of Detective Inspector Tony Leatham by way of Chief Superintendent Treddick and those forensic experts who had examined it in vain for fingerprints and other possible giveaways. By this time the lined paper, exercise book paper, was crumpled and rather limp. Leatham already knew what it said. A conference had been held solely for the purpose of discussing this letter.

Jason Stratford's father is Terence Wand, 5 Spring Close, Hampstead,

The writer evidently wanted them to believe this Wand had snatched his son and was keeping him hidden somewhere. The aim was probably no more than the vindictive one of wanting to cause trouble for Wand. Treddick, of course, believed Jason was dead and had been dead since the day he disappeared, had almost certainly been dead even before his disappearance was reported. He had been murdered and buried somewhere like the African child in Finchley, and one day, like that child's, his body would be unearthed.

For his part, Leatham wasn't so sure. He still thought it possible Jason had been abducted. Tough, hard, with little faith left in human nature, he nevertheless hoped for Jason. He was fond of children. Since Jason had gone, he sometimes found himself looking at his own sons with fiercely protective paternal feelings, something he hadn't consciously experienced before.

Treddick was gunning for Barry Mahon. He thought it was only a matter of time before he got him. One day Barry would betray himself, probably lead them to Jason's grave, and Treddick was patient, he could wait. Tony Leatham couldn't see they had a scrap of real evidence against Barry. The only offense he had committed, Leatham thought, was to write this letter. He was nearly sure Barry had written it. Treddick was too. He said it was an attempt on Barry's part to turn the heat off himself.

Leatham didn't care much; he was losing

interest in all of it. What he would have liked was to find Jason alive and in good shape – preferably for *him* to find him – and then let bygones be bygones. Another case he had been involved in back in the summer affected him more. The man in question, a bank robber, had broken prison while on remand, escaped, and made his way halfway across the world. They had recaptured Monty Driscoll in Melbourne, and when the Australian government agreed to give him up, Leatham hoped to be the officer sent out to bring him back. It would be the kind of excitement that seldom came his way. He was pulling strings to get himself to Melbourne.

In the meantime this Terence Wand business had to be attended to. They couldn't just leave it.

Mrs. Goldschmidt rang up early in the morning. Could she come and have another look at the house, take a few measurements? Terence didn't want her there but he didn't know how to refuse. There were all sorts of risks attached to having anyone in the house except his own personal invitees. He took two Valium.

She arrived at ten-thirty, dressed this time in a pink leather coat with a fur collar. Each time Terence had seen her, she had been wearing animal skins. Today her short blonde hair was swept forward in wispy curls round her face, her make-up mauvish, with damson lips. She had the manner of someone on depressant drugs, downers, and her first remark therefore sounded sarcastic.

"I'm thrilled we're going to have your house."

She spoke in the gray monotone of someone commenting on continual bad weather or chronic illness. Terence walked about the house with her. In the bedroom, where the futon was, she took off her coat and dropped it over one of the low Japanese tables. Under it she wore a very short, pink, knitted dress with a bulky polo collar.

"That's better."

She stood on a stool to measure the window for curtains.

"Blinds are so cold on their own, don't you think?"

She put out a hand for Terence to help her down, even though the stool stood no more than a foot off the floor. Now in stockinged feet, she climbed onto the ottoman which filled the window embrasure in the master bedroom. She stretched up with her tape measure, lost her balance, and would have fallen had Terence not caught and steadied her. He caught her round the waist and, instead of a stiff, nervous body, found himself clasping a relaxed, even yielding, one. He asked himself what was going on. Something certainly was. Terence knew he was attractive to women — it had made a living for him, as having a flair for design or management might — but he didn't know why. He was a little below medium height, nothing so much to look at, and with the sort of coloring that in a woman is called "mousy." Carol Stratford had once asked him if he was a man or a mouse, and it was true he often felt mouselike, smallish and brown and nervous. Perhaps that was what the women liked.

He took his hands away from Mrs. Goldschmidt's waist, giving her a light pat on the flank. He was wondering what to do, what response to make if things hotted up — would refusal jeopardize the sale of the house or, on the other hand, would acquiescence? — when, glancing out of the window, he saw two men come into the court from under the arch and stand just this side of it, looking at the five houses.

Terence had not been able to make up his mind about the watcher of a few nights ago, but he knew these two were policemen. He was one of those people who have a nose for policemen. No one else had quite those tired, bleary eyes, rubber-mask faces, clothes that looked as if their wearers had lost weight, black shoes that needed polishing. They stood there looking at the five houses. Then they began to move across the courtyard towards number one. Terence let out his held breath. Mrs. Goldschmidt put out her hand to be helped down as if she expected him to kiss it first.

As they were on their way down, he took a look out of one of the slit windows that lit the staircase. The policeman had gone inside number one but the front door still stood open. Terence didn't like it. He wanted Mrs. Goldschmidt to go. She moved slowly and languidly ahead of him, trailing her hand down the banisters, once looking back over her shoulder to give him a vague, wistful smile. In the hall, by the statue with a hole for a head, she stood making notes on a pad in large backward-sloping writing.

"Oh, I forgot my coat. I left it upstairs."

She would go up to fetch it, he thought, and then call him, and then . . .

"I'll get it for you."

He leaped for the stairs. The bedroom window showed him the two policemen on the narrow stone terrace outside the front door of number three in conversation with the woman who lived there. He grabbed the pink leather coat. Downstairs again, he held the coat for her, actually took hold of her right arm and pushed it into the sleeve opening. It took all the meager courage he had to open the front door. The policemen were outside, about three yards away, staring at the door and now at him.

His throat closed up and his heart took a painful leap towards the middle of his chest. Somehow they had got onto him. Someone, one of those neighbors perhaps, had seen the house was up for sale, was a friend of Sawyer's, had had a letter from Freda...Mrs. Goldschmidt went slowly out of the door, down the steps, extending her swan neck, vaguely smiling. He realized the police weren't going to move or speak until she was out of the way. That was their brand of tact. As if he cared! It could have been her who put them on to him, for all he knew.

She turned back once. "Well, goodbye for now and thank you so much."

Don't call me Phipps, he screamed silently, don't call me Phipps!

"I may be in touch. I may want to come back."

It sounded inexorable; it sounded like a dour threat. He had nothing to say and couldn't have spoken if he had wanted to. His voice would have been a reedy pipe. She walked past the policemen as if they weren't there or were mere furnishings of the courtyard, additional trees or urns, and backed with tiny slow steps across the paving to gaze at the house she had just left. It was only when she turned away once more, smiling with unparted lips in Terence's direction, began on her measured stroll towards the arch, that the policemen moved. They walked up the steps and the older one, ruddy and fair-haired, in a flapping raincoat with dangling belt, said in a low, conversational tone to Terence: "Mr. Wand? Mr. Terence Wand?"

Terence nodded. He felt as limp as a leaf. The front door closed with a soft, dainty little click. They were looking round Freda's hall, at the statues, the Modigliana copy, the black spaniel carpet, the way policemen always do look as if they themselves were condemned by an ungrateful society forever to live in pre-war council houses. Terence opened the double glass doors into the living room. He wished he hadn't eaten those cornflakes, that boiled egg, and that croissant for breakfast because he was sure that any moment now he was going to have to make an excuse and go away to be sick.

They walked in. They stood looking curiously about them as if they too had come with a view to buying the house. Just as Terence was trying to frame the words that would get him out of there and into the bathroom, the younger one said: "Jason Stratford, Mr. Wand. Young Jason Stratford. That's why we've come to see you."

For a moment the name meant nothing to Terence. It was a shock only insofar as it was utterly distant from what he had expected.

"May we sit down?"

Again Terence nodded. He didn't sit down. He was holding himself still and tense because he was afraid he might retch if he moved.

"You'll be aware of course that young Jason is missing. I don't reckon there's many people unaware of that now. Am I right in thinking you're a personal friend of his mother, Mrs. Carol Stratford?"

Relief hit Terence like a soft, warm pillow pushed into his face. He could hardly breathe for it. Whatever this might be about it was nothing to do with fraudulent schemes to sell Freda Phipp's house. He wondered if he could speak but was still afraid to try.

"According to our information there's a possibility you're Jason Stratford's father."

If anything could have fetched a voice out of Terence it was this. It came very shrilly.

"Me?"

They didn't say anything. They went on looking at him, though not in an unfriendly way.

"Did she tell you that?" said Terence, articulate again and gruff-voiced with indignation.

"Well, no, Mr. Wand. We're not able to divulge our source of information, but I think I can tell you who it wasn't, and it wasn't Mrs. Stratford."

Terence didn't believe him. It would be just like Carol to tell them that. No doubt she was shielding Jason's true father because the guy was up to something shady or really had got the boy. It could be almost anything with Carol, she was very devious. He could see what they were up to. They'd called on the neighbors to find out if any of them had seen a strange child about.

"I didn't know the kid existed," he said. "That is, not until I saw on TV about him being missing."

They continued to look polite, impassive. Terence could tell that the bigger, fair one was wondering why he had been so nervous if he had nothing to hide.

"I don't suppose you'd object if we had a look over the house, would you?"

What a way to put it! The younger one said it was a nice place he'd got here. Terence didn't object, he knew that would be very unwise, but he went upstairs behind them. In the bathroom off the master bedroom they found Teresa's eyeliner pencil lying on the glass top of the vanitory unit.

"Married, now, are you, Mr. Wand?"

Terence shook his head. He didn't explain. The younger one's eyes shifted as if this only confirmed the likelihood of Terence's having bastards he didn't know about all over the place. Terence felt an increasing grievance against Carol Stratford. He'd make it his business to have a word with Carol over this.

The policemen didn't exactly search. They just looked into all the rooms. They asked to see his passport, which gave him a dreadful pang for a moment in case they had powers to confiscate it. But they handed it back without a word and soon after that they went. Terence took two Valium and poured himself a very stiff whisky. He sat down with his drink and asked himself seriously if he was going to have the stamina to carry things through. Not was it worth it. He knew very well it was worth almost anything to get his hands on £130,000. Not was it worth it but could he stand the pace?

Terence knew himself. He had the rare quality of knowing himself quite well. The agony of the morning had brought him fresh self-knowledge. His fear had been so great and also so prolonged that he wondered now why

293

he hadn't had a heart attack or fallen down in a fit. If he reacted like that because two policemen called on him, how would his body and his nerves behave when he had to sign that contract, receive that huge sum of money, draw it from the bank, and escape with it? How would he stand up to things while, with the money in a bag in his hand, he had to get to an airport and board a plane?

Suppose he dropped dead of fear?

Might it not be wiser, after all, to opt for the thirteen thousand odd of the deposit money and call it a day? Take Goldschmidt's check and vanish? Goldschmidt's check...A chilly tremor ran through Terence. He set his glass down.

This was something he hadn't thought of, something he had entirely neglected to think of. Goldschmidt's — or his firm of solicitors' — check would be drawn to John H. Phipps and would certainly be a crossed check. He, Terence, would therefore have to pay it into John Phipps's bank account. But he didn't have a bank account, he didn't exist.

There was nothing to stop Terence going to, say, the Midland in West End Lane and opening an account in the name of John Howard Phipps except that they would want a reference. They would want someone else, preferably an account holder with the same bank, if not the same branch, to vouch for him that he was a suitable, respectable and credit-worthy person. As John Phipps. He knew all about it. Jessica had opened an account for him at the Anglican-Victoria in the Market Place in Hampstead Garden Suburb and had of course herself been his referee.

Who was there in the world prepared to say that Terence Wand, posing as John Phipps, was respectable and trustworthy? Come to that, who was there prepared to tell a bank Terence Wand was John Phipps?

No one. There was no one he could take on as an accomplice. To do so would necessarily mean sharing the £132,000, splitting it down the middle, in fact. He would rather forgo it all than do that, he thought, far rather.

A little snow had fallen during the night. It lay like a thin, patchy sheet of gauze on roofs and the tops of cars, but where commuters and the postman had already trodden were wet brown footprints. A steady *drip-drip-drip* came from the house eaves. Over the Heath a gray mist hung.

When he had finished his breakfast, Jason sat on the floor drawing. He drew a picture of the xylophone and crayoned all the notes in in appropriate colors. It was a very good drawing indeed for a two-year-old, Benet thought; you could easily see what it was supposed to be.

She had dressed Jason in clothes she had bought for him, not James's. She cut the labels out in case they were clues. Jason wore blue velvet-corded dungarees with a blue-and-white striped tee shirt and a sweater in natural undyed wool. He had fawn socks and brown leather lace-up half-boots. Benet sat him on her lap to put his coat on, a brown tweed coat with hood and toggle buttons, lined in Black Watch tartan. She was rather worried about that coat. She had bought it in Hampstead, in an exclusive, expensive shop, and she and Jason had been in there for a long time while he tried coats on. Would the woman remember her? The point was, she really did want him to have that coat. He had to leave the rocking horse and the xylophone and the drawing things behind, but she wanted him to keep that warm winter coat.

He liked riding in the car so much he was never any trouble. She wondered how he would react when they came to Lordship Avenue, if he would remember. And would he remember this house in the Vale of Peace? Not to tell people now, of course; that was not what she meant. He had nowhere near the required command of speech. But one day when he was grown-up, would he, if he came to Hampstead and perhaps walked up from South End Green or down from Heath Street, have a sense of *déjà vu?* Would he think, I have been here before? And if they had told him of that six-week-long lacuna in his life, would he then ask himself if he had spent it here?

She had very little real apprehension that she herself was in danger. She was not the kind of person the police would suspect. If they had questioned women known to have lost a child, they would already have come to her. There could not be so many. No, they had either neglected to take this step or else considered her so unlikely – the well-known, well-off young writer who probably didn't know where Lordship Avenue was – as to be beyond suspicion. So if she had been beyond suspicion while Jason was missing surely she would continue to be so once he was found.

At red traffic lights she looked over her shoulder as she always did to speak to him.

"All right, Jay?"

"White," he said. "Snow."

"It's going fast but there'll be some more and you can make a snowman."

"Snowman," said Jason, liking the word. "Snowman, snowman."

She began to speak her thoughts aloud to him.

"I'm going to take you into the public library in Lordship Avenue, Jay, the branch called Winterside. You may have been in there before with your mother or – or Barry? I remember the library. I used to go there a lot when I lived in Winterside Road. There's a children's section with chairs set round a table. I'm going to sit you on one of those chairs and get you a book to look at from the shelf and then I'm going to leave you there. But first I'm going to pin a label on your coat that says who you are. I've done a label with 'This is Jason Stratford' on it."

"Coat," said Jason. "Jay's coat."

"That's right, pinned onto Jay's coat. And when they see you're on your own, the people in the library will read the label and know who you are and fetch your mother."

And the police, she thought. She tried to imagine it all, the hue and cry, but somehow she couldn't. With Jason's return the world ended.

"Mummy," said Jason in a pleasant, conversational tone. "Mummy."

She drove eastwards along Rudyard Gardens, looking for a place to park. Parking had got a lot worse since the days when she had lived there. There were double yellow lines all the way along Lordship Avenue now. She didn't want to be too far away from the library. Winterside Road itself might do, only there was no entry to Winterside from Lordship Avenue. She had to make a long detour, coming into Winterside Road from Canal Street, passing Woodhouse's garage and the house where they had had the attic flat. There was a parking space almost outside the garage, but suppose Tom Woodhouse were there and were to come out and see her?

The pollarded plane trees were a hideous sight at this time of the year, their trunks like old bones. The heavy gray sky looked full of snow. She had first met Edward during a snowy winter, and it had been a cold hard winter, spring rather, when she had parted from him. They had been living in Tufnell Park, and it was he who had left and found himself a flat or room somewhere round here. Brownswood Common Lane? Brownswood Dale? She couldn't remember, and he wasn't there now anyway. The address he had left her was Kentish Town. He had told her he hated her, she was hard as nails, that they had never been suited to each other, and then had done one of his about-faces, tried to get her into his arms and make her promise to go back to him, to marry him.

There was a slot to park the car in on the Winterside Down side of the street just by the footpath that led to the Chinese bridge over the canal. She put Edward out of her mind. He lived here no longer, he was the last person she was likely to see.

The lawns of Winterside Down were a bright December green. In the branches of a Norway spruce someone had put a network of Christmas lights. Benet took Jason's stroller, the original one, out of the trunk of the car and debated whether to return it with him. It was old and battered, but it was Carol Stratford's and she, Benet, had no right to keep it. On the other hand, they might stop her taking it into the library or suggest she fold it, and that would draw unwanted attention to herself. She decided to leave it in the trunk. The clothes Jason was wearing more than compensated for the cost of a new one.

She lifted Jason down out of the car. He looked towards Winterside Down, the rows of red brick houses, the white roadways, the single tall tower. His cheeks went bright pink in the cold air. As they walked along he kept his head turned towards the estate, his eyes fixed on it, his hand in hers dragging a little. Then he pointed. He looked at her inquiringly, putting the question in the form all his questions took.

"What's this?" he said. "What's this?"

"It's where you used to live, Jay. It's where you're going to live." She picked him up. He sat firmly on her hip. "I'm sorry about it all. It wasn't my fault in the beginning. You and I, we were victims of circumstance. Well, we were victims of poor Mopsa, who's ill. And later on – I couldn't do that to Mopsa, could I? I've no excuse for keeping you so long after she went home. I don't really know why I did. I'm a coward, I suppose, or else I'd take you boldly into a police station. I'd take you to your mother over there. But I can't. I haven't the nerve, I'm a coward. So I'm sorry about it, Jay, and I hope you haven't been unhappy, I hope there's been no harm done." He wasn't looking at her. He was frowning and his lower lip stuck out. "Go on," she said, "say something. One kindly word will do."

"Dog," said Jason, pointing at the Doberman sniffing packing cases outside a fishmonger. And then, shrinking up against her, "Mummy!"

The Winterside library was a Victorian building with a Dutch façade and the words PUBLIC LIBRARY carved in recess on a red sandstone plaque over the doors. Benet walked up the steps, carrying Jason. An elderly man, a pensioner with an armful of books, held the door open for her.

Two librarians, both women, stood in the area between the IN and OUT counters, one in the act of stamping a book, the other studying a catalogue. Benet saw that the book which the borrower put out his hand for was her own *The Marriage Knot* in its large, handsome hardcover edition. Her photograph was on the back of the jacket, a young, heart-shaped, half-smiling face, unrecognizable surely as the gaunt woman who had just come in carrying a child, her head tied up in a scarf to hide the mass of dark shiny hair.

The children's section of the library was still there, though changed, brightened up, the little chairs now painted a variety of colors, and pinned up on the wall a collage poster to make her stare and smile. Was this a recurring motif in current teacher-training courses? Or had one of those librarians a child who had been in the hospital where James had been? The poster, though less ambitious in its execution, though small, sparser, and less adventurous, was a tree of hands.

Finding it here seemed an omen. But of what? She didn't believe in omens. She sat Jason down on a turquoise-blue chair and found a picture book from the shelves for him. The library was silent now but for the faint footfalls of two borrowers moving between the bookcases and the sound of a man reading today's paper at a table clearing his throat. There was no one in the children's section but themselves. Jason turned the thick cardboard pages of his book, looking at pictures of a dog, a cat, a pair of shire horses.

"What's this?"

She laid a finger on her lips, then on his, the way she had of telling him to be very quiet. The hands on the tree were all like her own, thin, brown, ringless hands, all the same, all pointing downwards. Her own hands were like those as they dipped into her bag for the label and the pin.

Jason pointed at the book. He whispered because she had asked him to.

"What's this?"

"You know what that is; that's a dog."

He spoke the first real sentence he had yet uttered. It was slowly and perfectly articulated, and he must have been aware of his triumph, for his proud smile began as he spoke.

"I don't like dogs," said Jason and, in spite of the sentiment, gave a pleased giggle.

She held the label in her left hand, the pin in her right. She felt sick, almost faint. It had struck her, what she was about to do, the realization. And she saw what lay beyond, this afternoon, tonight, the desert, the loneliness.

She looked as if for the first time, yet with eyes which saw very differently from that first time, at the fair-haired, sturdy, small boy whose legs as he sat there were not quite long enough to reach the ground, who laughed with delight at his own cleverness, whose scars would never fade. Of course she wasn't going to label him like some sort of parcel and leave him here. She wasn't going to leave him at all. How could she have imagined it? How was it she hadn't understood what had been happening to her as the days with him became weeks and dislike became toleration, toleration acceptance, acceptance camaraderie, and at last...

Why, I couldn't live without him now, she thought. Jason was getting down off the chair. He handed her the book and put up his arms. He had had enough of the library; he wanted to go home.

17

Last Christmas, Carol had had Tanya and Ryan home. Barry wondered who else had been there with Carol, apart from Iris and Jerry and the children. Terence Wand perhaps or one of those others Maureen had mentioned. Carol didn't even want to talk about Christmas; she said she'd work right through the holiday, she hadn't anything to celebrate. What was the good of saying they'd have Tanya and Ryan home when most of the time she wouldn't even be there?

If his own job had been a bit more secure, he might have been able to persuade her not to put in so many hours for Kostas. But he wouldn't have liked to bet on his having a job at all this time next year. Ken Thompson hadn't any more work lined up once the Finchley job was over. And it was almost over. They were dragging their feet really, Barry knew, because after that unless someone came in with an order in the next couple of days, there'd be nothing. Ordinarily, of course, Ken couldn't get rid of him, couldn't sack him without very good cause, but it would be another thing if he could prove there wasn't the work about to justify employing him. He couldn't say to Carol to slacken off when any time he might be on the dole himself.

Ken was acting differently towards him anyway. It was hard to put your finger on it, but Barry noticed he had stopped calling him by his first name. It used to be Barry this and Barry that but now he didn't use any name to him at all. And sometimes, while they were putting the finishing touches to the managing director's office, Barry looked round and caught Ken looking at him. Not in any sort of vindictive or disgusted way, it wasn't like that. Barry thought Ken looked at him as one might steal a glance at something not quite included in humanity, a variety of ape perhaps or a picture of prehistoric man.

At least the police hadn't been back. Was his letter responsible for that? It seemed likely. He imagined Terence Wand being put through those long grueling sessions with Treddick or Leatham, Terence Wand asked if he saw himself as a nursemaid or if he beat up kids. It would shake him up a bit, being fetched away from that fancy house of his in a police car. Barry tried to imagine how anyone with Terence Wand's background could ever have come to own such a house. He must have started himself off in some business when he was very young. Barry knew that was the way it was done and longed to do the same himself, to have a house like that for Carol, a car, only the times weren't right for it, things were different, he'd heard, ten years ago. There was no use in him starting up on his own now when even Ken, who was a businessman and known, couldn't get the jobs.

Winterside Down was giving him the cold shoulder. The Spicers next door weren't acting the way the Isadoros did or the people in the Bevan Square shops, they weren't staring and then turning ostentatiously away, they were just pretending they hadn't seen him when they had. Barry had to do something in the evenings, he couldn't sit at home all the time on his own watching television. He took to going to the Bulldog for a drink round about seven. The Bulldog was far enough away from Winterside Down for the people in there not to know who he was.

He met Iris and Jerry, coming from the opposite direction, bound for the same destination. That is, he saw them coming a long way off. They were arm in arm, Iris taller than Jerry in her wobbly stilt-heeled sandals. Barry had never thought the day would come when he would be glad to have even Iris and Jerry to talk to. He didn't wave, he didn't feel they had ever reached waving terms, but he quickened his pace a bit. The Bulldog was on this side, only a few yards away now. The brewery had put up a new sign, a bulldog with a cigar in its mouth and a sailor hat on. Barry saw Iris tug at Jerry's sleeve and whisper something. They weren't anywhere near a pedestrian crossing but they crossed the road, getting halfway and having to wait on the white line, they were that desperate to avoid him.

Barry could hardly believe it. Carol's own mother! She couldn't think he'd murdered Jason. She was as much responsible as anyone for his disappearance, more than anyone really. He was in the Bulldog's doorway now, but he stopped, he didn't go in. He could see them on the other side of Lordship Avenue, pretending to look in a shop window, no doubt watching the Bulldog's entrance reflected in the glass.

Obviously Iris was thinking along the same lines as the rest of them. He could hear her state her reason, if reason it could be called, in that placid, indifferent whine of hers.

"There's no smoke without fire when all's said and done, is there, Barry?"

Only she wouldn't call him by his Christian name again, any more than Ken did. He began to walk rapidly on down Lordship Avenue. Put a mile between himself and Winterside Down and he wouldn't feel everyone he passed was thinking child-killer, child-killer. He'd go and have a drink in the wine bar, he thought. Carol would have something to say about Iris avoiding him like that. He imagined her anger on his behalf and her calling him "lover" in front of all those people.

It wasn't worth getting a bus now he'd come so far. You could see the wine bar's neon sign a long way off because it was on a curve where the road bent round to the right. It was funny, he thought, how he always saw her lights in the distance and was pulled by fast magnetism towards them.

The wine bar was on the corner of a little side street called Java Mews. Down at the bottom was a pub called the Java Head that was Ken Thompson's local. Barry didn't want to run into Ken now. The awkwardness and the constraint would be worse than at work. He didn't want to see Dennis Gordon either, but there was no avoiding it. The silvery-blue

Rolls, a diamond on a rubbish heap, was parked a little way down the mews and directly under a street lamp as if the lamp were there specially to highlight it. Dennis Gordon was getting into the car, was in the driving seat, though the hand with that great gleaming lump of a ring on it still held the door open.

He got out again and waved to Barry. There seemed no reason for his getting out unless it was to show himself off and the cream leather trench coat he wore. He raised his hand with a backward flip at Barry and then he bent over the windscreen to scratch a grain or tiny smear off the glass.

Barry didn't nod at him or acknowledge the wave. It didn't occur to him to be grateful to Dennis Gordon for deigning to notice him. The Rolls moved off quietly, with smooth elegance, like a lovely ship leaving a port that is necessarily squalid with docks and wharfs. Barry thought what a lot of people there were about who had money: Ken, Mrs. Fylemon, Kostas, Terence Wand, Dennis Gordon. Sometimes his longing for money or for the opportunity to make it was as great as his longing for Carol. It seemed somehow that if he had it he could keep her forever.

The wine bar was full of trailing plants, pictures of the sea, posters of ruined temples,

310

very Greek. Alkmini, round, dark, heavy-browed, dressed in unrelieved black, was serving behind the bar on her own. Barry was glad afterwards — insofar as he was glad of anything — that he hadn't betrayed himself by asking for Carol. He hadn't got as far as speaking a word. At the sight of him, Kostas, unsmiling, lifted a brown hand an inch or two off his knee. It was Alkmini who told him.

"You forget it's Wednesday, Barry?"

He said nothing for a moment. He felt something move involuntarily inside his chest. His face grew hot. He knew at once with the intuitiveness of the lover what Alkmini was implying. Carol still worked at the wine bar, had even taken on Saturdays, but she had given up Wednesday evenings. She had given up working Wednesday evenings and she hadn't told him.

"It went right out of my head," he said.

He hardly cared whether they guessed or not. Or even, when he looked back over his shoulder and saw Alkmini whispering to a customer, whether it was him she was whispering about — "That's Carol Stratford's boyfriend, that's the one."

If Carol hadn't told him, it was because she must be going somewhere on Wednesday evenings she didn't want him to know about. Of course he could guess where that was. He got on a bus, the first that came along, hardly knowing where it was going, anywhere to put distance between himself and Winterside Down. A curious idea came to him — but one he quickly pushed away — that she must love him, she must care for what he thought and felt, if she bothered to deceive him. She must still care about hurting him.

He tried to remember what she had worn that day. Even if he could have remembered, it would mean nothing. For going out with Terence Wand, she would have come home and changed after being at Mrs. Fylemon's. The Zandra Rhodes dress perhaps or the black-and-white zig-zag with the fake fur over it, it was cold enough for that tonight. He got off the bus in Camden Town and went into the tube station. At Hampstead, when he came out into Heath Street, it was snowing a little, the odd occasional flake of snow falling out of the black, smoky sky.

Hampstead was like a museum full of old things, beautiful, preserved, unreal. The richness of it, even on this mid-winter night, the money-breathing walls, depressed him. He made his way through winding lanes and little alleys to the walls that enclosed Spring Close as if it were a castle. Which, of course, it was, a rich man's castle guarded from the rough world. Barry stood under the arch. The lamplight in there was of quite a different kind from that which glared upon and bleached Winterside Down. It seemed to *stroke* the brownish-red bricks, the pale smooth stonework, the dark shiny wood, the glass. There was enough of it to throw a shadow of the tree onto the paving stones, a shadow like a piece of branched coral. The snow had stopped.

Terence Wand's house was in total darkness. They were out somewhere together, of course they were, though they might intend to come back here later. What could he have done anyway if they had been there? He couldn't march in, fight the man, seize Carol. He wasn't her husband. She hadn't even promised he might be her husband one day.

He walked round the perimeter of Spring Walk. Number five's garage was empty, the door standing open. They had gone out in the car. He went back into Hampstead, into Heath Street, down to the High Street for a drink in the King of Bohemia. It was warm in there and crowded. Carol would have to be home by eleven-thirty, he thought, if she wanted him to go on thinking she had been at the wine bar. It was getting on for ten now. The cold hit him, coming out of that warm bar. It was stupid going back to Spring Close, but he went back.

The arrival of a police car put an end to his vigil. It slid in under the arch, a little sleek blue-and-white car with the orange-colored illuminated sign on its roof. Barry was caught in its headlights like a wild animal on a country road. His first thought was that they wanted him again for another half-dozen hours of questioning, that they had followed him here observing all his movements, the transport he had used, and now were going to carry him off to the fresh humiliation of some interview room.

But the young uniformed officer who got out and came up to him only asked him quietly and politely what he was doing there. Barry didn't know what to say. He didn't know what he was doing there himself.

"I was just looking," he said and he heard a stammer in his voice. "I didn't know there were any modern houses down here so I came in to get a closer look."

"You're taking your time about it."

One of the neighbors had been on to them, Barry guessed. Somebody in one of the lighted houses must have phoned them to report a loiterer.

"I should get off home if I were you," the

policeman said. "It's getting a bit late to be hanging about looking at other people's houses. Let's see you on your way. Know where the station is, do you?"

No question of their mistaking him for a Hampsteadite! They made sure he went to the station. They watched him from the car, and when he was at the top of Christchurch Hill, he heard the car crawl up behind him, felt her lights flood his back. The time was after eleven-thirty. If he didn't make haste he could miss the last Piccadilly Line train out of King's Cross. He'd be late anyway. For once Carol would wonder where *he* was. The police car followed him down Heath Street and, when he had been seen to go into the tube station, went off down Fitzjohn's Avenue.

It was possibly the last train he got and it brought him to Turnpike Lane at nearly half-past midnight. He had a long walk from there. The only people about were young men of his own sort of age, walking alone like he was, or in groups. There wasn't a woman to be seen. The traffic was light. It had snowed a lot while he was in the train and the snow had melted into puddles. A young black man passed him, carrying a transistor playing very loud rock.

Barry turned into Winterside Road and went down the path to the Chinese bridge. He counted the houses from the corner, but with no joy in his heart this time. Her lights would draw him to her but not happily, not at a run.

They were on, upstairs and down. He began to think what he would say to her. He couldn't just let it go. The green lawns were khaki-brown in the sodium lamplight and the sky held its reddish London sheen, but the lights at each end of the footpath ahead were timed to go out at midnight. The passage itself was dark though light at the end, as the mouth of a cave is when looked at from the inside. Barry thought suddenly, suppose he'd been wrong all the time, suppose she'd given up Wednesday evenings only this week and she'd forgotten to tell him? Alkmini hadn't said anything that didn't fit in with that. And then after leaving Mrs. Fylemon she'd gone shopping somewhere, to one of the centers that stayed open till eight. It was something she often did. He had gone out himself at seven. She was in now. She might have been home waiting for him for hours, he thought.

Barry very much wanted to believe this. He thought that, if Carol told him the story he had just told himself, he would believe her, he would be happy. He entered the passage between the high fences and as he did so two men came in at the other end. Their bodies blocked out the light and he could see the shape of them only, not their faces. For a moment he thought nothing of it. Two men had come into the passage and were walking towards him, that was all.

He went on walking, slowing down when he realized there was something odd. The odd thing was that they were still walking abreast. One hadn't stepped behind the other to let him pass. They still walked side by side, the pair of them coming towards him as if they hadn't seen him – no, not that, as if they meant to come smack into him.

Barry was aware of a danger that raised prickles on the back of his neck. He turned round. Another man, thin, lanky, his black clothes glistening in the little light that showed in the mouth of the passage, had come from the path across the grass and entered the footpath on purposefully silent feet. He stood there, waiting, his arms folded.

Not men, of course. Boys. He recognized the one with folded arms, he could see him. It was Blue Hair. They had been watching for him, they must have been. Waiting for him to be out late on his own. He turned again in the way a cornered animal does and his face met Hoopoe's hot breath, kebab stinking. Black Beauty with him had pockmarks under his

317

cheekbones as if his face had once been peppered with shot.

"Let me pass," said Barry.

"Fucking baby killer."

Barry knew he was in for it. It wouldn't make any difference what he did, cringe, plead, or what, so he wouldn't cringe. He wouldn't argue. That this lot should set themselves up as keepers of a social conscience was a bitter irony. He lifted his right arm and elbowed Hoopoe out of the way. He used both his arms, elbowing. He did it so fast that it nearly worked with Hoopoe. Not with the black boy. The black boy grabbed his shoulder and wheeled him round and struck him in the face with the flat of his hand. Barry punched back. He punched hard at Black Beauty and kicked out at Hoopoe and the adrenalin streamed into his blood and, for a moment, a split second, it was good; he was kicking and lashing out and winning. But only for a moment.

Blue Hair, who had been waiting, took a leap down the passage like someone doing the long jump and then he ran and landed on Barry with both arms flailing down hard. He had leather gauntlets studded with shallow metal spikes. Black Beauty, who Barry had kneed in the groin, grabbed his arms and pinned them behind him while Blue Hair punched hard, mostly at his head and face.

Black Beauty held him long after he would have fallen. He held him for Hoopoe and Blue Hair to use as a punching bag. Darkness came down in a sagging curtain and Barry felt his mouth fill with blood as a tooth went. Black Beauty dropped him, perhaps to keep himself clean of the blood which was spilling down Barry's chin. Barry fell, hitting the fence, making the fence shake and vibrate. Hoopoe's pointed boot went hard into his side. But this was his right foot and Hoopoe was left-footed. He drew back his left foot and kicked Barry's ribs as hard as he could.

The last thing Barry knew was a window opening úpstairs in the house behind the fence and a voice calling something he never heard.

BOOK III

18

This agreement is made the —— day of ——
nineteen eighty —— between John Howard
Phipps of 5 Spring Close, Hampstead,
London NW 3 (hereinafter called "The
Vendor") of the one part and Morris Goldschmidt and Rosemary Catalina Goldschmidt his wife, both of 102 The Dale,
Cricklewood, London NW2 (hereinafter
called "The Purchaser") of the other part.

Terence's eyes wandered down past the first
two clauses to the vital point three:

The price shall be £132,950 and the Purchaser
shall on the signing hereof pay a Deposit of
£13,295 to Lewis & Plummer, Solicitors for the
Vendor, by Solicitors' Client Account Check,
Building Society Check or Banker's Draft.

Did that perhaps mean that this solicitor would hang on to Goldschmidt's check, investing it perhaps, until the whole transaction was complete? Terence wouldn't have been at all surprised, it was typical of people like that, sharks and money grubbers. In any case it would make a difference of no more than a month or so. If he didn't manage to get himself a bank account by the end of the month, he must by completion date.

No date had been entered. But the solicitor's covering letter which had arrived with the contract suggested 15 February and would Mr. Phipps indicate in his reply if this suited him? Terence phoned. The man himself wasn't there but he spoke to a secretary.

"It would be usual practice for such a deposit to be held by the vendor's solicitors until completion date, Mr. Phipps."

Terence didn't want to arouse any suspicions by hinting he was in need of funds, though he was. He rang off. It had occurred to him that it would be wise to buy a plane ticket a week or so before completion to be used on completion day. What sort of a day was 15 February? Hanging up behind the kitchen door was a calendar for this year but nowhere in the house was there one for next year. He had to work it out on his fingers. February 15, thank God, was a Tuesday. Imagine if it had been a Friday, with Goldschmidt paying the money in the afternoon and him not being able to get at it till the Monday.

Would he dare wait to buy a ticket for a flight to, say, South America until that Tuesday? It was cutting it fine. Terence, whose anxiety neurosis derived rather from the anticipation of frightful fear than from fear itself, could picture the jelly-like, tongue-tied abjectness of his condition as, with a suitcase full of cash, he went from airline to airline attempting to buy a ticket. His tremulous glance would hardly dare to take in anything but that which lay straight ahead, for fear of the encroaching law. His throat would be too dry to speak, his hands shaking as he fumbled with the catches on the case. No, he must secure his seat in advance. His self-knowledge told him he would sail more or less serenely through such a purchase because at that point he would scarcely have done anything illegal. At any rate he wouldn't have laid hands on a penny of Goldschmidt's money.

But without Goldschmidt's money, how was he even going to buy a plane ticket? A one-way ticket to anywhere as distant as he intended to go to would hardly be less than £500. He wasn't going to mess about with charter flights you had to pick up in Amsterdam. The sum of

£500, which he had randomly seized on as likely, suggested to him the credit limit allowed him on his Barclaycard. He hadn't used the card since moving out of Jessica's house. Barclaycard didn't know of his change of address and the card would no longer be valid anyway.

Or was there a chance it was? Terence hadn't the faintest idea where the card might be except that he was sure he wouldn't have thrown away anything that might, however remotely, be a source of money. He went upstairs and hunted about. In the cupboard of the room where the futon was he had hung most of the clothes he brought with him after flitting from Jessica's. He went through all his pockets. Nothing but a few valueless copper coins, a dirty tissue, and a piece of chewing gum. Books had never been much in his line and he possessed none. What had become of the suitcase he had "borrowed" from Jessica to bring his things in?

No doubt it was with the rest of the luggage in the big store cupboard next to the guest bathroom. He looked in there and found it, a brown Revelation suitcase with a zip-up compartment inside the lining of the lid which he could feel was full of papers. . . . He undid the zip and took out a copy of *Knave* magazine, a letter from Freda, indiscreetly sent to him at Jessica's, a bill from Brian of Brook Street for two shirts, a bank statement — and the Barclaycard. The expiration date was February of next year. He remembered now. Jessica had got him the card in the early spring nearly two years ago and three or four months later he had left her. He could hardly believe his luck. What he must do was write at once to Barclaycard and inform them of his change of address so that they could send him a new card in time for the expiration date of this one.

Once he had the new card things would be easy. The fact that his credit limit was only £550 mattered not at all. He could buy a one-way ticket through a travel agent, paying the deposit on the ticket out of one month's credit and the balance out of the next month's, Barclaycard's accounting always taking place, he remembered, round about the twentieth of the month. And this way he wouldn't even have to make the requisite percentage repayment of ten or twelve pounds, for this percentage installment would not be demanded before the eighteenth of the month following the first credit and on the fifteenth he would be away.

Terence went back to the writing desk and wrote to Barclaycard, giving his change of address and requesting a new card. Only just in time he stopped himself signing the letter John Howard Phipps. He wrote to his solicitor, confirming 15 February as completion date, and then he braced himself for the signing of the contract. Thank God a witness wasn't needed.

A drink would be a good idea. Just one, though. One to steady his hand and calm the ravening anxiety that gripped him whenever he contemplated taking this step which would commit him to selling Freda's house. One and a half inches of whisky and the same of water. The Valium he had taken after lunch had more or less worn off by now. He sometimes thought he had taken so much of it that it didn't really work well any longer. It was starting to get dark, though still afternoon. He put on some of the lamps with black shades and some with white shades and paced up and down on the black spaniel carpet, drinking his drink.

Outside in the courtyard the fairy lights someone had put in the catalpa tree winked and sparkled. First of all the green and yellow lights came on, then the blue and red, then the white, then the lot together. Terence walked purposefully to the desk, sat down, and signed the contract. He took two or three deep breaths, grasped the pen firmly, and signed the document with the signature of John Howard Phipps. It was the best signature he had ever done, almost better than the genuine article, if that were possible.

The post wouldn't go out till morning now, but he might as well take his letters to the box and have a drink in the White Bear on the way back. He had a couple of quid left. It was while he was in the pub, minding his own business in a corner over a half of Foster's lager, that he remembered the bank statement he had found in the zip-up compartment of Jessica's suitcase. So excited had he been over the discovery of the credit card and finding it still valid that he hadn't even bothered to look at that statement. Suppose there was some money still in the account? Suppose there was as much as twenty pounds? There might be. He had never drawn anything out after leaving Jessica. Some kind of wariness had stopped him. At any rate he must check up on it. The last thing he wanted was to leave the country having made the Anglican-Victoria bank in Golders Green a substantial money present.

First thing in the morning he would go there and ask his discreet question. Equally discreetly the girl would let him know what the account contained by writing the sum on a scrap of paper and passing it face-downwards to him under the grill. Not tomorrow, though. Tomorrow, he remembered, would be Christmas Day.

Next week, then. He still had to think how he was going to establish somewhere or other a bank account for John Howard Phipps. The mean underhandedness of the solicitors had staved off the need for an account for a while, but only a while. The banker's draft for the balance of the £132,000 Goldschmidt would produce on 15 February had to be paid in somewhere. Terence couldn't ask his solicitors to convert it into cash for him. Or, rather, he *could* but he knew he wouldn't dare, he wouldn't take the risk.

And then suddenly he saw. He saw how it could be done. He was gazing into the clear golden liquid in his glass with its light swirl of foam, as if into a crystal. It became the elixir of life or a fount of wisdom. He drank it down and asked for another.

"Merry Christmas," he said to the girl behind the bar, though he didn't go so far as to buy her a drink.

The dream of a Christmas party for Jason had come to no more in the end than three infant guests and their mothers confronted by more food than twice as many could have eaten and a bewildering display of decorations and presents. But it had been a success too. They had enjoyed themselves, and Chloe and her two-year-old daughter Kate, who hadn't seen James for six months, were in no doubt Jason was him. The others, a boy and girl and their mothers living in the Vale of Peace, had of course no idea there was any doubt about it. They all called him Jay, though Chloe raised an eyebrow at the diminutive.

When they had all gone home and Jason was in bed, Benet sat in the basement room among the dirty plates and cups, the present wrappings and the glittering litter, and looked at the two trees, the Christmas tree hung with lights and the tree she had painted on the wall and adorned with green and yellow and scarlet hands. Each hand had held — or had had cunningly hooked onto it — a tiny present for Jason: a toy car, an orange, a marble, a magnet, a packet of nuts. She knew she had gone overboard with excess. A more temperate climate must prevail in future. She mustn't spoil him just because they had so blissfully found each other. But this first Christmas with him, she had been unable to help herself. It had been a celebration of her own joy as much as for his pleasure. Pleasure for him there had been, enormous delight. She thought for the rest of her life she would remember his slowly dawning, gleeful smile, his advance upon the tree, and his last-minute glance up at her for permission to help himself to what the hands held. Nevertheless it was for herself she had done it, to see that look on his face, to exult. Since that day in the library she had been warm with joy — literally warm. It was as if she couldn't feel the cold of dark sleety December. Often she found herself going out wearing only a light jacket, she was so heated by inner happiness.

For the rest of that day when she had taken him to and snatched him from the Winterside library and for a day or two afterwards, she had been beset by fear amounting sometimes to terror that she had betrayed them both, had been detected, and that the police would come. And her fear had no longer been for publicity or disgrace or retribution but solely that Jason would be taken from her. But when no one came and when at the same time all references to Jason seemed to disappear from the newspapers, a happy calm succeeded the fear. She moved into a lovely never-never land which had no past and no future beyond next week and which allowed for no thought about the impossibility of continuing like this or the inevitability of eventual discovery. She was happy, she was serene, and she was working. She knew that no rebuff and no rejection could hurt her, and it was in this frame of mind that she rang the hospital and asked for

Ian Raeburn to invite him to the Vale of Peace.

He came that same evening. Jason had been in bed about an hour. It was curious what happened. Benet had never had such an experience before. It was as if they both knew what they must do, as if this was the way they had greeted each other for a long time now at each of their lovers' meetings. They went into each other's arms and held each other and kissed passionately. What they were doing surprised them equally. They hadn't expected this, it had seemingly been involuntary, and they looked into each other's faces and smiled. But the smiles were brief because passion, until it is old and customary, is not amused. They held each other and kissed and Benet knew they wouldn't speak or explain or excuse but go up, still holding each other, to her bedroom up that long staircase. Only Jason cried. He screamed out in his frightened nightmare voice:

"Mummy! Mummy!"

It broke what had existed between her and Ian. Running up the stairs to Jason, she knew it had broken it only for a while, that one day soon what they had begun would proceed to consummation, but not this evening, not now. She picked up Jason and held him against breasts that ached, a body where half-forgotten little pulses beat. But when she came down-

333

stairs and found Ian in the basement room, it was only to take his hands and sit beside him. And it was better so, better to go forward with caution into what she began to feel might be for a lifetime.

He asked her if she were fostering the boy called Jay with a view to adopting him and she clutched at this straw and said yes. Yes, she was.

"He isn't a replacement of James. It isn't that at all. I don't know if you can understand."

"I'll try."

"It's as if I had two sons and one of them died. I'll never forget him and there'll always be an empty space in life where he used to be. An empty chair at the table, if that doesn't sound too sentimental."

"Not to me."

"I suppose the truth is you can't replace someone. You can just have other people. I won't say my feeling for Jay is greater or less than my feeling was for James. It's not even different. It's the same kind of love but for a different person."

"I'm glad for you," Ian said. "You've done something very wise and clever for yourself, haven't you?"

She had a momentary shivery feeling of what would he think if he knew the real facts? It passed, swallowed by her happiness.

"We're going to see each other all the time now, aren't we, Benet?"

"All the time," she said.

"And this is *it*?"

"Oh, yes, I think this is it, don't you?"

They laughed at each other. Benet said: "Every evening?"

"Every lunchtime and every afternoon," he said. "Just for the next fortnight anyway. I'm on nights."

"And I was forgetting I'm writing a novel."

"Could I make you forget *that*?" he said.

Since then they had met every day — with Jason. Ian had had to go home for Christmas to his parents in Inverness. At nine he would phone her. She began clearing up the basement room with the radio on playing light country music. The new novel was going well. She wrote contentedly at night after Jason was asleep, sometimes on until midnight. Of course there would have to be some changes there when Ian came back and went on day duty. . . . In the glass, pausing with a tray of crockery in her hands, she saw a fuller and younger-looking face, though there were a few white hairs among the dark, about an inch long they were, or two months' growth, and she knew they had come when James died.

She picked up the phone and dialed her parents' number in Spain to wish them a happy New Year. Mopsa answered.

"It's unlucky before the Eve itself," said Mopsa.

"Nonsense." Benet astonished herself by speaking so robustly. "I'll probably be out on the Eve enjoying myself."

There was a silence; then, "I only wish I had it in me to be as selfish as that." Mopsa paused for a reply and when none came said, "How is James?"

Benet's heart turned over, and for a moment she couldn't speak. It was to her father only that she had spoken when last they had been in touch a week before Christmas, and he, of course, couldn't be expected to know. But Mopsa! I must not hate my mother....

But the explanation was simply that Mopsa had forgotten. Her actions in the matter of kidnapping Jason had not been well received, still less applauded, so in the way she always reacted to any censure or criticism she had blocked the whole experience off with whatever mechanism of her curious mentality handled these things. She had forgotten. Memory for her had always been like the writing on a blackboard, which any kind of unease would wipe away at a single stroke.

"He's well," Benet managed to say. "We've had a party."

"I don't remember getting an invitation."

"Well, of course not. You'd hardly come eight hundred miles to a children's party."

"When your father's managing director's daughter got married in Santiago, she sent us an invitation and that was more like eight *thousand* miles."

Benet knew the uselessness of pursuing this. She spoke to her father, who sounded tired and subdued. Mopsa refused to come back to the phone. She said the line was so bad it hurt her ears.

I must not hate my mother. . . .

And suddenly, at last, Benet understood that she didn't hate Mopsa anymore. That she would never have to adjure herself with those words anymore. She would be eternally grateful to her and that was only a step from love. For without Mopsa she would never have had Jason. Mopsa had stolen him for her, knowing with a wisdom unsuspected in her that given long enough Benet would come to love him. And to this end she had risked what was most frightful to her, incarceration – indeed, forced imprisonment – in a mental hospital. She had stolen Jason and given him to Benet and, rather than be the only witness to this abduction, had with her methodical madness forgotten all about it.

"It doesn't matter," Benet said to her father. "Say goodbye to her for me. And give her my best love."

The chill, damp limbo that occupies the spaces between the high holidays of Christmas was making itself felt in Finchley High Road. On this the twenty-ninth of December, half the shops were still closed but not of course the banks. Buoyed up by a small whisky and two Valiums, Terence found ample parking space in Regent's Park Road for Freda Phipps's car. The few people about with shopping bags looked bemused, stunned by recent festivities.

Terence walked along rather slowly. He had passed the Westminster Bank and Lloyd's and the Midland and Barclay's and was beginning to fear (also in a way to hope) that there was no branch of the Anglican-Victoria here, that the phone book had been wrong or the branch had moved, when he saw it ahead of him, its A and V monogram on the orange signboard sticking out between the post office and a building society. He hesitated. He stood gazing into the darkened and barred window of a men's boutique as if the dimly discerned yellow pullover and beige cords in its shadowy depths held an obsessive fascination for him. There was no help for it; he had to go into the bank. It was either going in there or else giving up the whole thing, abandoning the project.

Eleven-thirty and the pubs were open. He was rather well off for actual cash, having, since the discovery in Jessica's suitcase, bought a good deal of his food, meals out, and drinks on the still valid Barclaycard. He could easily have run to a couple of Scotches. But he was scared of slurring his speech or of making a mess of John Howard Phipps's signature should he be asked to produce it.

What could they do to him in the bank after all but refuse him? They weren't going to send for the police because he asked for a bank account in the name of Phipps. It wasn't a crime to call yourself by a different name from your own; you could call yourself what you liked in this country. And he had found a foolproof way of getting round that reference business, hadn't he? They could do nothing but refuse him. . . .

Terence had often tried these methods of combating paranoia, these recognized ways of reassuring oneself by repeating such handy aphorisms as "Most of the things you've worried about have never happened" and "There is nothing to fear but the fear itself" and "They can't eat you" and so on. But they had never helped much; they had never seemed to get through. They were just things you said which sounded good. They didn't probe into the core of fear, still less start the process of breaking it up. There in Finchley High Road, in the gray gloom of a post-Christmas morning, a dreadful wave of depression flowed over Terence as he understood, staring unseeing at a pair of fawn trousers, that he was going to be beset by fear all his life, live in it and be paralyzed by it, and there wasn't enough Valium and whisky in the world to keep it at bay. It wasn't worth it, he thought, there was no way it was worth it. But what did he mean by that? What was worth what? Did he mean that life itself wasn't worth the fear it took to live it?

Thinking along those lines wouldn't do at all. He had no alternative now anyway; he'd gone too far. He had signed the contract and committed himself. In for a penny, in for a pound, in for one hundred and thirty-two thousand pounds. He walked into the bank and in a hoarse sentence, split by a clearing of his throat, asked to see someone about opening an account.

"Phipps," he said when they asked his name.

He was told to take a seat and did so in one of the orange leather chairs that stood about. After a minute or two someone came out and said the assistant manager would see him. Terence went into a very small office, also done up in orange, and shook hands with a man who said his name was Fletcher.

"I want to open a bank account." Terence's voice was back to normal though his body felt rather as if he were treading water. "With fifty pounds," he said, aware of what a small sum this sounded these days. It was the utmost he had been able to amass out of three weeks' Social Security.

Fletcher looked, if anything, relieved. It occurred to Terence that perhaps he had thought his visitor was a customer who had wanted an overdraft. "That shouldn't present too many problems, Mr. Phipps."

He produced a form which Terence scanned quickly, his throat constricting afresh. There was nothing really to dismay him. A specimen signature was required and, under Fletcher's eye, Terence signed "John Howard Phipps" with a hand that desperate concentration made steady.

Then came the bit about furnishing the name and address of a referee.

"You could apply for a reference," said Terence, "to someone who has an account at your Hampstead Garden Suburb branch. Would that be all right?"

"I should think that would do very well, Mr. Phipps."

So Terence wrote in the space provided, "Mr. Terence C. Wand," and underneath it, "14 Gibbs House, Brownswood Common Lane, London N15," which was his mother's address.

19

The gun wasn't the kind of thing Barry had expected. A pistol of some sort, he had speculated vaguely, a revolver, the kind of thing Dennis Gordon must have shot his wife with. This looked more like a rifle someone had messed about with and made a botched job of at that. But the man called Paddy was prepared to take £40 for it and Barry knew that wasn't much for a real gun.

"You're sure it works?" he said.

"Sure," said Paddy.

The room he lived in was one of the nastiest places Barry had even been into. He hadn't known such places existed in the Hornsey, where he had been brought up and where his parents still lived. It had no furniture but a mattress on the floor and an old meat safe with a wire front, and it smelt of unwashed clothes and hamburgers and urine. It was from this meat safe that Paddy had brought the gun.

"What sort is it?" Barry asked warily.

He wanted to be told one of those famous names familiar to all lovers of violent movies and fiction — Luger, Smith & Wesson, Beretta.

Paddy gave him a sidelong look.

"It's a sawn-off shotgun, isn't it?" he said.

He was a big, burly, fair man, not a bit Irish to look at and surnamed Jones. Or so he said. He hadn't much of an Irish accent either, Barry thought. His voice was a zombie drone. But he guessed that Paddy wouldn't have talked to him in the pub or brought him back here or be offering him the gun if he hadn't heard Barry's Irish name and noted in him the black hair and blue eyes and white skin of Connemara.

Barry thought of himself as English — well, British. And sawn-off shotguns he equated with terrorism. But he had to have the gun; he was never going to cross Winterside Down after dark again unarmed. A replica wouldn't satisfy him. His brother had said to get himself one of those replicas, they'd never know the difference, but Barry himself would know, he had thought. Besides, they cost nearly as much as the real thing.

"I don't suppose we could try it out?"

"Like where? In here? Down the High Street?"

Barry had thought of Alexandra Park but even that wasn't really big enough for experimenting with guns. When fired it would no doubt make a terrible noise.

"You have to trust me," said Paddy.

He suddenly looked – well, *political* was the word. Like one of those Irish National Liberation Army people whose faces were always being shown on the news. Barry took the thin roll of notes out of his jacket pocket. They were practically all he had in the world, nearly all his last week's pay, and it *was* his last week now Ken Thompson had gone bust and been obliged to send him away.

Paddy wrapped the gun in a piece of rag, part of an old gray undershirt. He put it into Barry's hands as if he were making him a rare and delicate gift.

He said simply, in his dead voice, "Kill English."

That made Barry's blood run cold, those light eyes staring at him and that numb tone and the deadly hate in it. He couldn't get out of the house fast enough, but he made himself move nonchalantly until he was beyond Paddy's sight. The last thing he saw of the vendor of weaponry was that chunky, puffy face with the unblinking pig eyes watching him over the banisters as he went down all those flights of stairs.

It was too late now to go back to his parents' house. Carol would be home in half an hour. This was the first time he had been out in the evening since coming out of hospital. He had sworn he wouldn't go out until he had the means of protecting himself. Blue Hair and Hoopoe and Black Beauty had taken a tooth from him and cracked two of his ribs, and for a while the doctors thought they had ruptured his spleen. They weren't going to get the chance of that again. He fingered the gun in its gray rag wrapping inside the plastic carrier. It was cumbersome to carry, but he would take it with him everywhere he went now. He smiled to himself, thinking how he would fire over their heads and see them run.

The day after he was taken into hospital, the police had come to see him, a sergeant and a constable he hadn't seen before. They asked him if he knew his attackers, and he hesitated for only a second or two before saying no. No, he couldn't identify them, he wouldn't recognize them again, he didn't know their names or where they came from. What was the use of telling? Blue Hair and the rest wouldn't go to jail. They'd be given suspended sentences or sent to psychiatrists and the first thing they'd do was revenge themselves on him.

"I never saw them," he said. "It was pitch dark. I never had sight nor sound of them till they were on me."

He could tell from the look on the sergeant's face that he thought what had happened only rough justice. The police couldn't touch Barry, they hadn't the evidence, so where was the harm if a bunch of yobbos gave him the private treatment? A few more questions were put to him but their tone was half-hearted. Maybe the doctors also thought he had killed Jason. And if his spleen really had been ruptured, maybe they'd have let him die and seen it as the best thing.

He and Carol would have to get away, they'd have to move. Perhaps they could get an exchange with a council house in another area. Crouch End, he would like, or Palmer's Green, but no further west than that, nowhere remotely near Hampstead. Wherever they lived it would be as far as possible away from Terence Wand.

Had she seen him while Barry was in hospital? He didn't know and he hadn't asked. In spite of the pain — his body had felt as if on fire and racked with stabbings for days — Carol's care for him, her shocked horror at his injuries, had brought him a blissful happiness. That first day she came in at visiting time, ran to him, and threw herself onto the bed and into his arms with a little hysterical cry. The pressure on his bruised side and arm and thighs had been an intense agony but his joy had outweighed the pain. He hadn't uttered a sound of protest even though she lay on top of him clutching at him with her fingers, and he whispered to her to get up only when the sister was coming and he was embarrassed.

After that first day she hadn't been able to come in all that often. Visiting times were also the times she had to be at work. Naturally he understood that. He had lain there thinking about Terence Wand and wondering if the police had ever done anything about that letter he had sent them. It had been in some ways a silly letter to write. After all, it wasn't of taking away Jason that he suspected Terence Wand, was it?

Maureen came in one evening. He was surprised to see her. She wore her long raincoat and her hair was scraped back in an elastic band. She didn't ask him how he was. His right arm, with the pajama sleeve rolled up, was lying outside the bedclothes and she lifted it up by the wrist as if it were some inanimate object, a branch, say, or a piece of piping, and examined impassively the by then brown and yellowish bruises.

"At any rate," she said, "you're still here."

She meant he wasn't dead.

"They didn't murder me, if that's what you mean."

"Mum says the trouble was he came between you."

"Who did?" he said, though he knew. "Who came between who?"

"Jason."

He looked at her, at the plain, round face that was still somehow Carol's face with a broadening here, a flattening there, just sufficient to deny it beauty. The vacant blue eyes met his. What she said took his breath away, a frequent effect of Maureen's utterances.

"Maybe it's just as well. Maybe it's all to the good. The fact is no one wanted him and he's best out of the way."

He knew then that she also believed him a murderer. The difference was that she believed but didn't care. She continued to stare at his bruised arm and made as if to pick it up again. He had a creepy feeling that she was capable of taking it by elbow and wrist and snapping the forearm bone in two. Quickly he withdrew it under the sheet, and after a while she got up and left, saying as she went: "I wouldn't hurry to come out if I was you."

He had sometimes wondered what that meant.

Coming out of hospital, he knew. He was not welcome in the hostile world of Winterside. The revenge taken on him somehow confirmed his guilt. People still spoke to him but no one used his name, and their eyes looked at him as if he were different from they, as if the unspeakable thing he was accused of doing set him apart from even the worst of them forever. That Carol stuck to him, that he still lived in Carol's house, was a wonderful thing, something to be treasured. He was stupidly grateful. Stupidly, he thought now, because he had done nothing, had never laid a finger on Jason, had in fact been one of the few who were really fond of him. They were all wrong in their suspicions and he was right. Even if no one in the world believed in his innocence, he would still be innocent, he still would not have killed Jason. Yet he was learning how hard it is to stand alone, how hard to hold to the truth in isolation, so that one even begins to doubt if it is truth. Several times in hospital and back at home he had dreamed he was in the garden of one of those condemned houses in Rudyard Gardens, burying Jason's body.

Awake, it was a street he always avoided. Getting off the bus, he walked down Delphi Road, past lighted houses, some of which still had Christmas trees and decorations in their windows. Two or three boys in leathers were sitting on the seat outside the public library. The muscles of Barry's stomach tightened; there was a constriction in this throat. He took the gun out of the carrier and put it inside his zipper jacket. He thought he would slit the pocket lining so that he could keep the gun in there and easily reach for it.

But the boys on the seat were not Blue Hair or Hoopoe or any of them. They were strangers who scarcely looked at him, who hadn't yet learned to know by sight the murderer of Jason Stratford. He made himself enter Winterside Down by the Chinese bridge and the path across the grass, the way he had gone on the night they attacked him. Sooner or later it had to be faced and sooner was best. The gun made a difference.

The night was less dark than that other night and it was much earlier. The grass had a sheen on it in the moonlight and frost painted the tops of the fences phosphorescent. With a leap of the heart he saw that lights were on in Carol's house. Just to make certain he counted the houses as he came across the green to where the footpath ran between the houses, one, two, three, four – yes, eighth from the corner the lights were on.

And the passage between the fences was

empty. He walked quickly through, keeping himself from actually running, passing the place where they had knocked him down, wondering if in daylight the stains of his own blood were still there on the concrete and the fence.

He didn't show Carol the gun or even tell her about it. She might have reproached him for spending the money when he was out of work. She was watching television with her feet up, a bottle of red wine from which she had drunk a couple of glasses beside her. He poured himself a glass of wine and sat down next to her. She let him kiss her and her mouth quivered a little under his.

The dress she was wearing was the black and white zig-zag one. Her black lacy tights he remembered her saying she had pinched from a stand in a fancy news-agent's up in Highgate. Had she also stolen the watch on her left wrist that looked as if it were made of diamonds?

There was a long angry bruise on her arm where the sleeve was rucked up. The watch covered the end of the bruise. Barry remembered with a kind of inner wince that time she had wanted him to strike and hurt her, how she had seemed to enjoy pain. She was laughing now at something on the television, reaching for her cigarettes. He knew he wasn't going to be able to ask her about the bruise and the watch any more than he had brought himself to ask her where she was that night the motorbike boys nearly killed him.

20

Terence lay in bed on the futon with Mrs. Goldschmidt. Both of them had fallen asleep and she still was. Waking, he didn't know where he was and scarcely who he was, let alone who the naked blonde with her face buried in the pillow was. For a few seconds he guessed Carol Stratford but that was wishful thinking. This was Mrs. Goldschmidt – or Rosemary, as he knew from the contract and only from the contract – with whom he had gone to bed some hours before. She slept on, occasionally giving a light girlish snore. Terence now wished very deeply and passionately that he had not succumbed to her.

She had called unexpectedly. Terence was increasingly alarmed by these surprise callers. After a morning spent writing a reference for the bank for John Howard Phipps in the name of Terence Wand, he naturally expected when the doorbell rung that it was the police. His stomach squelched. He made himself go to the door and open it, clenching his teeth but unclenching them into a sickly smile when he saw who it was. She wore a pale-green knitted dress with, over it, a fur coat made of innumerable tiny skins as if uncounted thousands of mouse-size creatures had given their lives to make it.

This time there was no ambiguity about the reason for her visit. She walked upstairs, Terence following. At the top she put her arms round him and kissed him with silent voracity. She proceeded to the room where the futon was, took off her coat, and let it fall to the floor. It lay there like a slumbering bear. Terence had a feeling of being borne helplessly along on one of fate's tides. Sometimes he thought it was his timidity which attracted him to them, what Freda had called his "feebleness," which made him theirs to do as they like with, to boss or mother or eat up.

Mrs. Goldschmidt ate him up. But what choice did he have? If he had said no perhaps she would have gone home to her husband and told him not to sign the contract, she had changed her mind. He had had some experience of the fury of women scorned. On the other hand, he couldn't now help thinking, she might be one of those who confessed to their husbands, in which case Goldschmidt's own fury would stop him signing.

He looked at her despondently. Rosemary. The name didn't suit her. His gaze had its effect and she opened her eyes, got up, and made her way to the *en suite* guest bathroom. Terence put on his underpants and went downstairs. He put the whisky bottle and a bottle of Perrier from the fridge and two glasses onto a tray. At the point where the stairs turned at a right angle, he paused and looked out of the window into the court. The lights on the catalpa had been taken down the week before. Someone had dropped a white plastic carrier onto the cobbles and the wind was blowing it about, in and out between the light and the dark, finally pasting it up against one of the low walls. The sky was a brownish-purple with a few smudged stars showing. Terence hadn't set foot out all day but it looked cruelly cold. Under the arch a young man was standing, looking up at the house and towards Terence so that it seemed to him as if their eyes met. He quickly turned his away. The watcher resembled the younger of the two policemen who had called on him, but he couldn't be positive they were the same.

Mrs. Goldschmidt was dressing, the lights on and the window blind up. Terence pulled down the blind.

"I thought you'd like a drink, Rosemary."

"Katie."

"Pardon?" said Terence.

"I'm called Katie."

He nodded, remembering her second name was Catalina. It didn't suit her any better than Rosemary. She slid her feet into bronze high-heeled shoes.

"Would you consider parting with any of the furniture?"

He was nonplussed. He lifted his shoulders helplessly.

"Only I'd take that futon off you if the price was okay."

They had their drinks. Terence screwed his courage to the sticking place and asked her if she and her husband had yet signed their contract. It was waiting at home, she said. It had come by the second post that morning and they were going to sign it tonight. In fact she thought she had better get off home and sign it. Terence wasn't going to quarrel with that. She wrapped herself in the multi-mouse coat, remembered about the futon, and wrote him a check. He was glad of the money, though it did rather give him the feeling he was being paid more

357

directly than usual for his services.

The first time Jason picked up the phone to answer it himself, the caller was Ian. It was Ian who heard him shouting, "Mummy, Mummy, there's a man!" So that was all right. The next time it was John Archdale from Marbella, and when she came to the phone, Benet thought she heard wonder in her father's voice and a kind of relief. He would accept the fact of the child now, no longer think of him as some sort of monster or skeleton in the family cupboard.

The first night she spent with Ian, she felt guilty because Jason was in the house. Waking very early with Ian's arms still round her, still holding her close to him spoon-fashion, she thought at once of Jason, of how it would be if he were to walk in and see them there together. It was strange because she wouldn't have felt like that if James had lived and it had been he sleeping in the next room. When she had had a child, she had not planned on remaining celibate until he was old enough to leave home. She got up and went into Jason's room.

Immediately it struck her how he had changed. His own mother doubtless would know him still. No one else would. She had had his hair cut the day before and the trim symmetry of the cut changed him from a toddler into a little boy. Yet in an odd way, she thought, he looked *younger*. His body was thinner and taller but his face had become more soft and full. Except to a mother's knowing intuitive eye, Jason Stratford had disappeared as entirely as might a person who has had plastic surgery. In that moment she knew he would never be Jason to her again. Letting down the side of the cot, she bent over him and kissed his firm, round, pink cheek.

When she came back with the tea on a tray, the cot was empty and he was in bed with Ian. Her life seemed suddenly full to overflowing and she caught her breath. She hesitated only for a moment before getting into bed with them, Jay between them, snuggling up.

In the middle of the morning the phone rang. It stopped so she knew Jay had answered it. But when she came downstairs the receiver was back and Jay was playing the xylophone. She asked him who had phoned.

He smiled. He used a made-up word, a combination perhaps of "ugly" and "ghastly." "Gugly," he said.

With a faint sinking of the heart, she guessed what he meant. "Jay, do you put the phone back without telling Mummy if you don't like the person's voice?"

"Yes," said Jay and he nodded vigorously to

give more emphasis. "Gugly man."

That made Benet laugh though it left her uneasy. Probably she had been wrong in thinking he had answered the phone only twice before. There might have been many times when he hadn't liked the sound of the caller so had simply replaced the receiver. Any brusqueness or even embarrassment would do it, she thought. She took Jay on her knee and explained carefully to him that he must always tell her when someone phoned. If she were upstairs and the bell was switched off there, she might not hear it and then she wouldn't know who had called her. Did he understand?

Later in the day the publicity director from her publishers phoned. They wanted her to go on a promotional tour of the United States in May to coincide with the American paperback publication of *The Marriage Knot*. Benet asked if he had phoned before. Yes, once, he said in his rather sharp, abrupt voice, but her little boy had answered and then cut them off.

Benet was immediately relieved, though she didn't quite know why.

The woman whose shape he had seen at Terence Wand's window Barry was certain wasn't Carol. She was dressing, raising white arms above her head, and her hair was short and blonde. There were too many hours in the day for him and not enough to do with them. Or that was what he told himself was his reason for taking himself over to Hampstead.

He hadn't been able to get another job, though Carol had. An additional one to Mrs. Fylemon and the wine bar. Part-time hotel receptionist. Barry was a little overawed. It seemed such a middle-class thing, verging on a profession really. He scarcely knew anyone who had been trained for anything, who sat at a desk answering the phone and filling in forms.

"Did you answer an advert, love?" he said to her. "You never told me."

She was vague. "This guy who runs it saw me in the wine bar. He told Alkmini he thought I was a model."

Serving drinks on trays? Barry thought this but he didn't say it aloud.

She had her Diagem watch on and a ring with a red stone she said she'd got at Christmas at Iris's. It was like no ring Barry had ever seen come out of a cracker. "He said he'd be willing to pay the earth to have someone like me at the Rosslyn Park."

"I hope he is," said Barry.

To look in and see her, he should have turned left out of the tube station, not right and up the hill towards the Heath. But he hadn't come to

Hampstead to see Carol. Why would he do that? She'd think he was checking up on her. He turned right and went up the hill and into Spring Close instead. It was soon afterwards that he had seen the woman dressing. That was why he hadn't stopped there long. Once he had seen her, he left, a bit excited and a bit embarrassed. It wasn't Carol, he knew it wasn't Carol, and surely he ought to know, he had seen her dressing and undressing often enough. Yet when he was in the tube again and later when he was crossing Bevan Square, he couldn't help asking himself how he was so sure it wasn't Carol. What single thing was there about that woman he could positively say made her not Carol? Wasn't it just that he didn't want her to be Carol?

Hoopoe and Stephanie Isadoro and Black Beauty and a couple of other kids were sitting on the seats in the square eating Turkish take-out out of waxed paper cartons. Whenever Barry saw Hoopoe, he remembered the feel, like an electric pain, of that pointed boot kicking his ribs. None of them took any notice of him. He put his hand into his jacket pocket and through the split lining and felt the gun. He wasn't going to need it, but it was a comfort feeling it there, just as a wad of money in one's pocket was a comfort or a word of love remembered.

Had it been Carol in Terence Wand's bedroom? He had been sure at the time it wasn't but he wasn't so sure now. Perhaps he had been certain it wasn't only because he knew Carol was at the reception desk at the Rosslyn Park Hotel. His eyes went to the phone on the shelf with the framed photograph of Dave beside it. He didn't know the number of the Rosslyn Park but he could ask Directory Information. If she were there now, of course, that wouldn't do anything to prove she had or hadn't been in Spring Close an hour ago.

He dialed Information and got the hotel number, but that was as far as he went. It was a mystery why he should suddenly feel so enormously cheered up to be told the phone number of the Rosslyn Park, almost as if he hadn't really believed in its existence.

Barry changed the sheets and vacuumed the bedrooms and took the washing round to the laundrette.

When he had been told contracts were exchanged, the deposit in the hands of Goldschmidt's solicitor and the completion date confirmed for 15 February, Terence went into a travel agent near where his mother lived to book a flight to Singapore on that date. When it came to the point, Terence's courage, such as it was, failed him at the idea of being alone with a suitcase full of money in Central or South America. He would go to Singapore and there board plane or ship for Bali.

All this would depend, of course, on what time the Singapore flight left. Goldschmidt's banker's draft would come into John Howard Phipps's account at noon on the fifteenth, and that gave Terence three and a half hours before the bank closed to draw it out again. He had to allow for that and for getting to Heathrow. The idea of spending the night of the fifteenth in London appalled him; his nerves wouldn't stand it. The Goldschmidts' moving van full of furniture would arrive at Spring Close soon after lunch. The house would be full of furniture too, Freda's furniture, and Freda's car in the garage. That would matter a good deal less if, when they made this discovery, he was already on his way to the airport.

It was therefore, a relief to find that the Qantas flight, stopping at Bahrain and Singapore, left at nine forty-five in the evening. He booked himself a seat, economy class, and at a reduced rate owing to his paying for it a month in advance. His new Barclaycard, which had arrived that morning, took care of that. By the same post his solicitors had sent him a document called "Transfer of Whole," which was something to do with land registration and required his signature. His and another's, for this time a witness was needed. Terence drove down the hill to the wine bar to have lunch there with Carol Stratford. He had given her a ring as soon as he saw that transfer.

"No news, I suppose?" said Terence.

"Not a sausage." Carol was used to being asked, as a preamble to any sort of conversation, if she had had news of Jason.

"He wasn't mine, you know, Carol."

"I never told the fuzz he was. I'm not saying I don't know who did it, but it wasn't me."

Terence shrugged. He told Carol he had sold his house and asked if she would mind witnessing his signature to a document. He reasoned that Carol was the only person he could possibly ask, the only person he knew who, if questioned about it – before 15 February that is, for after that who cared? – would lie stoutly for the mere sake of lying, the only person who wouldn't look too closely at the document itself, knowing by a sort of nose for that kind of thing that there was bound to be something fishy about it.

The fishiness was that Terence had photocopied the document at an instant print place on his way over. He intended to sign it in his own name in her presence. What he wanted was a specimen of Carol's signature to copy on the real transfer when he signed it later on in the name of Phipps.

She signed in her round, backward-sloping hand but not before she had proved him wrong and read it, pausing at and rereading the bit where the price was given.

"Three years ago," said Carol, "you were as skint as me."

"I've had a bit of luck," Terence said vaguely.

She asked him what he was going to do with the money and Terence told her he was going round the world. "You fancy coming along?"

"You're kidding," said Carol, all round doll's eyes and baby curls.

Terence admitted that he was. He was really. It would be more of a business trip than pleasure. But she'd come out and have a meal, wouldn't she, the night before he went? Barclaycard would pay, he thought.

21

Over dinner in the Villa Bianca, Ian told her about the job he had been offered in Canada. It was the first time Benet had been out in the evening since Jay came. She had phoned one of the babysitters from her Tufnell Park days, an eighteen-year-old who had last sat for her when James was fourteen or fifteen months old. Jay was in bed and asleep anyway by the time she came.

"It would be a great opportunity for me," Ian said. He smiled. "My big chance. The hospital is new. It's equipped as a matter of course in a way that would be just a dream here."

"When would you go?"

"I don't have to let them know definitely for another month." He hesitated and she found herself holding her breath. "Would you consider living in Vancouver, Benet?"

Would she? When her parents had gone to Spain, she had categorically declared nothing would persuade her to live outside England. She hadn't known then that she would fall in love and that would change everything. Then, as always now when she contemplated any plan or change, she thought of Jay. The last risk of his being identified would be removed if she took him half across the world. But to commit herself utterly, and so soon...? She laid her hand over his on the table.

"Let me think about it. Give me a little time, will you, Ian?"

He said, "I'll give you all the time I have. I was sure you'd say no. You've made me ridiculously happy by not just saying no."

They were a little later getting back than they had told Melanie they would be and she was ready to leave. Benet had time only to pay her and thank her before Ian drove her home. She found the note by the telephone in the basement room: *Edward Greenwood phoned 8:30.* Reading the words, Benet knew now why she had felt uneasy about Jay answering the phone and not always telling her. She was afraid there had been phone calls from Edward. It was a month now since she had seen him, but thoughts of him had been niggling there under the surface of her mind. To go to Vancouver would be to escape him also. . . .

She said nothing of any of this to Ian when he returned. It was their last night together before he went back on night duty. She tried to rid her mind of Edward and believed she had succeeded, but she dreamed of him, a bad nightmare in which he threatened her with a knife and tried to persuade her to enter into a suicide pact with him. She awoke screaming, terrified, looking for Ian. The other half of the bed was empty. She put on bedlamps and called for him in a panic of fear. He came rushing in from Jay's room.

"He started yelling first and then you joined in." He took her in his arms. "What's got into the pair of you?"

"I don't know; I don't know. What would I do without you?"

"You don't have to do without me," he said.

In the morning when Ian had gone and they had arranged to meet and have tea somewhere, Benet steeled her nerves and dialed the number Edward had given her. She thought she might finally get rid of Edward by telling him she was getting married and going to live in Canada. There was no reply. Very likely there wouldn't be at eleven in the morning. No doubt Edward had some sort of job and had to go to work. Had she phoned him at eleven because she know: wouldn't be there? T_____ some pricking of alarm and disquiet, to be able to say to herself, "I did phone him, I did try"?

She was upstairs at the front door giving a pound to someone who had called collecting for charity when she heard the phone ringing. It rang ___ ce and stopped. Jay must have answered __. No small shrill voice called, "Mummy, Mummy!" Benet ran down the passage and the basement stairs. Jay was on the rocking horse, swinging vigorously.

"Phone ring," he said and he gave her his widest, most radiant smile.

Edward wore his thin clothes and the thick long scarf wound twice round his neck. His face was red, with a bluishness about the lips. Jay's face would go like that, Benet thought, if he were really cold. He was behind her now as she opened the door, clutching onto her skirt.

"If you'd sent him to answer the door," Edward said, "I'd have had it slammed in my face."

All day she had somehow known he would come and had been bracing herself for it. "Come in," she said. "It's freezing."

He took her to imply he was letting in the cold. "Forgive me for making a draft."

"Edward, you know I didn't mean that. Don't

always made me out such a bitch. When you phoned, I'm afraid Jay was playing with the phone and didn't always tell me, I'm sorry."

"You shouldn't let that little devil answer the phone."

Benet said nothing, though she didn't like hearing Jay called a little devil. Jay himself, silent, was staring with fascinated wonderment at Edward in the way very young children stare at those they dislike. It was the middle of the afternoon. Having had lunch with Ian, Benet had been about to take Jay out for his walk in the stroller and, on the way, make inquiries about the play group she wanted him to join two mornings a week. She wondered why Edward had come, and as they went down the stairs to the basement room, two answers to that came to her mind. He wanted money. He wanted to bring some sort of action against the hospital for negligence leading to James's death. Well, she could handle that. She could handle either or both of those contingencies.

The tree of hands, denuded of course of the packages the hands had held, still hung on the wall. She saw Edward look at it and then, with the same mild reflective distaste, at the piles of toys which filled this end of the room. Ringed by a zoo of cuddly animals lay the two drawing blocks she had bought Jay while they were out, the top sheets of which he had already covered with shapes of birds and flowers and trees in bright crayon colors. Having had his fill of gazing at Edward, he returned to his work, selecting with a smile a hitherto unused colored pencil in a brilliant shade of veridian green.

"You shouldn't let him scribble on that," Edward said in exactly the same tone as he had admonished her for letting Jay answer the phone.

Suddenly Benet remembered that, the last time Edward had been here, nearly two months ago, she had told him she was minding Jay for a friend. Eight weeks was a very long time, an unheard-of length of time, to mind someone else's child. She filled the kettle and plugged it in. She set cups on a tray and opened a jar of orange juice for Jay. Edward would say something about that any minute now, he would ask why Jay was still here, and she would have to have a reasonable answer for him. He had seated himself in the rocking chair where he could watch Jay. After a moment or two he got up again and picked up, first, the drawing block Jay wasn't working on and then, murmuring something to him, the one on which Jay was filling in with his bright green pencil the outline of a tree.

Jay didn't cry out or scream. He simply

stood up and stared in stupefaction. It was Benet who wanted to yell at Edward. She made a mammoth effort at self-control. She explained to Edward that she thought Jay had a real talent for drawing, that he should be encouraged in every possible way, knowing as she did so that the words she spoke made her role as a mere temporary minder of Jay less and less likely. His lips had begun to quiver now. He started to cry and, putting up his arms, threw himself against her skirts. Picking him up, holding him, she waited for Edward's inevitable comment: "Who is this child? What is he to you?"

It didn't come. Edward shrugged and put the drawing blocks back on the floor. The blood, drawn into the surface of his skin by the cold, had receded and he seemed paler than usual. His face had a concentrated look. Benet wiped Jay's tears and put him back on the floor.

"Gugly," said Jay to Edward, who fortunately had no idea of the significance of this word.

Benet made the tea, putting the single flat teaspoonful of sugar into Edward's cup.

"You remembered," he said.

"Well, of course. You don't forget something like that."

He was silent. Jay finished his tree and started drawing a strange bird with large feet and red legs. Benet found she had nothing to say. There was absolutely nothing she could think of to say to Edward to fill this silence. It became embarrassing, almost tangible. He filled it with an abruptness and with a subject that astounded her.

"Benet, I want us to get together again, be as we once were. I want to come back and live with you. It's the natural, obvious thing to do. There hasn't really been anyone else for either of us — at least there hasn't for me." He added a kind of envoi that made her stand up and take a step or two away from him: "We belong together, Benet."

"It isn't possible," she said. "It's out of the question."

"Why is it? We're older now. I'm older, if you like. I wouldn't resent your success and I've lost any ambition of my own. I'd be content to take any routine job I could get. There's a course going teaching English to foreign students. I could get in on that. I've got a degree. I'd be quite content for you to go on in your high-flying way and be a humble teacher myself."

She nearly laughed, but it would have been unkind. She was less in danger of uttering the base retort about relative incomes which came to her. He had said nothing yet to deserve that. And she was so enormously relieved that he hadn't come here to talk about Jay that something like real affection warmed her, moved her back to sit beside him and lay her hand gently on his.

"It really isn't possible, Edward. Dear Edward. It's not your fault any more than mine. Maybe it's more mine. I know I did you an injury." She didn't want to name that injury, confident he would understand what she meant. "But it's too long ago." Should she mention Ian? There was no need, not yet. "I've changed — and not in a way to bring me closer to you."

"I can't see any change in you." He hesitated. "We could have more children, you know. I could put up with children for your sake."

Her heart hardened again. Jay was watching them in silence, aware without understanding it of the emotion with which the room had become charged.

"I couldn't do it, Edward. I've already said it isn't possible."

"Perhaps I didn't make myself clear, Benet. I was suggesting we get married. I'm asking you to marry me."

He said it with the air of one conferring a great benefit. He said it pompously. An enormous compliment was being paid, a reward bestowed. This time she did laugh.

"A proposal isn't necessarily something

women feel passionately grateful about these days, Edward. I can't think of any good reason for marrying you and I've one very good reason against. I don't want to."

He bowed his head, looked down at his hands in his lap, then up at her, into her eyes.

"I'll tell you a good reason." He cocked his thumb in Jay's direction. "Do you think a judge would allow you as a single woman to adopt that child over there?"

Something clenched and chilled inside her. She felt muscles stiffen. Had she told him Jay was a child she was fostering and hoped to adopt? She was sure not. The last time she had seen or spoken to Edward she was still — incredible as it now seemed — bent on finding a way to return him to his family.

"That's what you want, isn't it?" he said. "That's what you're planning on?"

She nodded, held still, mesmerized, by his eyes. What he said next made her feel faint. The room darkened and she thought she would fall as she had fallen in the hospital when they told her James was dead. But she stood still, she held her shoulders back, driving her nails into the palms of her hands.

"I know who he is, you know," Edward said. "I put two and two together. It wasn't difficult. He's Jason Stratford, the missing boy."

22

Afterwards she wondered why she hadn't denied it. She could have bluffed it out. But she hadn't had the nerve or been cool enough. She hadn't been cool at all. By asking him how he knew — and that was the first thing she did — she admitted everything.

"How did you know?"

"You calling him Jay, for one thing. You don't use shortened forms of people's names. You're the only person I know who's never called me Ted. Then his coloring. He's been described often enough in the papers as fair-haired and blue-eyed. Your situation — it's women who've lost a child that abduct a child. And then the place he comes from. You used to live round the corner." Edward looked pleased with himself. "Satisfied?" he said.

It was a strange word to have used. She felt

dry and hollow inside. She thought of the true explanation of Jay's presence, but was there any point in relating all that to Edward? It was all the same now as if she had taken him herself, all the same as if she had set out deliberately to steal him. Besides, there was only one thing she was interested in and that was what he was going to do about it. Yet already she knew that his knowledge in itself was bad enough. He knew. He wouldn't forget as Mopsa had forgotten. His knowing was almost the end of the world.

"What are you going to do about it?"

"I imagine you've been living in some sort of fool's paradise, but you must have known you weren't going to get away with it indefinitely. What did you think was going to happen in the future?"

She had never looked to the future beyond a day or two. "I suppose I thought he would change as he grew older and no one would recognize him. I thought of taking him away, a long way away...." Had she? She realized she was thinking of it now. "I don't think anyone but his mother would know him now." She was trying to keep cool but her voice cracked. Her voice was hoarse with fear. Edward was looking at her like a judge, leaning forward, frowning.

"What steps were you going to take to protect yourself?"

"What do you mean, steps? I'd kidnapped him, abducted him. I haven't any rights at all, I know that."

Jay chose that moment to put down his crayon and come to her, holding up his arms to be lifted onto her lap. The feel of him in her arms made her give a little sobbing cry which she stifled with her hand. Jay began to hug and squeeze her with a small child's surprising strength.

"Jay, you're choking me, no, darling..." She was determined not to cry in front of either of them. Her face and eyes felt burning and swollen. "Please, Edward, tell me what you're going to do?"

He said rather scornfully, "You make me sound like a blackmailer."

Wasn't he one? She understood that was what she had been thinking. "Edward..."

"I knew you'd taken against me but I didn't know you rated me as low as that."

She held Jay. It was as if people had actually come to take him from her but she knew they wouldn't do it by main force, they wouldn't physically tear him away. At the same time she was aware of the picture of demented, misplaced maternity she must be presenting to

Edward. Gently, yet with a more gargantuan effort than she ever remembered giving to any task, she made herself lift Jay down and set him on the floor.

"I'm sorry," she found herself saying, "but you frightened me. You must mean to do something or you wouldn't have come here."

"Don't you think he ought to have a father?"

"No doubt he has one somewhere. I've never thought much about it."

Edward was looking at her with a curious emotional intensity. His face was sharpened with it.

"You see yourself as his mother. If I were your husband we could be his parents. We'd be highly suitable *adoptive* parents, Benet. You've got money and this house. We're the right sort of age. Neither of us has been married before. I'd say we'd quite easily get an adoption order made if we applied to the court."

"You must want to marry me an awful lot," she said dryly.

"That's right. I do."

Her eyes rested reflectively on Jay. I wonder how long it would be before *you* started beating him up, she thought. You *hate* children.

"It's impossible anyway. He's not up for adoption; he's got parents. I *stole* him. I thought you understood that, that's what you've been telling me."

Edward said, "I spent the whole of yesterday in the newspaper library at Colindale reading up on the Jason Stratford case. It's obvious his mother doesn't give a damn for him. Her other two children are in care and Jason would have gone the same way in a year or two. She's a barmaid and her boyfriend's out of work. Don't you think there's a good chance she'd sell Jason to you?"

Hope came back, intruding itself, wriggling in like a small finger pushing through a crevice. She saw a clean, innocent, above-board world in which everyone knew the truth and everyone was happy, the death of James proclaimed and the existence of Jay announced, she and Edward having drunk perhaps some blinding love potion, living together and seeing each other as they once had with the eyes of illusion. The finger crept in and a door closed on it, not with a slam but with decisive firmness.

"I thought of offering her twenty thousand."

"It doesn't seem much," Benet said drearily. "It seems very little for him. I paid five times that for this house." She felt the warning signs of a hysteria she rigidly suppressed. "A house in Hampstead costs five times what a child costs. There's something wrong with that somewhere, Edward."

"Could you go up to fifty thousand if I had to?"

Everything I have, she thought. This house, all the money from all my sales, everything I have. Of course. It goes without saying. Why doesn't he know that?

"Suppose she won't have anything to do with it? Suppose she just goes to the police?"

"That's a risk you have to take."

"Why do I, Edward? Why do I have to take any more risks? You could walk out of here now and put it out of your mind and we need never meet again."

"To put it at its most basic, leaving out emotion, I'd know, wouldn't I? All the time you'd know I knew. Why don't you think about it, Benet? You can have three days. I've made a date to meet Carol Stratford, but she doesn't know why, she only knows it's something to do with money and she likes money."

"You were very sure," she said in a low voice.

"I was sure, yes."

Three days to get away in, three days in which to escape with Jay. She felt almost glad that he had given her a chance. The police wouldn't have done that.

The night Carol didn't come home at all Barry phoned the Rosslyn Park Hotel at midnight. He had drunk a whole bottle of wine and was past caring what people thought of him. There were always bottles of wine in the house these days, brought home by Carol. The answering voice told him Carol wasn't working late, they hadn't given her a bed for the night because of the snow and the bad roads — a straw clutched at by Barry — she hadn't been working that evening and in fact she didn't work there at all. Barry fell asleep at last on the sofa in the living room.

He didn't see her all next day. Late in the afternoon a man with a posh voice phoned and asked for her. Barry was going to ask if he was Terence Wand, but the man put the phone down before he had a chance. After he had been to the Job Center to see if there was anything going, but of course there wasn't, he went for a long walk for something to do, the gun knocking lightly against his chest as he tramped the streets.

Carol was there when he woke up next morning. She was in bed with him — that is, they were in the same bed. She lay on the extreme edge of the mattress and it was only the way the bedclothes were tucked tightly in that kept her from falling out. It was late in the morning, ten or eleven, he thought. He went down to make tea.

The first things that caught his eye when he went back into the bedroom were the diamond watch and the ring with the red stone in it, which she had taken off and laid on the bedside table. She was awake now, lying on her back, her blue eyes wide open.

"Hi," she said and then, when she saw the tea tray, "Are there any cigs in the house?"

He shrugged. He didn't know. Mysteriously he had given up smoking a week or two before without willing it or scarcely even noticing it had happened. One day he had been smoking twenty or thirty and next he hadn't smoked at all. He didn't miss it.

Carol said in Iris parlance, "You've got a face like a wet week. What's got into you? If it's on account of me getting back late, we had an emergency at the Rosslyn Park. I missed the last bus and I had to wait for a lift."

"You don't work there," Barry said. "You've never worked there."

"OK, so I don't." She was still in a good humor. He could smell stale brandy on her breath after all those hours, but her face was a little girl, dewy, satiny, pink and white and innocent. She sat up and he saw that she was quite naked, her breasts resting softly on top of the sheet. "If you didn't ask questions," she said, "you wouldn't get lies. What's it to you anyway where I go? You're not my husband. You're as bad as bloody Dave, you are. Where were you? Who were you with? Where've you been?"

He felt he was on the brink of terrible revelations. Never before had she given him a hint that Dave had been anything but totally loving and beloved. An intense red color showed in two spots on her cheekbones.

"I don't ask you to account for your movements," she said in a higher voice. "I don't follow you about, spying on you. I don't ask where you've been morning, noon and night, by Christ I don't!"

"Carol," he said, "you were with that fella that's Jason's father, weren't you? He's a rich man, I know that. You didn't nick that watch and you didn't get that ring out of a cracker at your mum's."

She got out of bed. There was a bruise of loving teeth marks on the side of her neck. He thought for some reason of the bruises on Jason, who had that same fine white skin.

"Run my bath, will you?" she said.

Her hard voice, both mocking and commanding, made him tremble. But he didn't move. He stared at her standing there naked with her mouth set and her fists clenched and for the first time he noticed imperfections in her, the droop of flesh on her inner thighs, the child-bearing stretch marks. It was as if lengths of old gray elastic had been inserted in the white silk skin.

"He's Jason's father, isn't he?" he said.

As if she'd had a fuse and he'd lit it, Carol blew up. She was little and a woman and naked but she wasn't afraid of him. She came to him and put up her arms and clutched his shoulders and yelled into his face. She yelled into his face in Iris's raucous broken voice.

"You want to know? Is that what you want? You want to know who his father is? Well, I'll tell you. I don't know who his fucking father is. I don't know and nobody bloody knows. The week I reckon I fell for him, I had eight men in seven days and it could be any one of them. See? Any one of them or maybe one of the seven or eight I had the next week. I don't know and I don't fucking care."

"Carol," he said. "Carol . . ." He got hold of her by the neck, squeezing the sore place where someone's teeth had bitten. "That isn't true, say it isn't."

"Of course it's true. Take your hands off me!"

He slackened his hold. He was aghast, as if he had opened some forbidden door and seen carnage inside. She twisted out of his grasp and ran out of the room. He heard the surge and splash of the bath taps turned on too hard. Suddenly he was afraid she would lock herself away from him in the bathroom. He followed her and stood in the doorway, holding the door.

She was bending over the bath, pouring in a trickle of herbal essence. A smell that was like a mixture of rosemary and Dettol rose from the steaming water. As she turned round slowly, straightening up and standing up, to look at him, he was hit by a wave of powerful desire for her. In spite of what she had just told him, he wanted her. It was humiliating and in a way shocking, but he wanted to take her in his arms and drop that warm, naked, white body among the tumbled towels on the floor, caring nothing for the sea-watery smell on it of another man.

"What happened to us?" he cried. "What went wrong, Carol? Can't we make it right? It's not too late. I love you, I want to marry you, I still do."

"You must be joking," she said and she spat the words. "Still do," she said. "I like that. I should co-co. I expect you 'still do.' I expect you *still* think I'd marry the man who murdered my Jason."

"What?" he said. It was as if she had struck him. "What did you say?"

"You heard."

If she had struck him, he could have handled it, but not this. Had his ears really sent that message to his brain?

He spoke like a child unjustly accused of some classroom crime. "*You* can't think that. Not *you*. You know I didn't, I couldn't have. Whatever the rest of them say, you know I couldn't have."

"Of course you did," she said, "only I was too dumb to see it." She turned off the taps with a squeak. There was a jug standing on the bath rim she used for washing her hair. He was too stunned to realize what she was doing when she bent over and dipped the jug into the hot water.

She jumped up with a very swift twisting movement and flung the jugful of water into his face. He gasped. She pushed at him with both hands and slammed the bathroom door.

23

Every day she saw Ian, and each time they met, she meant to tell him. She intended to confess everything and throw herself on his mercy. A small voice inside her whispered that if she did that two people would know, not just Edward. Or by tomorrow Edward and Carol Stratford.

Besides, Ian would immediately advise her to give Jay up, hand him over to the police. He was that sort of man. He wouldn't connive at what she was doing. The irony was that she wouldn't want the sort of man who would connive at what she was doing. That was another reason why she didn't want Edward.

Ian was on night call and she was glad of it. Her nights were nearly sleepless but sometimes she slept, always started awake by a violent dream. Edward came back on Sunday evening. She found him in the study room reading a page of manuscript.

"How did you get in?"

He smiled and held up a bunch of keys. The smile wasn't triumphant or presumptuous, still less menacing. He had come home again, it said; he was taking it for granted he was accepted back.

"You don't look well, Benet."

She shrugged. She said nothing.

"There's nothing to worry about." He tried to put his arms round her. She stood stiffly in his arms. "If she says yes, we're in business, and if she says no, you're no worse off than before."

"If she says no, she'll also tell the police."

"People like her are very loath to tell the police anything, Benet. I've read the newspaper stories, remember. It was a day and a night after he'd disappeared before she went to the police."

"I don't want you to see her, Edward," Benet said. "I want you to go away and leave us alone. If I was prepared to give her money..."

He let her go. "Don't turn me into a blackmailer."

She went into the living room, took out two glasses and the whisky bottle. She poured one for him and one for herself. Her hands were shaking, Jay was upstairs asleep, two floors away at the top of the house, yet she sensed all

390

around her his even, tranquil breathing.

I will take him away, she thought. I'll take him away where no one can find us. Edward's plan would never work; his reasoning was faulty, for if Carol said no, the police would trace Jay through Edward, and if Carol said yes, Jay would inevitably have to be produced and for a time returned to her. If for a time, why not for good, since the buying of a child was illegal? Edward would offer her a sum of money to agree to the adoption, and the balance when the adoption was completed. She would take the first payment, Benet thought, and then go to the police. I will take him away to avoid that happening, I will take him out of the country, a long long way, to the Far East perhaps. I'll use my money to hide him, not to buy him.

She handed Edward his glass. "You must do as you please," she said. "Do whatever you like."

After he had gone, she marveled that she, who was a middle-class, law-abiding person, who until a few months ago had envisaged her only possible brushes with the police as being the outcome of traffic offenses, should have become — and so easily and inevitably — a kidnapper, a felon and a fugitive. She went upstairs and into Jay's room and looked at him.

He had tossed and turned in his sleep, thrown off the covers, and slipped his pyjama top off one shoulder. Even in the half-dark she could see the burn hole the cigarette had made, an inch away from his spine. She overcame an hysterical need to pick him up and clutch him. Gently she covered him up. She began in a haphazard, feverish sort of way to pack clothes into suitcases.

By the first post, next morning, Jay's passport came. She had forgotten about that, she had forgotten they couldn't leave the country without it. Still she hadn't decided where to go. The suitcases had been packed in a panic without thought as to whether their destination would have a hot or cold climate. Impossible, in the here and now, to imagine sunshine, warmth, clear skies! A light, dry, powdery snow had begun to fall. She found her own passport and put it in her handbag with Jay's new one. Jay woke up late. She dressed him and gave him his breakfast.

"Snow," he said, pressing his face against the window. "Make a snowman."

"We're going a long way from the snow, Jay."

She wrapped him up in his duffel coat, put his boots on, wool hat, warm scarf. While she loaded the car, he played with snow, throwing handfuls into the air. The cold reddened his cheeks and the tip of his nose, and she remembered its similar effect on Edward's face. An idea came to her that was suddenly appalling and she thrust it away with a violent act of inhibition.

By Monday morning Carol still hadn't come back. It was Valentine's Day. Buying a birthday card for Carol soon after they had first met, Barry had thought about this day, had looked forward to it and even made a mental note of the particular Valentine's card he would buy to send her. A card did come for her by the morning's post in a large, pale-pink envelope. Barry opened it, looking for Terence Wand's name, but it was signed only with a row of crosses.

Snow was falling in a steady fine mist. By midday Winterside Down was white once more and the house filled with pale, radiant, reflected light. Carol had been gone since Saturday. Round and round in his mind went the things she had said. That there had been a hundred, a thousand, men in her past no longer really mattered. He could bear that. But that she too could accuse him of being Jason's killer, she who had met him on the afternoon Jason disappeared and run to him and kissed him and pirouetted in her new dress!

He hated her for that. Nothing mattered,

not the men, not the lies, not her using him as if he were her servant, but that mattered. While she believed in him, he hadn't cared about the rest who didn't. He sat in the living room that glowed with snow light and thought of what she had said about not marrying the man who had murdered her Jason. An overwhelming desire took hold of him to be away from her, never to see her again, to be away forever from Winterside Down and back in the comfort and caring of his parents' house. It was childish, it was immature, he knew that, but he didn't care, that was what he wanted.

But at the same time he didn't. At the same time he loved her. He was learning on Valentine's Day something that had never hinted itself to him before, that it is possible to hate fiercely and love fiercely at the same time. When he made this discovery he made a sound. He heard himself groan aloud and at once, though there was no one to see or hear, he clapped his hand over his mouth.

What he had to do was see her, be with her again. He had to get her to retract what she had said, to admit she had said it in the heat of the moment, that it was false, false as hell. A snowball slapped against the window and he jumped up, sure it must have been vindictively thrown. But it was only little kids out there,

Isadoros and Kupars and O'Haras, and their snowballs were simply handfuls of snow that contained no stones or pieces of glass.

The sun had come out and a thaw already begun, *drip-drip-drip* off the gutterings. She would come back if he waited long enough, she would have to, but he couldn't bear the inactivity. He was putting on his jacket and slipping the gun inside it when the phone began to ring.

Barry answered it. He thought it might be Carol and he held his breath. A man's voice asked cautiously if Carol was there.

"No, she's not."

"Will she be at Bacchus?"

It was so long since Barry had heard it called this that he had almost forgotten the wine bar's proper name. "Is your name Wand?" he said.

There was a silence, whispered into by the sound of indrawn breath. Then the receiver was replaced.

Carol would of course be at the wine bar on a Monday at lunchtime, Barry thought. She would be there until three.

The Channel had been icily calm. Benet wondered if Jay had ever seen the sea before. He stared at the sea with a long, concentrated gaze, then turned his face to hers and laughed. It was only during those few early years, she thought, that we laugh with delight at what pleases us. After that, laughter is strictly for amusement only.

They were coming into the harbor at Calais, in a chill gray mist, when she understood where it was she was going. Down to the tip of Spain to Mopsa and her father. She was their daughter and she had a son. Their neighbors, their circle, would know that now. What could be more natural and acceptable than if she and their grandson came to stay with them?

Britain had no extradition treaty with Spain. Or from there she could easily go on to North Africa. She saw herself fleeing with Jay to infinite distances. He was too small for a piggyback; he sat astride her shoulders, shouting, "I like the sea, I like the sea!"

When she got to Paris, she would phone her parents and tell them she was coming. Or perhaps, when she got to Paris, she would abandon the car and take a flight to Marbella.

The house was in darkness. Coming in under the arch, Barry could have sworn he had seen a light in one of the narrow slit windows on the left-hand side, but now he thought that what he had seen had probably been no more than the reflected image of one of the streetlamps.

He was going to ring boldly at Terence

Wand's door. If she was there with him and they tried to beat him up between them, he didn't care. He had to find her and see her and have his confrontation. If need be, he would use the gun to threaten. For Terence Wand he no longer had any feelings. The man might be Jason's father and he might not. Barry wondered why he had ever cared who Jason's father was. He rang the doorbell, once, twice, then insistently. It might only be his imagination that there was someone in there lying low, refusing to answer. How could you tell? There was no sound; the silence was total. Trying to see into one of the windows showed him nothing but the filtered light from a lamp in the close striking silky dark carpet and the bronze limbs of a statue. He went round to the back and looked through the window of the garage. The car was there. He tried the garage doors but they were locked.

Piles of snow, yellowish or rimmed with grit, were stacked against fences. It had become very cold. Ice glittered where before there had been black wetness. Barry went down to the station. He would try Maureen, he thought, and, if he had to, Iris.

As he came off the Chinese bridge onto the crusty remains of snow that lay in islands on the sea of grass, he saw lights on in Carol's house. His heart jumped as it always did, but heavily this time, with pain. Although he knew it was her house he counted from the end to make sure: two, four, six, eight. . .

He had the gun so he wasn't even apprehensive about going through the passage in the dark. Before he entered the black tunnel, slippery underfoot tonight and the fences on either side of it silvered, he got out the gun and held it clutched in both hands the way Paddy Jones had shown him. But he met no one and no one followed him in. He came out into the street at the other end and from there he could see the light from her living-room window shining onto the little bit of front garden. Then the light went out. He couldn't be sure if all the lights in the house went out; he couldn't see from there.

A woman came out of Carol's house. For a moment he thought it was Iris, the way she clutched her coat round her, the quick, almost scuttling walk. The light from a street lamp showed him her hair, the pale, gleaming, natural curls. It was Carol herself. She was wearing Mrs. Fylemon's fake fur and sandals with very high heels. Sometimes, he remembered, she would come home with her feet blue with cold.

She darted quick glances about her as if she

were afraid of something or someone, afraid perhaps that someone might be following her. He didn't flatter himself that she might even be afraid of him, but he followed her. There seemed nothing else in the world to do, no other occupation for him. Looking about her but never directly behind her, she came into Bevan Square. Black Beauty and Blue Hair were up at the top end of the square, on the corner of the row of shops, draped negligently over their bikes as if the saddles were bar stools.

Barry had replaced the gun inside his jacket. He held on to the butt of it but he didn't get it out. One of them said something, a muttered, indistinct, probably obscene word he didn't catch. Carol thought it was directed at her. She turned, quick as a flash, and shouted at them to piss off. He admired her nerve. The two of them sniggered. Carol was heading for Lordship Avenue.

He slackened his pace, uncertain what to do. It occurred to him that she might merely be going to Iris's. But she too was walking less quickly, and at the corner where the entrance road ran in between the two blocks of flats, she stopped and waited. Or, rather, she paced on one spot, turning round and round on those nearly bare feet, her arms folded and wrapped round her. A little snow, fine as dust, stingingly cold, needled onto his face and the backs of his hands. He pushed his hands inside his jacket. The cold was biting, yet the sky was the color of smoke from a burning rubbish heap.

The car turned in from Lordship Avenue. It turned in, looped round, and stopped at the left-hand curb. Barry couldn't see the driver but he thought the car was the one he had seen an hour before in Terence Wand's garage.

Carol darted across the road as the passenger door swung open. She jumped in — she almost dived in to escape from the intense cold — and the door slammed. The car slid out into Lordship Avenue once more and moved off down the hill.

It had disappeared by the time Barry came out into the main road, but he thought he knew where it had gone. There were people standing round something by the curb looking at something that lay there. A woman stepped back and began to walk away, leaving a gap in the crowd. Barry saw that a van had run over an animal and its driver was arguing with one of those bystanders who mysteriously spring out of the ground when an accident happens. The thing in the road, black, lean, sleek, apparently unmarked, dead, was the greengrocer's Doberman. The sight of it made him feel slightly sick.

He meant to walk, but a bus came as he reached the stop outside the pub. The gun was sticking out, pushing out the front of his jacket as if he had a deformed breastbone. The woman in the seat opposite stared. He pushed the gun down and held on to it.

They weren't in the bar. He could see that, he didn't have to ask. Alkmini was serving. Kostas sat at a table with a group of middle-aged Greeks like himself. Dennis Gordon, three parts drunk, his face dark and swollen, hung slouched against the black, curvy counter. He looked at Barry and their eyes met, but neither of them said a word. Then Barry saw the other man's eyes move. Glazed and blood-shot, they strayed back to where they had previously been fixed — on Kostas's black glass clock, whose hands pointed to five minutes to nine.

Barry had the bare price of a drink on him, but he didn't spend it. He went back outside. In Java Mews, Dennis Gordon's silver-blue Rolls was parked as it had been the other night. Barry heard the side door of the wine bar swing open and shut with a slam, but he didn't look behind him. His instinct had been wrong and she wasn't there, and he wondered where to look for her.

Probably, instead of coming here, they had

gone down to the West End. Go home, the sensible voice inside him said, go back to where you were before you met her. Sooner or later you'll have to, so why not now? A solitary bus appeared over the crest of the hill, rounded the curve in the road with its lumbering galleon-like motion, a red double-decker bus going up to Hornsey that passed the end of his parents' street.

He let the bus go. They might be in a pub instead. They might be down there in the Java Head. Barry didn't approach it from the mews but from around the block, walking round the square formed by Lordship Avenue and the three small streets, looking into parked cars.

It was dark, with lamps only at the corners. He wasn't in danger here, no one knew him here, but the two boys waiting under a corner lamp looked too much like Hoopoe, were too much on Hoopoe's style, for comfort. He held the gun and felt a quickening, strengthening surge into his blood. The boys didn't even look at him.

He was almost at the pub, he was entering the pool of light under the saloon bar window, when he heard the first shot. He was still grasping the gun through the lining of his jacket and for a wild moment he fancied that it was he who had made the shot, fired the gun. Then there came a volley of shots and a scream that split the cold, thick air. Barry began to run. The pub doors opened behind him and people poured out. He ran up the mews, not knowing whether he was running away from the shots or towards them.

There was one more shot. He saw Dennis Gordon on the pavement ahead of him, a blind, staggering, King Kong shape, a silhouette as black as a gorilla. The little gun half the size of Barry's was in his paw of a hand and he flung it in an arc away from him.

Barry didn't know where all the people had come from. The cold had kept them in and blood and screams and the heat of violence had brought them out as if melting their doors. The mews was full of people and their noise.

He saw the bullet hole in the wing of the car before it registered with him whose car it was. He pushed his way through, he elbowed the crowd out of his way. The passenger door he had seen opened for Carol stood open again, and thin threads of blood came out over the edge of the seat and in winding narrow rivulets over the rim of the door.

There was a lot of blood on the floor of the car, a lake of it forming. Barry had often wondered how he would feel, what he would do, if he saw Carol in another man's arms, in, say,

Terence Wand's arms. He witnessed that sight now and knew the total negation of feeling that shock brings. Impossible to say whether they had been embracing before they were shot or had fallen into each other's arms in death. There was no blood on Carol's golden baby curls. The shot that had killed her had made a round hole just below the lobe of her left ear, where the clotting blood formed an earring like a cluster of dark jewels.

Barry turned away and elbowed through the people to the end of the mews. He walked up the hill like an automaton or a contestant in a walking race. Police cars with sirens blasting and a useless ambulance came past him through red traffic lights. The night was suddenly filled with the howls of sirens. Barry felt nothing, but all the time he could see Carol's face with that red jewel just below her ear and he fancied he could smell limes as he had smelled them in the mortuary. Mechanically he walked, the gun moving rhythmically like a fifth limb.

At the top of the hill he leaned over the bridge and dropped the gun over the parapet into the canal. The water rings from the splash were still widening when he got onto the Hornsey bus.

24

The taxi set him down in Golders Green. That was far enough; he could get a tube from there. He felt curiously carefree and light of heart. Light of body he was too. He had weighed himself before leaving and found he had lost eleven pounds since Christmas. All his troubles seemed left behind with his discarded past. He was so relaxed that he bought an evening paper in the station for something to read in the train.

Going down the steps to the platform, he glanced at the front page lead. Glanced, then stopped and read. The shock gripped and twisted his insides. If he hadn't phoned Carol yesterday afternoon to say he couldn't make it, it might have been him with her in what the paper called the "death car." So his nerves had come in useful and saved his life. If his nerves hadn't told him that the only way he was going to get through his last night in Spring Close was alone and on a stupefying mixture of tranquilizers, alcohol, and sedatives, it might have been him! He and she would certainly have spent part of their time together in the wine bar. One always did with Carol. He hardly took in the name of the murdered man, Edward Greenwood, whoever he might be. His hand was trembling so much that the one good clasp on the brown suitcase shook undone.

Rather late in the day, he spared a thought for Carol. Poor old Carol. Suppose he had taken her out last night as they had originally planned? Even if he hadn't got shot, he would doubtless have been involved in some unpleasant way in all the fracas that went on between her and this jealous guy with whom she'd apparently been living on and off. The one he'd spoken to on the phone yesterday perhaps. The result would have been all the business of Freda's house coming out and his getaway with the money prevented. Terence decided he must have a guardian angel after all.

He got out of the train at Euston and walked to the small hotel where he had booked a room for the night in order to have the use of it during this afternoon and evening. There he counted the money. Two thousand or so fifty-pound notes wouldn't have taken up all that much room, but the bank manager hadn't been able to let him have it all in fifties, and so at least half was in twenties and tens. In fact the case was hardly big enough to contain it. That was why the clasps kept coming undone.

He dared not leave the money in his room. He took the case with him and walked along Tottenham Court Road. There, in a shop that sold leather goods and souvenirs, he bought a canvas strap to put round the suitcase and — as an afterthought when he was leaving the shop — a nylon fold-away bag.

Back at the hotel, he surprised himself by the amount of intense anxiety he seemed to find it necessary to devote to the packing of these bags and the disposal of the money. He had packed them both and re-packed them over and over and finally got all the money in the nylon bag, and the few clothes he was taking and his toilet things in the other, when it occurred to him he might very likely be permitted only a single item of hand baggage. The nylon bag only, then. It was the kind on which the zip goes almost all the way round so that when empty the bag could be opened out flat, folded into its own pocket, and reduced to handkerchief size. It weighed practically nothing and was more capacious than he had at first supposed.

He realized as he emptied both bags once more that his nerves were screwing up again. Carol, he thought, Carol, trying to feel sad and upset but succeeding only in thinking about 5 Spring Close and the Goldschmidts' removal van arriving to find it full of furniture and Freda's car in the garage. That would have happened by now. What would they do? Go to Steiner and Wildwood and get Mr. Phipps's forwarding address from Sawyer. That would be care of Wand in Brownswood Common Lane, Tottenham, and Terence knew for a fact his mother would be out all day visiting her sister in Palmers Green as she always was on a Tuesday.

But even if the Goldschmidts were at this moment trying to trace him to get his furniture moved out, that wouldn't make them suspect him of never having owned the house in the first place. That and its implications would very likely not dawn on them for a week or more. Just the same, he was on tenterhooks as he re-packed the bag and watched the time creep very slowly towards seven-thirty, and it was an enormous relief to be in the tube at last with the nylon bag on his knee and a one-way ticket to Heathrow Central in his pocket.

Detective Inspector Tony Leatham had a

rather smart overnight bag, not leather but as good as, a dark-cream fake pigskin. He'd wangled it so that he'd be stopping two nights in Melbourne. Monty Driscoll had been there three months anyway so a couple more days wouldn't do him any harm, while a brief twenty-four-hour stopover would have been cruel on the jet lag. He had never been further abroad before than the Costa Del Sol.

He was going to enjoy himself. No tube for him. They let him have a car to take him right up to Terminal Three. Like all tyro travelers, Leatham was early and one of the first to check in on the Qantas flight that went out at 9:45. He had a cup of coffee and bought a paperback. Not *The Marriage Knot* you saw on display everywhere, he didn't think that was quite his line, but a new collection of twelve horror stories. Then, because there seemed nothing left to do, he presented his passport, and went through the gate from which there was no returning this side the air.

The girl was his type, with a little round face and blonde curls, though hers were permed. She was surrounded by stacks of luggage. He didn't know how on her own — for the little kid with her would have been more hindrance than help — she had managed to hump it into the train. She was wearing jeans and a brown fur jacket, rabbit probably, and at first he thought she must have an enormous bust, unnaturally huge on so small a girl. It was only after he had been talking to her for a few minutes – or she had been talking to him, she had cottoned on to him fast the way they did – and told him her name was Jane that he realized it was a baby in a sling she was carrying strapped to her chest. She bent forward and he saw its round, nearly bald head where he expected her cleavage to be.

Two kids and all that baggage! Terence didn't want to get involved, but it was too late. She had already read the label on Jessica's suitcase that said Singapore and the name of the hotel he was going to. He could see in her eyes the greedy relief that she had found herself an escort and a porter for the next twenty hours. It would distract his mind, there was that to it. Talking to her would stop him dwelling on the Goldschmidts. And when they got to Singapore...

"Bill's going to be stuck in Penang till April," she was saying, "but he's got an ayah all lined up for me."

Terence understood vaguely that she meant some sort of nurse for the kids. He thought he could do worse than enjoy her undivided companionship for a day or two if that was what fate had in store for him. The older child, sexless in velour dungarees and crew cut, though called Miranda, climbed on to his knee and began fiddling with the zip of the nylon bag. Terence hoped the ayah would be waiting at the airport, preferably on the tarmac.

He carried three cases, pushed one that was on wheels, the nylon bag hooked over his left wrist. Jane carried the baby and two more cases while Miranda hung on to the hem of her jacket, grizzling. There were no policemen loitering around the check-in desks – one of Terence's fears. Relief at getting rid of the cases was succeeded by anxiety at going through baggage scrutiny. And for Terence it was a literal scrutiny. He thought it was all up with him when they said they wanted the nylon bag opened and then opened it so that half the contents fell out. But no one said anything. They turned over the wads of notes with the same indifference as that with which they had handled Jane's package of disposable napkins. He saw Jane looking at the money, but she didn't say anything.

They all went into the duty-free shop, where Jane bought perfume. Terence didn't buy anything. One hour to go and he wouldn't need whisky anymore; he had never really liked the taste. They had coffee and Miranda had a packet of potato chips, and while they were sitting at the table wondering whether to have a sandwich or wait for food on the plane, Qantas announced that boarding was about to begin on their flight QF2 for Bahrain, Singapore, and Sydney. It was only the first call; there was a long time to go yet.

Jane said she thought she ought to go to the loo, or rather to the mothers' room if they had one, and change the baby's diaper. She might not have another chance for hours. Everyone knew what it was like queuing up on those flights. Terence thought she would take Miranda with her but she didn't, and as soon as her mother was out of sight, Miranda knocked over a nearly full cup of coffee. The coffee flooded over Terence's nylon bag. He ripped open the bag, through which coffee had begun to seep, and as he did so, Miranda, contrite perhaps or merely frightened, jumped onto him and locked her arms round his neck.

Passengers were now getting up all round Terence and flocking towards the gates. He decided to go too and to hell with Jane and her kids and her bags and her ayah. He struggled to his feet, still holding or being held by Miranda, and as he tried to pry her off found himself looking into the face of Detective Inspector

Leatham. Recognition was mutual, immediate. Terence experienced the same sick, dizzy feeling of faintness he had had when Leatham called on him in Spring Close.

Leatham had been sitting at a table three or four yards away. He got up and came slowly towards Terence, looked at Terence and at Miranda, and said:

"Jason Stratford, I presume?"

The words were audible to Terence but they didn't register as more than sounds, as an unknown foreign language might. His nerve burst and frayed open like a too tightly stretched string. He let out a low inarticulate cry. He thrust Miranda off him, grabbed the open bag, and ran. The bag peeled itself inside out and the contents tumbled out behind him like the laying of a paper chase: razor, newspaper, underclothes, toothpaste, tranquilizers, a hundred and thirty-two thousand pounds...

25

They were taking the book back. Holding Jay's hand, Benet went into the Winterside library on a March morning, handed the book across the counter, and tried to explain how she happened to have it. Though not a member, she had happened to be in the library some months before; her little boy had picked it up and inadvertently...

The animal picture book was large and gaudily colored, hardly an unconsidered trifle. But the librarian seemed glad to get any missing book back, on any terms. Benet could have returned it by post. She had made herself come here to this corner of Tottenham, to Lordship Avenue and Winterside, because she felt that if she didn't do it now she might never have the courage again, she might avoid it forever, making elaborate detours whenever it was necessary to cross this part of London. The book was only an excuse to fetch her for a painful but cathartic look at the neighborhood where Edward had died and Carol Stratford with him.

As on their previous visit, she had left the car parked in Winterside Road. It was a sparkling, icy day, daffodils out but not a leaf bud showing, not a breath of spring in the air. Jay was growing out of his duffel coat. He might need a new one before the warm weather came. She strapped him into his seat and drove the car into Woodhouse's garage to fill up with petrol.

A young girl served her. Benet went into the office with her to pay with a credit card. Tom Woodhouse was sitting at a desk, talking into the phone. She looked at him, in two minds whether to declare herself when he put the receiver back or to let it go, and then she looked harder. A curious feeling that was a mixture of wonder and of intense embarrassment washed over her. It was almost like an unexpected and unwelcome encounter with an old lover. Yet, of course, Tom Woodhouse had never been her lover. He had been Carol Stratford's. There was no doubt of that.

The resemblance was uncanny, something to send a shiver down the spine. The man on the phone had a high forehead, sea-blue eyes, a hook of a nose, and a long chin. His eyebrows were blond thatch eaves and his hair a sandy fair. The first time she had seen Jay, hadn't he forcibly reminded her of someone else she had once known? She signed the chit mechanically. Tom Woodhouse said goodbye into the phone, put the receiver down, wrote something on a pad, slowly raised his head.

Benet took her receipt and, keeping her head turned, walked quickly out of the office. The last thing she wanted was to renew her acquaintance with this man who was Jay's undoubted father.

It was a week since she had seen Ian, and the departure for Canada was less than a fortnight away. He rang the doorbell at seven, just after Jay had gone to bed.

"I'm not coming with you," she said, moving out of his embrace. "But you know that, you've guessed, haven't you?"

His face wore the same heavy look of sadness that had been there when she told him that it hadn't occurred to her to tell him she was going to Spain, that she had forgotten him. She had been three days with Mopsa and her father, the news of Edward's death had reached her, before she remembered to phone Ian. And yet it hadn't been a lack of love, only that fear drives out all other emotion.

"I know you're not, but I don't know why," he said.

She was going to tell him a lie in order to avoid all the lie-telling of a future. Any future for them without those lies would be impossible, for he would never connive at what she had done. On the other hand, a future of lies in which she passed on to him one invention and prevarication after another to account for Jay's presence, legal status, continued situation as her son, was equally unthinkable. The relationship would be destroyed even if he believed her — and she didn't think he would believe her for long.

Some future lover, some man in time to come — if such a man ever appeared — would know nothing of her history, would be content with a word or two of explanation. But Ian was the only living person who knew Jay could not be the James Archdale of his passport, the only person who had known James and knew that he was dead. So she had to make a choice, and she had made it. Ian or Jay — she had chosen. And first she had to tell that lie.

"I'm sorry, Ian. I just don't care enough for you to follow you half across the world. I thought I loved you and I do, but not enough."

He wouldn't accept it. "We could try six

months' separation. You could see how you felt after that."

"I shall feel the same."

She knew she would never see him again after that evening. "I'll buy your books," he said. "If I can't be anything else to you, I'll be your constant reader."

She cried after he had gone. She poured herself a drink and sat in the study room and took cold comfort from the fact that her last obstacle was gone. It was she herself who had chosen it, who had deliberately mapped out her life on these lines. Cold comfort in a lonely midnight house.

Jay woke up and cried for a drink of water. She might as well go to bed, she thought, and not come down again. She sat him on her lap and gave him the cup of water to drink. He went back into the cot willingly, closing his eyes even before she had covered him up. A little ruefully and with a lot of hope she looked at him. Some words of Edward's came back to her.

"Well, Jay," she said, "it looks as if we're in business."

THORNDIKE PRESS HOPES you
have enjoyed this Large Print
book. All our Large Print titles
are designed for the easiest
reading, and all our books are
made to last. Other Thorndike
Press Large Print books are
available at your library,
through selected bookstores, or
directly from the publisher. For
more information about our
current and upcoming Large
Print titles, please send your
name and address to:

THORNDIKE PRESS
ONE MILE ROAD
P.O. Box 157
THORNDIKE, MAINE 04986

There is no obligation, of course.